Ready to be Loved by You

ENEWEROME

Scriptures used in this book are taken from;

THE HOLY BIBLE, NEW INTERNATIONAL VERSION ®. Copyright© 1973, 1978, 1984, 2011 by Biblica, Inc.™. Used by permission of Zondervan.

Manuscript edited by Leah Taylor

Cover designed and illustrated by Quadri Ayinde

For more information, contact;

storiesforchrist@gmail.com

Ready to be Loved by You

ENEWEROME

For my daughter, Zioraifechukwu.
May you grow up to love the Lord unapologetically and live for
Him unashamedly, no matter the cost.

Author's Note

When the Lord first laid the idea of this story on my heart, I didn't know where or how I would begin. So, like a child needing their parents for survival, I held on to God—the one who gave me this story, for wisdom and the strength to see it through. Today, Ready to be Loved by You is in your hands and I do not take credit for any of this. I also couldn't be more thankful to God who made this story find its way to you.

Dear friend, I hope that you enjoy Ready to be Loved by You as much as I enjoyed writing it. But most importantly, I pray that it draws you closer to the one whose love we truly need, without which we won't be complete—Jesus Christ.

All my love,

Enewerome.

Glossary

Abeg - **Please**

Abi - **Or/Right?**

Ahan - **Used to express shock or admiration**

Ankara - **A type of cotton cloth featuring brightly colored patterns produced by means of a wax-resist dye technique, associated especially with West African fashion.**

Aproko - **An indiscreet gossip.**

Aso ebi - **A uniform dress or dressing code/style that is traditionally worn by the Yoruba people at special occasions as an indication of cooperation, camaraderie and solidarity**

Bololo - **Bald headed**

Cut cap for you - **An expression which means you respect someone for their skill or achievements**

Danfo - **A yellow minibus that carries passengers for a fare as part of an informal transport system in Lagos, Nigeria.**

Eba - **A stiff dough made by soaking garri (dried grated cassava flour) in hot water and kneading it with a wooden baton until it becomes a smooth doughy staple. It is often eaten with rich soups and stews, with beef, stockfish or mutton**

Ehen - An exclamation in pidgin that means by the way, or that's more like it, or really?

Isoko - **A tribe in Delta State, a Southern part of Nigeria**

Gele - **A type of elaborate headdress worn by West African women for special occasions**

Ke? - **Used to add emphasis to a question asked**

Ma binu si mi - **It means don't be angry at me in Yoruba language**

Men-will-stain-your-white - **A popular phrase used to show how men will end up embarrassing women who reciprocate their love interest**

O - **Used for emphasis**

Ofada rice and ayamase sauce - **Ofada rice is an indigenous rice from a small community in Western Nigeria called Ofada. Ayamase sauce is a stew made with unripe habaneros, locust beans (iru) onions, lots of meat parts, eggs and palm oil.**

Oga - **Boss**

Omo mi - **My child in Yoruba language**

O wa - **Used to let a bus driver know you have arrived at your destination**

Oya - **Come on**

Pele - **Sorry in Yoruba language**

Peppering - **Used to mean someone is uncomfortable**

Seafood okra - **A Nigerian Okra stew dish made from Okra, a variety of seafood and spicy pepper sauce.**

Sha - **Though**

Shege - **Suffering**

Shey kosi - **Hope no problem in Yoruba language**

Wahala - **Problem**

Wetin - **What**

Wo - **Look in Yoruba language**

Wrapper - **A traditional attire, usually a long piece of fabric made from embroidered George or any other type of fabric, worn by both men and women.**

Yoruba - **A tribe in the Western part of Nigeria**

Content Warnings

Death (loss of a loved one), memorial service, accident, grief and therapy, attempted suicide, mention of miscarriage and stillbirth, sickness-acute liver failure.

Playlist

Theme song: Ready to be Loved - St. Lundi

Fear is not my future - **Chandler Moore, Kirk Franklin, Brandon Lake & Maverick City Music**

Olufunmi - **Style Plus**

Uptown funk - **Mark Ronson & Bruno Mars**

Daddy dada - **Daniel Bentley**

I like me better - **Anthony de la Torre & Lana Condor**

Anyone else but you - **Anthony de la Torre & Lana Condor**

Worth the wait - **Spencer Crandall**

Scan the QR code to listen to the playlist.

Chapter One

Levi

Waves of excitement and nervousness washed over Levi as he got out of bed. Waking up before his alarm could ring at 5 A.M. was no surprise because today was unlike any other Saturday where he worked as an event coordinator with his boss, Ms. Preye. It was the day he would show her how capable he was of pulling off the perfect wedding ceremony and reception for an expat bride and her husband and that he deserved more opportunities like this. This was his first shot at overseeing the entire planning and coordination of such a high-profile wedding, something his boss had never done since he started working for her.

Levi loved every aspect of his job. Right from the discovery call with the clients to mapping out their vision for their events, sourcing for vendors, and getting the best deals, to seeing the entire vision come to life and receiving feedback from his clients. However, what he looked forward to most was the wedding ceremonies and receptions where he could watch the couple looking so in love with each other. Every time he helped couples plan and organize their wedding ceremonies, seeing how happy they were on their big day fueled his desire for love and a happy marriage even more.

He walked into the bathroom whistling the popular "Blessed Assurance" hymn, catching a glimpse of his crucifix necklace in the mirror as it bounced off light. Singing was something he did to calm his nerves, and right now, they were all over the place. He had about an hour to leave the house so he could get to the church by 8 A.M., at the latest. That would give him ample time to make sure everything was in the right order.

As usual, he had to spend some time praying and studying his Bible before leaving the house, so he took a quick shower and dressed in a white button-down t-shirt, leaving the top button undone so his crucifix necklace showed. Midnight blue was one of the wedding colors, but since he didn't have pants in that color, he wore his navy blue ones.

He went to his prayer corner and opened his devotional. The topic for the day was dealing with anxiety, which was something he had been battling with ever since his cousin, Joshua, passed away four years ago. The anchor Scripture for the day was Philippians 4:6.

"Do not be anxious about anything, but in every situation by prayer and petition, with thanksgiving, present your requests to God."

After his cousin's death, Levi went to therapy for a year to help with his anxiety and panic attacks. Coupled with prayers and affirmations from Scripture, his condition significantly improved and the panic attacks stopped. Still, he had to deal with having constant knots in his stomach whenever he felt tense about anything—today was no exception. Levi's mind drifted to the wedding, and he was about to reach for his iPad to check his To-Do list when he caught himself. This was his devotion time, and God deserved his full attention.

He read through the devotional one more time and highlighted the key areas he needed to work on, one of which was learning to stop the need to control everything even though being a perfectionist didn't help matters. If he was being honest, he didn't like living with the feeling that something could go wrong at any time. What was funny was that a majority of the time, his worries were unfounded. Even though he had been working on learning to make peace with things not going as planned or people not doing things exactly the way he would have wanted, today's devotional was the perfect reminder and encouragement for him to allow God to take the lead. Levi looked at his wristwatch and saw that he had forty minutes left of his devotion time. He would use this remaining time to pray about his anxiety and commit the day's job to God's hands.

"Heavenly Father, thank you for today. I thank you for my life, for sending your son, Jesus Christ, to die for my sins so I can have this beautiful, growing relationship with you. My Father, I thank you because you are concerned about even the minutest detail of my life. Thank you for helping me overcome this spirit of anxiety over the years." He paused and then continued.

"I know that you have healed me of this spirit that threatens to steal the joy and peace you have lavishly given to me. I decree in the name of Jesus that I am no longer anxious for anything, regardless of the situation. Therefore, I commit my day and this job to your hands, Lord. I ask that you guide my path and help me do my job excellently from a place of rest, Lord. Let my performance at work and my behavior toward everyone I meet today bring glory to your name. Thank you, glorious Daddy, for answering my prayers in Jesus's name."

He prayed in tongues for a few minutes and felt the peace of God wash over him. All he had to do now was remain conscious of God's peace in his heart to fight against anxiety. As Levi walked out of his house, he made a mental note not to allow any situation or anyone to rob him of his peace. While he fished for his car keys in his pocket, the smell of rain hit his nostrils and his heart skipped a beat. He looked up at the marble mix of dark and light clouds in the sky and couldn't tell if it was going to rain or not. Subconsciously, he clutched the crucifix pendant on his necklace and prayed.

"Lord, please, let it not rain. Please! I can't afford for anything to go wrong today."

Trust in me with all your heart…

Proverbs 3:5 popped up in his heart, and he let go of the crucifix pendant, knowing God had his best interest at heart. The first thing Levi did when he got into his car was to turn on the radio. If he wanted to maintain his peace, he had to ensure the atmosphere around him was right. Much to his surprise, a crude song blasted out of the speakers and he hurriedly lowered the volume.

"Just imagine the nonsense they are playing this early morning."

Levi sighed and started his car to warm up the engine. He scrolled through his phone to search for a worship song. He needed a song that would fill him with hope and the expectation of God's goodness. So, he played the latest addition to his worship playlist, "Fear is Not My Future" by Chandler Moore, Brandon Lake, Kirk Franklin, and Maverick City Music, which was becoming his favorite song. He drove out of his compound with the music on full blast, and each time the song got to the chorus, he would sing loudly and sway his head.

It was just 6:30 A.M. and the roads were already busy with pedestrians and vehicles of all sorts. There were people already hawking their wares along what was left of the road motorcycle and tricycle drivers hadn't bullied pedestrians for. The frequent cacophony of car horns blasting into the chilly air made Levi wonder how he survived this madness daily. He would often joke that any Christian living in Lagos needed a double dose of the fruit of the Holy Spirit to live a sanctified life. Levi stopped in front of a red traffic light with other vehicles and watched as the countdown began.

As soon as the red light turned yellow, vehicles started revving up their engines. One truck in particular emitted so much carbon monoxide that Levi could still smell it in his wound-up air-conditioned car. Some drivers even attempted to move forward with whatever little space they could maneuver their vehicles into. This made them honk persistently at those who refused to make room for them. Soon, they had about thirty seconds more to wait until the yellow traffic light turned green. In the middle of the chaos going on,

Levi lifted his right hand in worship and sang the chorus loudly again.

"Hello, peace; hello, joy; hello, love; hello, strength; hello, hope. It's a new horizon (fear is not my future)!"

When the timer got to five seconds, he put his hand down and got ready to move. The light turned green and all the drivers charged forward, each one trying to overtake the other. Levi was about to move when a tricycle cut in front of him and he stepped on his brakes abruptly.

Is this man crazy or something?

He wound down his window and honked loudly, intending to give the crazy driver a piece of his mind if he looked back.

Levi, don't.

He huffed and wound up his window, thinking about how lucky the man was. Eventually, he caught up with the tricycle driver, who had cut him off earlier, at a junction. Levi watched the man turn to look at him, and he bit his tongue. He was still tempted to ask if the man was crazy by twirling his index finger above his temple, but he remembered the Lord's instruction, so he kept quiet and continued driving. Usually, whenever an erring driver turned to look at the person they had offended, it was with a what-are-you-going-to-do-about-it look. But not this man. He waved at Levi and clasped his hands together to show that he was sorry before driving off. Levi heaved a sigh, glad he hadn't said or done anything harsh to the man.

"It's hard not to insult people in *this* Lagos. Lots of mad people everywhere!"

As soon as the words left his mouth, a Scripture he knew too well popped up in his heart, and he knew it was God schooling him again.

Let your conversation be always full of grace, seasoned with salt...

He sighed and said, "Yes, Lord."

One hour later, he was on the Third Mainland Bridge where people drove a lot saner than on the mainland. Twenty more minutes and he would be at the church. His mind wandered to his To-Do list, and he needed to be sure everything was going as planned. He paused the music and called the head of the logistics department. The line rang but there was no answer. When it stopped ringing, he dialed the number again. After what seemed like an endless wait, the person answered.

"Hello?"

"Bayo, *what's up now? Where you keep phone wey person dey call, you no pick?*"

"*Oga Levi, no vex. Na those people wey dey design the flower arch I been dey talk to wey carry my mind go.*"

"*Ehen! That na why I even call you. I hope say una don arrange the flowers the way I show you for that picture?*"

"*Yes, sir!*"

"*Okay. Una don put the arch for the front of the altar abi?*"

"*Yes. Since.*"

Levi nodded, relieved that things were going as planned. This flower arch had given him cause for concern because they had only found one to rent just yesterday. Now that the flower arch issue was settled, the next thing to take care of would be the seating arrangement. But that would have to wait till he got to the church.

"*No problem. I dey on my way now. I go soon reach church.*"

"*Okay, sir. Till you come*"

"*Thank you, Bayo. Later.*"

"*Yes, sir,*" Bayo said and hung up.

"*Wait! What of the…*" Levi hadn't asked if they found maroon roses for the arch decor. He would have to find out when he got to the church. After all, he was only fifteen minutes away.

As Levi got closer to an intersection leading to a street adjacent to where the church was located, he saw a *danfo* turn into the lane he was on from another street. Levi couldn't believe his eyes because it was a one-way road and an accident was bound to happen because of this driver's recklessness. He slowed down his vehicle and made way for the impatient ones behind to overtake him. If they could see the oncoming bus and still decided to forge ahead, he wouldn't stop them. But one thing was sure, he wasn't going to risk his life.

He switched on his caution lights and watched from his side mirror as another *danfo* sped past him. The bus driver overtook and sped past other vehicles. Before he could blink, a desperate squeal of tires and crunching metal pierced through the air. It was the *danfo* driver who had just overtaken him and the other one driving on the wrong lane.

Time stood still and Levi froze. Flashes from his accident four years ago reeled through his mind and left him in a daze. It was the loud honking from other vehicles that brought him back to reality. Both *danfo* drivers got out of their vehicles, charging at each other in ferocious rage. Other drivers honked incessantly as they tried to squeeze their way out of what was now a roadblock. A part of Levi wished he hadn't slowed down when he saw the driver initially. But he couldn't have, not when his heartbeat had doubled out of fear.

Somehow, he summoned the courage to follow other vehicles as they maneuvered their way out of the traffic jam. As he drove past, he heard the ongoing argument between both drivers about who was at fault for the accident. Neither of them was willing to take responsibility for their actions, especially the driver who had driven in the wrong lane and clearly caused the accident. They continued hurling insults and threats at each other while their *danfos* remained a nuisance to other road users. Levi was thankful he had left his house early enough to avoid the horrific traffic jam this accident would later cause.

"I just feel bad for people who have to pass this road later today," he said.

Levi played the music he had paused earlier. He would arrive at the church soon and needed to get in the right frame of mind quickly. Since he stepped out of his house, it had been from one drama to another, and he hoped this was the last. A crack of thunder pierced through the sky and rain droplets spread across his windshield.

"Great!" Levi said through gritted teeth.

By the time he turned into the street leading to the church, the drizzling had gotten a little more intense, each drop beating down on his windshield in a persistent, rhythmic sound. He parked his car and jogged inside the church. Bayo, who always wore a smile, was the first person to welcome him as soon as he got inside.

"Oga, Levi. Welcome, sir."

"Thank you, Bayo. How the work dey go?"

"Fine, sir. We don already finish. Come, make I show you," Bayo said, leading Levi to where the flower arch was.

As Levi followed Bayo, the contrast between the brightly lit church and the gloomy sky was staggering. There was a floral archway of maroon roses and dangling greenery at the entrance door; he could also see that Bayo had done a cascading floral arrangement of the pew flowers just as he had instructed and they looked stunning. Still, something about them didn't feel right, but he couldn't put a finger on it. A sickening feeling engulfed his stomach like a grim prophecy, and he didn't like the anxiety that came with it.

When Levi saw the flower arch, he couldn't believe his eyes. He looked at Bayo and back at the arch. He let out a dry laugh, scratching the back of his head.

Lord, what kind of temptation is this?

"Oga? Any problem?" Bayo asked.

Levi bit his lip and drew in a ragged breath. He thought of the best way to tell Bayo that not only had they disappointed him, but that it was too late to fix their massive error.

"Bayo, if na the arrangement of the flowers for this arch, you get am well well. But this red for the rose wey you use no be the type wey I show you now. Wetin happen?"

Bayo explained that he had checked with many vendors but couldn't find maroon rose flowers. Those who had them didn't have enough to sell, and he thought combining two different shades of red was a terrible idea. This was one thing Levi could agree with him on, but he wasn't happy that Bayo hadn't informed him earlier.

"Bayo! But why you no tell me since? Now we no fit change am because e dey too late."

"Oga, Levi, no vex abeg. I been think say our vendor go still fit see that maroon wey you talk. But she no see am and the wedding been dey near, I come say make she supply us this one like that. No vex."

Levi couldn't say anything. He was too frustrated and disappointed to utter a word. Ms. Preye had entrusted this wedding to his hands, and if he had already messed up by getting the wrong shade of red roses, Levi wondered what else wasn't going according to plan. Right from his school days, he never liked group assignments because he would have to delegate tasks, and some people couldn't care less about doing things properly.

To date, he still felt the same way, but it was impossible to be successful as an event coordinator if he didn't delegate tasks. Planning and executing events wasn't a one-man job, and he would be a liar if he said delegating tasks wasn't beneficial to him. Nevertheless, he would take a more active approach to being on top of things. Whether it was cross-checking a million times if he had to or asking for the proof of tasks done. He would do whatever it took to prevent future letdowns like this, even if that meant he became an overbearing boss.

Levi walked a few steps away from the arch to check if it was right in the middle. Since he couldn't get exactly what the bride wanted, the least he could do was make sure they had perfectly placed the arch in the middle.

Just a little shift to the left and this flower arch will be perfectly in the middle of the altar.

"Bayo, make you and Chuks shift this arch go left small. Small o!"

"Okay, sir. Chuks abeg, come help me."

Levi instructed them on how far they should push the arch. After a few wrong attempts, they finally got it.

"Thank you. Una don try well well," Levi said.

Chuks smiled and went back to cleaning the seats while Bayo walked to meet Levi with a beaming smile. He made a comment about how beautiful the arch looked, and Levi affirmed it. Levi opened his iPad, took some pictures of the arch, and moved on to tick things off his To-Do list.

"Oga, but this color take style resemble that one wey we been want o," Bayo said, sounding upbeat in a way that annoyed him.

Levi looked up from his To-Do list, giving Bayo the stink eye. Bayo cleared his throat and said something about going to check on those arranging the seats.

"No, leave am. I go tell Chuks to handle am. I want make you go where we go do the reception go see wetin dey happen for there," Levi said.

"But Oga, rain dey fall," Bayo said.

Levi looked outside and chuckled. *"Bayo, when rain never serious, we dey call am drizzle. This type no dey wet clothes like that sef."*

Bayo arched his brows and nodded his head as he listened to Levi. Levi had gotten used to seeing Bayo act this way—paying rapt attention and learning something new. Despite being older than him, Bayo was teachable. It was also one reason Levi couldn't stay mad at him. Besides, he was good at his job and knew when to take responsibility for his actions.

"But anyway, na you drive company van come here abi?" Levi asked.

"Yes, sir."

"*Good. Drive go the reception make you organize things for there. Anything wey fit spoil inside rain, abeg carry am go inside the hall. When the rain don fall finish, we go bring the things outside again.*"

"*Oga, you say this one no be rain. Na drizzle.*"

Levi chuckled. "*Na true.*"

"*Make I dey go. If you want make I come back here, call me for phone,*" Bayo said.

"*No problem. But make sure say you look inside the van well, remove anything wey we go need for this church before you go abeg.*"

"Okay, boss," Bayo said and turned to leave.

Levi looked at his list again and saw that he hadn't confirmed if they had brought the rug for the aisle. He was thankful for his To-Do list because he wasn't sure he would have remembered to ask with the thousand and one things running through his mind.

"*Bayo! Where the white rug?*" Levi called out to Bayo who was about to walk out of the entrance door.

"*The rug dey with Chuks,*" Bayo said.

"*But why you never set am for the aisle now?*"

Bayo jogged back to meet Levi before answering. "*Oga, drizzle dey fall and you know say that rug na white. Make person no carry dirty stain am. I don tell Chuks to spread the rug once time na ten minutes to the wedding. That time, nobody go dey inside to dirty am.*"

Levi couldn't believe the blunder he would have made had Bayo not been thoughtful. God was indeed mindful of him, even down to the minutest detail.

Thank you, Father, for saving me from this huge mistake. What would I have done if the rug had gotten stained?!

"*Bayo, God go bless you. Thank you!*"

"*Boss, I dey here for you. No dey worry too much.*"

Levi smiled, and Bayo jogged out of the church. As always, his worry was unfounded. Also, for someone who left his house determined not to let anything make him anxious, he was certainly doing a terrible job at it. He could blame it on the events of that morning, but he wouldn't. A big part of learning to walk with God and trusting Him involved taking responsibility for one's actions, picking one's self up after a mistake, and asking for God's grace to do better. He also knew that if he wanted to continue the day without any worries, he would have to lean completely on God and not his organizational skills. A good example was God using Bayo to remind him that even his most thought-out plan could still fail if he didn't rely on God for help.

Levi breathed a sigh of relief as he glanced at the checkmarks on his To-Do list. Every major thing he needed to prepare for the wedding ceremony was ready. His next course of action was to pick up the wedding programs from his car and hand them over to the usher in charge. Levi looked round the church, and it was so beautiful that it made him wish he were the one getting married. But if wishes were horses, he sure would be riding one to meet his bride.

He ticked off laying the carpet on his To-Do list. Now there was only one thing left to do on his list.

Chapter Two

Vivienne

Lip gloss, ATM card, cash, chewing gum, powder puff, compact powder, purse, shoes, handkerchief, pocket perfume… Am I forgetting anything?

Vivienne checked that she had indeed packed what she needed for the wedding as she rummaged through the gift bag on her bed. On a normal day, she would feel excited to attend a wedding because it was the one time she could dress up extravagantly, dance as much as she wanted, and eat and drink to her fullest without paying for it. But today, she honestly wasn't in the mood to attend any party, especially not after what she had heard her father say about her to her mom over the phone. However, she couldn't disappoint Oluchi, especially not after collecting a hundred dollars to attend the wedding.

Back in school, Oluchi was just an acquaintance and coursemate. Their conversations never went beyond saying hi to each other and borrowing or lending notes. But after they graduated, Oluchi started following Vivienne on Instagram, liking her posts, and even leaving nice comments. At first, she found it strange and creepy because it felt like Oluchi was stalking her. But after a while, Vivienne got used to the compliments and even followed her back. That was when she learned Oluchi had traveled to the United States for her postgraduate studies. They kept in touch occasionally through DMs so it wasn't a surprise when Oluchi reached out to her a few days ago. Vivienne assumed it was their normal catching up, but Oluchi said she needed her help.

"Vee babe, please, I need you to attend a wedding on my behalf."

Vivienne's brows furrowed in confusion as she wondered what kind of strange request Oluchi was asking of her.

"Why? What happened?"

Oluchi explained how she was supposed to be her cousin's maid of honor that weekend but fell ill a day before her departure date. She asked to call Vivienne on video so she could explain better, to which Vivienne agreed. When Oluchi came on, she could see IV fluid connected to her free hand.

"It's this serious?" Vivienne asked and Oluchi nodded.

Oluchi was light-skinned, which made the dark circles under her eyes even more visible.

"Sorry, Oluchi. How did this happen?"

She explained how she hadn't been feeling quite like herself two weeks before she fell ill but had rationalized it by saying it was school and work stress. Besides, she would rest when she got to Nigeria. Then the previous night, she'd had dinner and went to bed only to wake up in the middle of the night with a sharp pain in her stomach. Shortly after, she started vomiting and had developed a fever.

"When they brought me to the ER, I was already weak and could barely talk. They said it was food poisoning and dehydration. I should be out of here by tomorrow though."

"Sorry about that. Please get well soon."

"Thanks, dear. Enough about me, Vee babe," Oluchi said and tried to sit up straight. "My cousin's wedding is this Saturday, and it's Thursday already. They won't discharge me until tomorrow, and there is already a six-hour time difference. Ultimately, I won't attend the wedding, which saddens me deeply because Amara is one of my favorite humans in the world. Still, I want to do what I can to help make her day as beautiful as she has always imagined."

"So, if I understand you correctly, you want me to be her maid of honor in your place?"

"Exactly, Vee babe."

"Uh… I have never done this before and I don't want to mess things up."

"Don't worry, I will guide you."

"Sure?" Vivienne asked, and Oluchi nodded, saying it wasn't a big deal.

"But what will I wear? And why did you even choose me out of everybody you know to do this for you? Don't you have other friends?"

"Which friends? The ones who stopped speaking to me since I traveled out, or which? I chose you because I see your wedding guest pictures and you always look so stunning. More so, I remember back then in school how you were always determined to finish difficult group projects, even if you had to do them alone."

"Really? We were not close, yet you know this much about me. Were you stalking me?" Vivienne asked with a small smile playing on her lips.

"You wish," Oluchi said, laughing.

"Amara is an only child and isn't close to our other cousins. She has been crying since I told her about my situation. Please, Vee babe."

"Okay. I'll do it."

"Oh my goodness! Thank you so much! You don't know what you have just done for me. Has anybody ever told you that you are Godsend?"

Oluchi, the only people who will agree with you are my mom and sister. My dad thinks I am a failure.

Vivienne let out a forced chuckle and said, "You're welcome. So, what's the plan?"

They went over the plan for Vivienne to attend the wedding and what she would do for Amara when she arrived. Oluchi also wired her the money for a new dress, shoes, makeup, and transportation fare to the wedding venue while they were still talking. Just before they ended the call, Oluchi went over the details of the type of dress

Vivienne was to buy, her makeup style, and her duties as the maid of honor again.

"Vee babe, please, buy a dress with a veil just in case they see something wrong with the dress so you can use it to cover up."

"I won't forget. This is the third time you have said it."

"Really?" Oluchi said, feigning ignorance, and Vivienne rolled her eyes.

"Thanks a lot for doing this, Vee babe. I deeply appreciate it."

"You're welcome. I have to go now so I can withdraw the money you sent and change it today. Then I'll go to the market to look for a dress tomorrow. I'll keep you posted too."

"All right. Talk soon."

"Oluchi, wait. What about my hair?" Vivienne asked, and Oluchi stared at her blankly.

Just in case she didn't hear her the first time, Vivienne added, "My hair's currently in afro ringlets and I dyed it ginger."

"Oh, I forgot to tell you. Amara doesn't mind. She's currently wearing a pixie cut hairstyle and is using it for her wedding, so it's just perfect."

"Okay then. I'll talk to you later."

"Bye," Oluchi said and ended the video call.

Later that evening, Vivienne got a call from Amara thanking her for coming to her rescue, and it made her wonder if she knew Oluchi had *paid* her to attend her wedding.

The next day, Vivienne spent hours under the scorching sun, searching for the perfect midnight blue dress in the bustling Balogun market. The best one she found was a cowl-neck spaghetti-strapped dress that was a little tight on her bust. Vivienne sent a picture to Amara on WhatsApp, who called her almost immediately on video and couldn't stop gushing about how stunning she looked in the dress.

"What about the cleavage? Are you sure it won't be a problem?"

"I mean, I think it will. But you've spent hours searching for a dress, and this is my favorite of all the ones you showed to me." Amara's American accent cut through the loud pidgin voices in the shop.

"So, what do we do? What if I still look around to see if I can find something else?"

"No, that's okay. You can always use the veil to cover up if anyone bothers you about it."

"Then I guess this should work," Vivienne said and draped the veil over her neck.

"Yeah. But Vivienne, do you like the dress?" Amara asked, watching Vivienne closely.

"Actually, I do. It's my favorite one as well."

"Perfect! If I had noticed the slightest dissatisfaction, I would have allowed you to look for more options. But thank God you love this one. You're so stunning, and I'm so excited to see you, Vivienne."

She felt warm that someone she'd just met valued her contributions and even cared about how she felt. Although Vivienne thought the dress wasn't worth the price, she grudgingly bought it because she didn't have a choice. Besides, the money wasn't technically hers. She also bought a pair of four-inch strappy silver heels and a silver clutch purse. She was a petite five-foot-five woman who needed the extra support.

While she tried to think of what she might be forgetting, Vivienne peered into the bag one more time before going back to her vanity to touch up her lipstick. She chuckled, remembering how Amara had gushed over her in the dress. If Amara thought she was stunning then, she should wait until she saw her all dolled up. If only her father would be a little excited about her existence. Not that she cared, though.

"Is your lipstick now funny?" Fisayo, her twenty-year-old sister, asked.

"Haha!" Vivienne rolled her eyes and continued applying more lipstick.

Despite Amara telling her to wear her makeup as she liked, she decided to go with Oluchi's suggestion, which was subtle eye makeup and bold lips. Still, she didn't know if she was doing too much. She stepped back from the vanity and looked at herself in the mirror. So many thoughts ran through her mind, and she didn't want to ruin Amara's perfect wedding by not looking good enough. It also didn't help that her father's words had put her in a dump. Knowing how much his words affected her, Vivienne knew she had to snap out of her sad mood if she wanted to do her best for Amara.

Is my hair not fighting with this lipstick for attention? Is this color even right for the occasion? What if Amara doesn't like how I look? Maybe I should wipe this one off and wear my Barbie pink lipstick instead.

Immediately she thought of her pink lipstick, and she remembered what she had forgotten.

"Ah! The wedding present."

Until now, she couldn't count how many people have treated her with warmth and respect without knowing her. They always judged her because of her hair and ear piercings. So when Amara had talked to her with so much warmth and kindness, it touched a spot in her heart and made her want to reciprocate the kind gesture. When she saw a vendor advertising the cutest table picture frames as she scrolled through Instagram on her way home from the market, it just made perfect sense to get one for Amara as a wedding present.

Vivienne ordered a pink one for Amara and a white one for herself. Amara and her husband were traveling back to the US after their wedding and she didn't want to give them something that would become a burden for them to travel with. Also, since she wasn't rich enough to give them money as a wedding present, the picture frame would have to do. She had even made a mental note to print their family's last year's Christmas photo and put it in the frame she'd gotten for herself.

Vivienne opened the top drawer of her vanity, where she thought she had kept the frame, but it wasn't there. She opened her closet and combed through the clutter, but she didn't find the frame. She tried to recall where she had kept it after the dispatch rider dropped it off the previous day, but couldn't. Vivienne slammed the door and let out a loud, exasperated hiss.

"What are you looking for?" Fisayo asked.

"A small picture frame. It's wrapped in a white wedding-themed wrapping paper."

Vivienne opened the drawers in her vanity again, but the frame still wasn't there. Her armpits were sweating and her palms were clammy. She didn't want to go to the wedding without the present, so she had to find it fast.

Fisayo stood up from the bed and went to the living room as Vivienne watched her walk away, wondering why she wasn't helping. Normally, Fisayo would help her search for her missing stuff, but not without draping her with a few sarcastic comments. Today, she just ignored her.

Right now, Vivienne's priority was to find the frame and make it in time for the wedding. Later, she would address Fisayo's behavior.

"Here," Fisayo said, holding the wrapped frame in front of her.

Vivienne hadn't even noticed when her sister walked back into the room.

"Where did you find it?" she asked, wide-eyed.

"On the dining table where you left it with the scissors and Scotch tape you used to wrap it," Fisayo said dryly.

Vivienne squealed with delight and jumped onto her sister. "Thank you!" she said and planted a big kiss on her cheek. "I thought you didn't want to help me look for the wedding present when you left the room."

"When have I never helped you look for something? You know that without me, your life is an enormous ball of chaos, right?" Fisayo said and thrust the wrapped frame to Vivienne.

"I know, and that's why I love you," Vivienne said, grinning.

She collected the frame from Fisayo and carefully put it inside the bag. She looked at the time on her phone.

6:30 A.M

There was still enough time for her to decide whether or not she should change her lipstick before heading out.

"You look stunning, Buks," Fisayo said with so much admiration as she watched Vivienne hold the red and pink lipsticks close to her hair, trying to decide which one complemented her hair color better.

Buks was Fisayo's nickname for her, while their mother called her Buks Buks when she wasn't scolding her or being a typical Nigerian mom. They coined her nickname from Oluwafiebukunmi, the Yoruba name her father gave her as his first daughter which meant God used you to bless me. Aside from thinking that the name was a mouthful, she preferred to be called Vivienne, as she didn't want to be reminded of her dad each time someone called her name.

"Really? You don't think my lips are too red or that I should wear this pink lipstick instead?"

Fisayo shook her head.

"So you're saying the red lipstick works better with my hair?"

Fisayo nodded again.

"What about my dress? Does it look good on me? I also think my cleavage is showing a little too much. What do you think, Fifi?"

Fisayo put down her phone and scowled at her sister. "Buks, the dress is a perfect fit and you are stunning! Yes, your cleavage is a little out in the open," Fisayo shimmied and they both laughed, "but that's why you have the veil. Hope you carried it?"

"Yes," Vivienne said, pointing to the veil beside her bag.

"Great!" Fisayo clapped. "Then you are good to go and should already be booking a cab."

"That's what I'm about to do. Let me type in the address of the hotel where Amara is lodged. I just hope it won't be more than my budget because it is on the Island."

"Don't forget that today is a Saturday. There is usually a surge in cab prices, and it looks like it may rain. That also affects the price."

Vivienne paused and looked out the window. She shook her head and said, "It's March, Fifi. It doesn't start raining until April. Besides, how many times has it looked like it would rain yet nothing happened?"

"That may have been the case years ago when the effect of global warming hadn't kicked in. My friends in other states keep talking about having regular rainfall. Just go with an umbrella in case it rains."

"I can't. It's too much of a hassle."

Vivienne typed in the hotel's address and waited for the estimate. Going out in Lagos wasn't child's play, especially when it involved leaving the mainland, where she lived, to the island. The division of Lagos into mainland and island made it a rich-versus-poor, sane-versus-chaos thing. People often considered those living on the island to be financially better off than those on the mainland, even though that wasn't always the case.

"Nine thousand, five hundred naira from Ikeja to Victoria Island! *For what now?*" Vivienne exclaimed.

She couldn't fathom why they would give her such a ridiculous estimate for a ride they said would take just an hour. There was also no weekend price surge, which was sketchy but not the point. She had a little over three hours to get to the wedding ceremony scheduled for 10:00 A.M. Since she had enough time on her hands, she would go by bus and still be right on schedule regardless of how many stops the bus had to make for passengers to alight at their different bus stops. Worst case scenario, it would take her two hours to get to TBS, which was a stone's throw from the hotel.

"That's a lot, Buks. What are you going to do?"

"I'll just use public transport. I'm on a skinny budget."

"I don't get it. Didn't Oluchi send you money?" Fisayo looked confused.

"She did, but I have other bills to sort out."

"Like what?"

"Like the money you asked me for. Where do you think a jobless girl like me got ten thousand naira to give to you?"

"Oh," Fisayo said, unsure of what to say next.

"Mm-mmh," Vivienne replied.

She gathered her things, wore her slippers, and walked out of their room into the living room. Vivienne was about to leave the house when she remembered she hadn't worn any perfume, and she knew just the right one. Her mom's Zara perfume. It was the perfect boost of confidence she needed.

"Why are you going to Mommy's room?" Fisayo asked.

"To use her perfume. What else?"

Fisayo let out a dry laugh and said, "If Mommy asks who touched her stuff, I will not lie."

"Whatever," Vivienne said, rolling her eyes.

The perfume was in its usual spot on her mother's vanity. Knowing her mother, if she had suspected someone else was using her precious perfume, she would have hidden it. But it was still there, so she was safe. She sprayed some on her neck and wrists and kept the bottle as she'd met it. She was about to leave the room when something on the vanity caught her eye—a red book with the words *prayer journal* written on it.

Vivienne regularly entered her mother's room, but it was her first time seeing the journal. She picked it up, wondering if journaling was something her mother had recently started doing or if she had been doing it for a while and just forgot to keep the journal in its hiding place.

Her mother prayed a lot, especially at night, so it made no sense why she would still keep a prayer journal. Vivienne opened the first page. It was blank. Then she flipped the page, and on the next page was the date her mother bought the journal: 07/10/2021. Three days to Vivienne's twenty-first birthday.

She was about to flip the next page when Fisayo shouted, "You're running late, Buks!"

She put the journal down and walked straight to the entrance door of their living room.

"Where did Mommy say she was off to again?" Vivienne asked once she got to the door. "I thought she wasn't feeling too well?"

"There's a wedding in church today, so the sanitation unit has to tidy up earlier than their usual time. Mommy also said a little malaria cannot stop her from serving God," Fisayo said and bit into an apple.

Vivienne sighed. She would never understand her mother's relationship with God, even after everything she had gone through because of Him.

It was already 7:00 A.M., and she had to leave immediately.

"Tell Mommy I'll try to be back before 8 P.M. She knows where I'm headed," Vivienne said and walked out the door.

"Bye. Love you!" Fisayo said with her mouth full.

"Love you too."

Vivienne stepped out of the house, and the cold air embraced her. It was such a welcome feeling from the heat of the past weeks. The sky was a tie-dye mix of clear and dark clouds, and petrichor hung thick in the air. Fisayo was right. It looked and smelled like it would rain. Even though she had been praying for rainfall, she hoped it wouldn't rain today. Or at least, not until she got to the hotel. The last thing she needed was to arrive at the hotel looking like a drenched rat.

She got to the bus park just in time to take the last seat. It was the one beside the conductor, which she hated, but had no choice than to manage if she wanted to be on time. Vivienne adjusted the veil on her neck and gave the conductor, who had been ogling her, a stink eye. She planned to stop at TBS—Tafawa Balewa Square—and then board another bus to the junction closest to the hotel in Victoria Island. From there she would book a cab ride to the hotel. Going with this plan, she wouldn't spend more than three thousand naira in total.

Vivienne began scrolling through Instagram when she came across a father-daughter dance video. She felt a sudden tightness in her chest and clenched her jaw. Her father's words echoed in her heart, and she couldn't help but replay it repeatedly.

How can someone study chemistry education in the university and not expect to become a teacher? Bukunmi's rebellion against me is why she didn't study law and make something of her life. Even getting a job as an ordinary teacher has proven difficult for her. She never does anything right! At her age, all she knows how to do is go to parties, dance, and snap pictures. What a waste!

Vivienne released her jaw when it began to hurt. Unlike her, Fisayo had nothing to worry about. Her sister was Daddy's golden girl, studying to become a lawyer so she didn't have to worry about her tuition not being paid. Vivienne was glad her sister didn't have to face the hardship she endured in school.

It's been almost six years since she gained admission to the university and two years since she graduated from it. Still, the memories left a bad taste in her mouth and her dislike for her dad grew by the day. Not that he even helped matters with his constant derogatory remarks. Since her father said the only thing she was good at was attending parties, she wouldn't disappoint him.

"TBS, *bọ lẹ!*" the conductor croaked when they got to Tafawa Balewa Square.

Vivienne was so lost in thoughts that she didn't notice when the remaining passengers, who were seated at the back of the bus, alighted.

"*Fine girl, you no wan come down? Abi make I carry you go my house?*" the conductor said with a grin that revealed tobacco-stained teeth and a missing upper right incisor.

Vivienne hurriedly gathered her things and made her way to alight the bus. But the conductor had an arm out, blocking the exit. The driver, annoyed by the conductor's behavior, honked loudly, startling Vivienne. He warned the conductor that if he let Vivienne go without collecting her fare because he was flirting with her, he would deduct the money from his wage. When the conductor affirmed that he had collected Vivienne's fare, the driver shouted at him to let her through, then he began calling for passengers headed to their next destination.

As soon as Vivienne alighted the bus, it began to drizzle. She contemplated going ahead with her initial plan of boarding another bus to Victoria Island to save some money while risking getting drenched in the process or spending extra money to book a cab straight to the hotel and avoid getting wet. She decided getting wet wasn't worth it, especially because of her hair.

The estimated fare to the hotel was two thousand, five hundred naira—which was a thousand naira more than her budget—but it didn't matter. She could afford this.

She walked briskly towards a flyover to take shelter while she waited for her cab. Per the plan with Amara, she was to arrive at the hotel an hour before the wedding began so she could settle in and help the bride do the same. Then they would all go to the church together in the bride's rental car. The time was currently 8:25 A.M, which meant she even had an extra twenty minutes to spare for any contingency on the way going by the estimated ten-minute trip to the hotel from where she was.

"*Fine girl! Fine girl!*" the conductor from the bus she had just alighted shouted when they drove past her. From the corner of her eye, Vivienne saw him waving something at her, but she hissed, ignoring him, and crossed to the other side of the road where the flyover was. Why would he expect her to answer him after he had sexualized her?

Five minutes later, the drizzling had turned into full-blown rainfall and she was thankful she had somewhere to take shelter. Vivienne's cab also arrived. It was an elderly man whose salt-and-pepper beard made him appear to be in his fifties. She got in, greeted him, and asked if he would accept his payment by bank transfer. He agreed and they began their trip to the hotel.

Vivienne removed her slippers and put on her shoes. Despite not feeling as good as she looked, she was determined to give this maid-of-honor duty her best shot.

Chapter Three

Levi

What was a drizzle had turned into a heavy downpour. Levi had just gotten off the phone with Bayo, who assured him that everything was in order at the reception venue. He had also called the photography and videography teams to confirm that they were already at the hotel, filming the couple and taking pictures of them as they got ready for their big day. All that was left for him to do now was to check up on the bride.

"Hello, Ms. Amara. How are you doing today?"

"Hi, Levi!" Amara said, sounding elated. "I feel amazing! How are you?"

"I am well, ma'am. Thank you for asking," Levi said in an equally cheerful tone.

Amara was such a sweet and easygoing person. He was also thankful her wedding was his initiation into planning weddings independently of his boss. He even wished all his future clients would be easy to work with just like her. If only wishes were horses…

"I don't want to take up much of your time, but I just wanted to ask if everything is to your liking and to also let you know that you have nothing to worry about. Not even with this rain falling heavily. Everything is under control. The church and reception hall are both set, and your drivers will arrive in thirty minutes to bring you and Mr. Brandon to church," Levi added.

"That's perfect. And yes, my experience with you guys has been great. Everyone is so professional and they understood their assignments," Amara said.

"Awesome. I'm happy to hear this, ma'am."

"Thank you so much for giving me such a wonderful wedding experience so far, Levi."

"It is my pleasure, ma'am. You make this job so easy to do," Levi said, and Amara chuckled.

"Well then, I'll be sure to refer your company to my friends."

"Thank you, ma'am. We will appreciate the referral. I have to go now but I will call you again at nine thirty when your ride arrives at your hotel. Take care, ma'am."

"All right. See ya!" Amara said and ended the call.

That's done. What's next?

He checked his To-Do list and saw that there was nothing else to do except to go over everything again, and he would spend the next thirty minutes doing just that. Once everything was to his liking, Levi gathered the staff present to address them. While he was talking to them about how well they had done their jobs that morning, his boss, Ms. Preye, entered the church.

Apart from the click of her stilettos announcing her presence, her signature lavender scent danced around his nostrils. Ms. Preye, a young woman in her mid-thirties, was the fiercest-looking woman he had seen, but she was also one of the kindest people he knew. She took her job seriously and didn't tolerate mediocrity or disrespect. It was no wonder she had a successful event-planning business that catered to high-end clients in and out of the country. Being tall also helped her command respect as she could easily stand toe-to-toe with many of the men she worked with.

"Wow, Levi. This place looks amazing! You really outdid yourself *o*," Ms. Preye said as she looked around the church, nodding.

The other staff members greeted her, and she responded, waving at them. Levi excused himself from their meeting and went to meet her where she stood taking pictures of the church.

"Good morning, ma'am. Thank you," Levi said, smiling. He paused, not sure if complimenting his boss was stepping out of line. They weren't friends but they had a cordial relationship. So he just said, "And you look different too. But nice."

Since he started working for her, Levi had never seen her in anything other than denim pants and t-shirts. But today, her hair, which was a shoulder-length blonde bob, and makeup looked impeccably done. Levi wondered why she was dressed so elegantly, but it wasn't his place to ask.

"Thank you, Levi! I figured ditching my regular pants and t-shirt for a dress was a good idea," she said, beaming.

"It sure was," Levi said with a nod. "So, ma'am, everything is set. I have also called the drivers who are on their way to pick up the couple and bring them to church. Now, we just have to wait for the wedding ceremony."

"You have done well, Levi. I had no doubt handing this project over to you was the right thing to do," Ms. Preye said.

If you trust me to handle projects excellently, then why am I just getting my first one?!

"Thank you, ma'am. I appreciate it," Levi said with a smile.

"You're welcome."

"I should get back to my meeting with the guys."

"Right. And I'll be around taking pictures and videos if you need me," Ms. Preye said.

"Sure." Levi walked away.

He rounded off his meeting with his team and walked out to the veranda in front of the church to get some air. Levi mindlessly watched the rain fall, and a few wind-driven splashes landed on his shirt. The last time he intentionally watched rain falling was with his cousin, Joshua. This was six years ago, before his death.

They had gone for a walk around campus after a late-night study session when it began to rain without any warning. Both of them had taken shelter in the staff parking lot. When they had run out of things to laugh about, they just sat silently watching the rain, and he remembered Joshua saying, "Watching rain falling is so soothing for me. Do you feel the same way?"

Not anymore, Josh. Not anymore.

Levi shoved his hands into his pockets and stepped back a little. He had come outside to while away time and not drown in melancholy. He loved and missed his cousin deeply, but staying sad wasn't an option today. At least not until the reception was over.

"Young man, won't you catch a cold?" someone said, dragging him out of his thoughts.

"Oh," Levi said and turned to look at who just spoke to him— the elderly, heavyset usher he had given the wedding programs to earlier.

"I'm fine, ma. Thank you," he said, forcing a smile.

The woman nodded and went back inside, muttering about how the rain wanted to ruin such a beautiful day.

When Levi looked at his wristwatch, it was exactly 9:30 A.M. But before calling Amara, he called one of the couple's designated drivers to ask if they had gotten to the hotel. The driver affirmed and said he and his partner were waiting for the couple to come out. As soon as he got off the phone with the driver, he called Brandon to tell him his ride was waiting for him downstairs. Then he dialed Amara's number for the second time that morning.

"Hi, Ms. Amara. Your car is outside waiting to take you to church. Are you ready to go?" Levi asked.

"Uh, Levi," Amara said, and he heard the worry in her voice. Instead of asking her what was wrong, he waited for her to express herself.

"I'm not sure. I mean… I am ready, but I don't know if my maid of honor is."

"Huh? I'm not sure I understand, ma'am."

"My maid of honor hasn't arrived at the hotel. She should have gotten here thirty minutes ago, but I haven't seen her."

"Okay? Can you call her to confirm?" Levi asked.

"That's the problem. I have sent her a few text messages, but no response."

Levi worked his jaw, wondering who this maid of honor was and why she wanted to throw a spanner in his works. As much as he was angry at the incompetence of this anonymous lady, he couldn't let the bride know how he felt.

"Ms. Amara, today is all about you and Mr. Brandon. So, please take your mind off anything and everyone else. I want you to take a deep breath." He paused, waiting to hear her do as he said. When she exhaled, he continued. "Think about how excited you are to be getting married to the love of your life today. Focus on that positive energy and go meet your ride. I believe your maid of honor is already in church waiting."

Or maybe stuck in that traffic?

Levi frowned and shook his head, wondering where the crazy thought came from.

"The agreement was that she would come to the hotel first, and then we would go to the church together. But maybe she forgot and went straight to the church."

"Right! So, there's nothing to worry about."

"Whew! I feel relieved."

"Everything is fine; you'll have an amazing day." Levi nodded, convincing himself that he was right.

"Thanks, Levi."

"You're welcome, ma'am. See you later."

"Bye."

At the sound of the disconnection tone, Levi went back into the church to keep Ms. Preye updated on his call with the bride. As Levi waited for her to finish her phone call, he couldn't help but wonder how the bride's maid of honor could be so incompetent with such a crucial duty. In the past three years of working as an event coordinator, this was the first time he would experience a maid of honor not being present thirty minutes before the wedding procession.

Levi thought Ms. Preye was taking too long to finish her call, so he paced the floor to get her attention. His boss got the message and turned. When she saw the look on Levi's face, she said, "Desmond? Can I call you back later? Something urgent has come up."

There was a small pause on her end, after which she said, "Sure. Thanks." Then she ended the call.

"What's wrong, Levi?"

"Ma'am, the bride's maid of honor hasn't arrived yet."

Ms. Preye tilted her head and shrugged. This reaction was unlike her, and it took Levi by surprise. Knowing his boss, he had expected her to swing into action immediately, looking for a solution to this problem.

"Aren't you worried?" Levi asked. When she didn't respond, he continued. "Because I am. We have less than an hour before the wedding ceremony begins and the maid of honor still hasn't arrived at the bride's hotel. Can you imagine?"

Levi resumed pacing the floor, muttering to himself about how people who didn't take their duties seriously ended up ruining things for others. Different solutions to the problem raced through his mind, but nothing was practical. Ms. Preye sat on the pew closest to her and told Levi to stop pacing the floor and take a seat instead. Levi sat facing her, and she looked at him intently, which made him slightly uncomfortable. It also didn't help that he couldn't tell what she was thinking.

"Levi, you have done an excellent job coordinating this wedding, but you can't even see it because you keep obsessing over everything!" Ms. Preye sighed.

From experience, Levi knew she was frustrated. She leaned forward and brought her voice down to a whisper before saying, "I know how much you love your job, Levi. I have watched you bend over backward countless times just to make sure things are done well. Truth be told, Levi, your excellent spirit challenges me to do better. But oftentimes, you overdo things."

Levi's eyes widened and his mouth opened slightly. To say he was shocked would be an understatement, and he didn't even try to hide it.

"Yes, Levi," she said, leaning backward and resting her arm on the pew. "You've worked with me for three years. Don't you think I know you enough by now? Or at least your work ethic?" Ms. Preye asked.

This is a rhetorical question, right?

Levi stared at her blankly as he tried to make sense of all she said. Yet, what didn't make any sense to him was his boss thinking he was being obsessive by making sure things were done properly.

"Okay, now that you know the maid of honor isn't around, what can you do about it?" Ms. Preye asked, pulling him out of his thoughts. Levi shook his head mindlessly.

"Exactly my point! There is absolutely nothing you can do about it. So why are you constantly fretful about things you have no control over?" She paused then said, "Levi, to succeed in our line of business and more importantly, to protect your mental health, it is high time you learned how to let go of the things you can't control and do your best with what you can control."

Levi nodded, knowing his boss was right this time. He couldn't count how many times worrying over the quality of other people's work had caused him anxiety. Still, he wouldn't trade being in control of things and situations for anything.

"You know what?" Ms. Preye said.

Then she stood up and signaled for him to let her through. Levi also stood up and stepped out of the pew so she could come out.

"I think you need a break from whatever is going on here," she said, waving her meticulously manicured fingers around. "Go to the reception venue, get something to eat or drink, and just chill out."

"But, ma'am, I ..."

"No buts, Levi. I'll handle anything else that needs to be done here," his boss said, cutting him off. "Knowing you, I doubt there will be anything left for me to do here. Just go and relax."

Relaxing was the last thing on Levi's mind after being told to leave the church premises. Seeing couples exchanging their wedding vows was something he always looked forward to. In fact, it was his favorite part of weddings. Now, the opportunity to be present at the wedding ceremony he had so meticulously organized had been snatched away from him.

He tried to convince his boss that he would stop fussing over things, but she would have none of it. She told him he would have other opportunities to organize and attend future clients' wedding ceremonies, but this one was a no.

Levi replayed Ms. Preye's words to him as he jogged to his car in the rain.

Overreacting? Overdoing things? So getting kicked out is my reward for wanting to make sure things go as planned?

Levi thumped his head on the steering wheel and said, "I really wanted to be at this wedding, Lord."

He had no interest in hurrying out of the church, so he sat in his car and waited. The only sounds he could hear were the rain dropping on the roof of his car and his heartbeat. He thought of calling Ms. Amara to ask if her maid of honor had arrived, but he decided against it. There was no point calling the bride and making her worry about something he couldn't fix for her. Levi raised his head and looked outside the window. Just then, the bride and her groom arrived at the church in their separate vehicles. He watched Brandon come out of his vehicle to meet Chuks, waiting for him with an open umbrella. Before Brandon walked into the church, he blew his bride a kiss.

Levi caught himself smiling at the sweet gesture. Seeing this made being asked to leave the church not so terrible after all because he was sure he wouldn't have seen it had he been inside the church. Family members and guests of the couple began to arrive, and ushers with umbrellas filed out of the church to receive them. Once the groom had entered the church, the bride got out of the car and ducked under an umbrella the same elderly female usher he had spoken to earlier held for her. She was all smiles as she exchanged pleasantries with the usher who smiled back and patted her on the back.

Before they headed for the back entrance of the church, the bride lifted her dazzling white dress to reveal the white stilettos she wore. Levi thought he had never seen a more stunning bride than Amara, and it made his heart flutter with longing. For a brief moment, he pretended it was his wedding day and that a woman who looked just as beautiful was his bride. By the time his daydreaming ended, Amara and the usher had disappeared to the back entrance of the church. Levi started his car and the clock on his dashboard read 9:48 A.M.

"Just great!" he said.

Everything was pretty much set at the reception venue. He had made sure of it the previous day, which was why he couldn't imagine sitting down and doing nothing for the next three hours while they waited for the reception to start. He backed his car out of where he had parked it and headed for the gate, which doubled as both the entrance and exit of the church. This meant cars had to take turns to either enter or leave the church premises.

Levi was about to drive out when a car cut him off and sped into the church compound, parking very close to the front entrance door.

"For God's sake, why do people keep cutting me off this morning?" Levi said through clenched teeth as he stepped on his brakes abruptly and honked loudly.

He watched the car from his rearview mirror and saw a young woman sprint out of the back seat of the car he suspected was a taxi. The first thing that caught his eye was her bouncy, bright orange curly afro. Levi thought it was the prettiest hair he had ever seen. Though he couldn't see her face, he saw her sparkly shoes when she picked the hem of her dress off the floor. He wondered who she was and why she was in such a rush when the ceremony hadn't even started.

As he drove away, it baffled him how she could run in those high heels like they were nothing. But what did he know, when the only women he spent time with were his quinquagenarian mom and aunt?

Chapter Four

Vivienne

It was 9:50 A.M. when Vivienne hopped out of the cab and darted to the church entrance door. When she got closer, she saw that the door was locked and her stomach dropped. Her first thought was that the ceremony had started. But she didn't want to believe it as she was sure they wouldn't have started before the stipulated time. She looked around, trying to figure out what to do, but the only thing she saw was a group of girls dressed in the same maroon lace *aso ebi* and elaborate midnight blue *gele* trotting towards her. When they got to where she was, they stopped to shake off the rain drops on their clothes and fix their makeup.

As expected, they began to chatter away, and it made Vivienne so mad, she clenched her fist tightly because she couldn't think straight amid their noise. She paced the floor not, minding the weird stares she got from the girls. She looked at her phone and the time was 9:55 A.M.

I am done for!

Her pacing became more frantic and she felt hot all over despite the chilly air. One of the girls got on a phone call with someone and signaled for the rest to lower their voices, which they did.

"The back entrance door, yeah? 'Cause this one's locked," she said in an accent Vivienne couldn't quite place.

Oh, there's an entrance at the back?! Why didn't I think of this?!

Vivienne halted and paid more attention to the girl's conversation.

"Okay. We are headed your way," the girl said and hung up. Then she signaled again for her entourage to follow her.

Vivienne hurried past them to the back entrance of the church. The last thing she wanted was to be behind a bunch of chatterboxes when she was in a rush. She thought about how ridiculous it would sound if she told anyone that she could have made it to the hotel on time if it weren't for two *danfo* drivers who had hit each other and instead of finding a solution to their problem, left their buses in the middle of the road to hurl insults at each other, causing a traffic jam on the fastest route to the hotel.

An hour had passed before she left the traffic jam and continued her journey to the hotel. Since she was already late to the hotel, she decided that diverting to the church was wise, seeing that it was already 9:35 A.M. So she had changed her destination from the hotel to the church, without telling Amara so she wouldn't cause her to worry. What should have been a ten-minute trip from Tafawa Balewa Square to the hotel became a seventy-five-minute journey.

Vivienne slowed down as she reached the back entrance while peeking through the windows. She had never felt more relieved than she did seeing that they hadn't started the wedding ceremony. She took a deep breath and was about to enter the church when someone blocked her path.

"You can't enter this church dressed like that." An elderly heavy-set female usher stood, arms akimbo, before her.

"Ma, what do you mean by I can't go in there dressed like this?" Vivienne asked, wondering why the usher would speak to her this way when she had covered up with the veil.

The woman curled her lip upward and looked her up and down before settling her gaze on Vivienne's cleavage. Vivienne's brows arched as she tilted her head to the side. She knew what that look meant, and she was prepared to answer this woman appropriately.

Is this woman for real or can she really not see the veil on my neck? If she can't see it, I will show her.

Vivienne touched her neck, ready to yank off the veil and show it to the usher, but she couldn't feel it. Panic set in. Her fingers frantically ran through the width of her neck in search of the veil. But it wasn't there. She looked around her and her eyes scanned the path she had just walked. The veil wasn't on the floor either. Just then, the girls she had seen earlier arrived at the entrance and the usher allowed them in. Vivienne tried to squeeze her way in with them but the usher wouldn't have it.

"Young lady, step back!"

The usher's lip curled further, and she took a more defensive stance to block Vivienne's path as though she were a security detail guarding the president of Nigeria. Vivienne took a deep breath, knowing she had to calm down and reason with her if she wanted any chance at entering the church.

"Ma, please. I am the maid of honor and must be next to the bride. If you stop me from going inside, who will assist the bride, help her calm her nerves, and make sure she has a perfect day?"

"Young lady, I am not the one stopping you from going anywhere. Your indecent dressing is what is stopping you from performing your duties." The woman sounded more irritated, and Vivienne knew it wouldn't be wise to annoy her even more.

Vivienne checked her phone and saw that she had one minute to be next to the bride. She could also see the lock screen message notifications from Amara. The last one was ten minutes ago, and it was a simple but panicky, *"Where are you???"*

From where she was, Vivienne could see Amara with her bridal party at the beginning of the aisle. Amara kept turning back to look at the entrance door, and Vivienne could tell she was deeply worried because she, Amara's maid of honor, hadn't shown up. There was one trick that worked every time and never in her life did Vivienne think she would be the one using it. But desperate times called for desperate measures, and she was beyond desperate.

"Mommy, Mommy!" Vivienne said, poking the woman lightly on the arm. "Don't be angry, please," she said on slightly bent knees and her hands clasped together. "To be honest, I didn't know this dress would show any cleavage. I ordered it online and didn't know it wasn't my perfect size. I am sorry, Ma. Please, can you let me go in? I am already late."

The woman relaxed her shoulders, and her curled lip straightened. Vivienne did an internal happy dance because her trick had worked. How easy was it to get what you wanted if only you could massage a person's ego?

"Okay. You can go in, but you must drape a veil on your chest to cover your breasts."

"That's the problem, Ma. I had a veil hanging on my neck right from when I left my house. You may not believe me, but it's the truth. I must have left it in the cab I rushed out of when I got here."

"Hmm," the woman said.

"Yes, Ma. It's the truth."

The usher called a younger usher who had a maroon pashmina hanging on her neck.

"Lend her your scarf, please. I will make sure she returns it immediately after the wedding."

The girl nodded and handed the scarf to Vivienne. Then the elderly usher said, "In fact, hold on to her bag as collateral so she has a reason to return your scarf."

"Yes, Ma," the girl said and stretched her hand to collect Vivienne's bag.

Vivienne thought it was a good bargain, and she agreed to it. After all, she wouldn't be needing anything in the bag until after the church ceremony.

"Thank you, Ma," Vivienne said, adjusting the slightly damp pashmina on her shoulders in the most stylish way possible.

"Hurry up. The bride will soon walk down the aisle and you need to join her before she does."

"Okay, Ma," Vivienne said and hastened to where the bride was standing with her dad. She missed a step but quickly caught herself before she fell.

"Take it easy *o!*" the woman said. "*Children of nowadays* always want to do things their way. But when they get into trouble, we are the ones who come to their rescue," she muttered under her breath before cheerfully welcoming a group of attendees she said should have waited in their cars until they saw ushers with umbrellas.

Amara looked so relieved to see her, and it made Vivienne feel ashamed for showing up late. She apologized for coming late and said she would explain why later.

"All that matters is that you are here. At least nobody has to wonder why I am holding two bouquets."

Vivienne collected her bouquet from Amara with a smile. She also looked at the two bridesmaids, who she presumed were the cousins Oluchi had mentioned. They were busy snapping selfies that they didn't even notice when she joined them. She wondered how long they had been waiting to walk down the aisle if none of them could see that the lace from Amara's corset was undone at the bottom. From their attitude, it was glaring why Amara needed someone else to be her maid of honor.

Vivienne tied the lace, tucked it in neatly, and adjusted Amara's veil.

"Thanks, girl," Amara said and Vivienne nodded.

The organist started playing the "All Things Bright and Beautiful" wedding processional hymn. Amara and her dad exchanged loving looks. Then he asked, "Are you ready, baby girl?"

To which she answered, "Yes, Papa." Her voice was laced with so much emotion as she bounced on the balls of her feet.

Vivienne smiled wistfully as she fought back the tears that hung for dear life on the edge of her eyelids. For years she had longed for her father's affection to no avail. Seeing Amara's dad being so loving to his daughter tugged at her heart and exposed her hidden desire for her father's love. She wished they could go back to how they were before they fell out but the damage was too far gone and beyond redeemable. Vivienne shook the nostalgia away so she could focus on what was salvageable: her terrible start on this job.

Amara and her dad walked down the aisle to Brandon, who was wiping tears away while his best man patted him on the back. Vivienne couldn't understand the tears or happiness of marrying the love of one's life. She had never been in love and she didn't want to be. It was a waste of time and an inroad for someone else to cause avoidable hurt. All she wanted to be was successful, not in love.

Two hours later, the ceremony was over, and if Vivienne was being honest, it was beautiful too, even though she still thought the exchange of vows was quite cringey. The rain had also stopped falling, and the sun was already peeking through the clouds. What had been a gloomy, chilly morning was now a bright, sunny afternoon with cool fresh air. It was just the perfect weather. Right on cue, everyone gleefully filed out of the church, starting with Amara and Brandon. Vivienne lifted her face to the warmth of the sun, smiling as she spread her arms. For the first time that day, she felt alive, and it had everything to do with how things were finally looking up. The best man, who had been stealing glances at her throughout the ceremony, nudged her and said, "Beautiful day, huh?"

She wasn't in the mood for any small talk nor did she want him to think they would be the next couple walking down the aisle just because they were paired for the day to serve the bride and groom, if she might add. She put her arm down and told him to excuse her. While the couple snapped pictures, Vivienne snuck away to return the pashmina to the usher and collect her bag.

"Thank you very much for your scarf and for holding my bag," Vivienne said and checked that everything was still intact, including her new purse.

"You're welcome. But sorry about the damp scarf too. I had to *jump* buses to get here, and the rain caught up with me."

"Oh, that's fine. Without your scarf, I would have ruined the bride's day," Vivienne said.

The usher smiled and she smiled back.

"I have to go now. Thanks again." Vivienne turned to leave.

As she walked back to join the photo session, it hit her like a tonne of bricks that the reason the bus conductor had called her was to give her the veil she had left behind. The same one he had waved at her.

Chapter Five

Levi

Levi entered the driveway lined with lavender bushes and rose gardens. Beside it were the manicured lawns that housed sparkling fountains. It was still raining and he hoped it would stop before the guests arrived for the reception. He parked his car and looked out the window, taking in how gorgeously decorated the entrance of the hall was. There was a welcome roll-up banner with a picture of Amara and Brandon, dressed in Igbo royalty attire, at the bottom step of the veranda in front of the hall.

Beside it, on the extreme right of the entrance, was a huge flex banner of the couple dressed for a black tie event, decorated with midnight blue, off-white, and maroon flowers along with little gold decorative pieces. This flex banner was arranged strategically for the guests to take pictures outside the hall.

Levi hoped the bride wouldn't notice that the flowers they used for the church's decoration weren't maroon like the ones used in the reception venue. Or that even if she noticed, she wouldn't be too mad about it.

He picked up his iPad and checked the reception To-Do list. Like the wedding ceremony list, he had a lot to do and needed to get right into it. Before leaving his car, Levi mentally calculated how many steps it would take for him to reach the entrance door since it was quite a distance from where he parked. Moments like this made him berate himself for not keeping a standby umbrella in his car.

He got out of his car and jogged to the entrance, groaning each time splashes jumped out of a puddle he had stepped in. Thankfully, his pants were too dark to show any stains. When he got to the entrance, he stamped his feet on the doormat and walked inside.

The first thing Levi saw was a lush maroon carpet in the middle of the hall that ran from the door to the stage. The sight plastered a wide grin on his face as he remembered how stressful it had been finding someone to make a custom carpet for the hall. When he didn't find a supplier who could deliver within his time frame after a week of searching, he ordered directly from a factory in China. Thankfully, using Google translate had proved effective since the supplier got the exact color shade and dimensions.

Across the carpet on both sides were round guest tables, each surrounded by six gold chiavari chairs. The tables were covered with soft, midnight blue linens and adorned with centerpieces of maroon, off-white, and blue classic floral arrangements. There was fine china placed on gold charger plates carrying fancy food menus, with polished goldware and crystal glassware placed beside gold-colored damask napkins in front of each seat.

Levi scanned through the hall. It was the perfect union of classic and contemporary design. The high crystal chandeliers, accent lighting for the cake and head table, floor-to-ceiling arched windows, luxurious midnight blue silk drapes, polished white marble floors, and intricate corner pieces, all working in divine unison to create the most glamorous reception hall he had ever seen. Even though he had brainstormed and planned the entire decoration of the hall and other intricate details with the design team, he was still astounded by how stunning everything was in reality.

He took pictures and videos of everything, confident that Ms. Preye would be pleased. A part of him was itching to send them to her but he decided not to. He would wait for her to come down to the venue and see things for herself. This way, he could witness her honest first reaction. Levi swiped back to his To-Do list to tick things off it.

Guest table arrangement, check. Aisle runner, laid? Check. Head table arrangement?...

He looked up from his iPad to the head table to find the placecards at each seat. Still, he needed to be sure they were arranged exactly how the couple had intended for their guests to be seated.

Since he started working for Ms. Preye, this was the first wedding a couple had opted for a head table instead of the regular sweetheart table. Their reason was they wanted their bridal party and parents to sit with them at their table so they could all talk, get to know one another and have fun together instead of being so far away with the other guests.

Levi swiped his screen right to see the list the bride had sent to him. The couple was to be in the middle, and beside each of them was their best man and maid of honor, followed by an alternation of a groomsman and a bridesmaid, then ending with the moms on one end and the dads on the other end of the table. After moving a few placecards around, Levi was happy to move on to the next item on his list.

Stage…

He looked up from his iPad again to find only the head table on it. The cake table wasn't set nor was the cake anywhere to be found. At the extreme left of the stage was the DJ stand which was the only part of the stage, apart from the head table, that looked ready. Levi looked back at his list and added an asterisk beside the cake stand to remind him to find out from the decoration and setup team why their jobs were not done at past 10 A.M.

Then he called the DJ to confirm that she had the song arrangement in the right order. There were specific song requests by the couple that needed to be played at the right times.

"Mr. Levi, everything is in order. I will set up my equipment as soon as I get to the reception venue."

"Okay, see you soon." Levi hung up.

Even though he could cross the DJ off his list—since he had made sure she did a pre-wedding setup so they could fix any issues or buy whatever they needed before the wedding day—he didn't. Instead, he added an asterisk to her name too just to be double sure she didn't have any issue setting up her equipment when she arrived.

He let out a deep sigh as he glanced through the hall one more time. To say he was pleased with the work done so far would be an understatement. Everything was going so smoothly despite the heavy downpour, and he couldn't help but thank God for it. Just then he remembered Bayo. How silly was it that he had spent over thirty minutes in the hall but didn't remember to reach out to him?

"Bayo, how far? Where you dey?"

"Oga, Levi, I dey back dey show the caterer where him go take enter the hall," Bayo said.

In the background, Levi could hear Bayo shouting for someone to be careful so they don't trip and pour the food on the floor. His stomach took a deep dive at the thought of food pouring but he had to remind himself that nothing of the sort had happened yet. There were also other people barking out different orders. All of it sounded like music to Levi's ears because it meant one thing. Everyone was doing their jobs.

"Okay. I dey inside the hall, come meet me," Levi said.

"Ehen? You no go the wedding?"

"I no go," Levi said dryly.

"Okay. I dey come now," Bayo said and hung up.

Levi walked back to the entrance of the hall to wait for Bayo. The smell of smoky *jollof* rice hit his nostrils even before he saw Bayo, the caterer and his servers headed to the staging kitchen. There was no Nigerian party without smoky *jollof,* and the aroma made his stomach growl. It was a reminder that the last time he had eaten something was the afternoon before.

As staff of the wedding, they were entitled to a meal either before, during, or after the reception and it was at their discretion to eat whenever they wanted. Levi was tempted to go ask for a plate, but he didn't think eating now was best, especially since he still had a lot to do. Still, the thought of savoring even a bite made his stomach protest his decision.

Levi's eyes followed the chafing dishes to the staging kitchen, and he could taste the perfect blend of the distinctive smoky taste from the slightly charred rice at the bottom of the pot with the mildly sweet and tangy flavor from the tomato and red bell pepper sauce, the spiciness of the Scotch bonnet peppers, spices—thyme, bay leaves, curry powder, ginger, garlic—and seasoning. To crown it up, a well-seasoned grilled chicken and a cold drink.

"Boss!" Bayo's voice brought him back to reality.

Instead of going with the caterer and servers, Bayo asked a colleague to take them to the staging kitchen while he jogged to meet Levi.

"Oga, so true true you dey here?! I think say you been dey joke o," he said with a sheepish grin.

"Na Madam pursue me comot from church say make I come here. How far now? Why dem never arrange the cake table?" Levi asked.

"Na the baker say make we wait for her to come before dem do anything for the cake table."

"I no understand o," Levi laughed dryly and Bayo looked embarrassed.

"Wetin concern baker with decoration work? Na she wan decorate the cake table?" Levi asked.

"Oga, true, I tell her say na we dey design the cake table, but she no gree. She say she get design for mind wey she wan do. As I no wan argue with her, I just leave her," Bayo explained.

Levi couldn't believe his ears. Since when did a baker get to dictate wedding decor, especially when the bride had already picked out a design?

"*Which time you and her talk this one?*" Levi asked.

"*This morning when she come.*"

"*Wait o. The baker don come?*" Levi asked, clearly stunned, especially because he hadn't seen her since he got to the hall. So, where was she?

"*Yes, since. E no tey as I come, she sef drive come,*" Bayo said.

"*You know where she dey now?*" Levi asked.

"*Yes. She dey the kitchen.*"

"*Okay. Thank you. I dey go meet her now. But look for Anita and tell her say make dem decorate the cake table according to the design wey I give them now. That design go take time but I no care. They must finish in one hour. Tell them like that.*" Levi's voice was stern so Bayo knew he meant business.

"*Okay, sir,*" Bayo said, and turned to leave.

"*Bayo.*"

"*Sir?*"

"*Thank you. You really try for here,*" Levi said, meaning every word.

"*No wahala, boss. I dey here for you.*"

With that, he flashed a smile and jogged away. Levi couldn't believe the baker's audacity. Their plan for the wedding day was that she would get to the reception hall, set the cake on the already decorated cake table and add whatever finishing touches she needed to do. After which she would arrange the sweet treats in the stage kitchen for easy service during dessert. So he wondered what side of the bed she woke up on that made her decide to change things. He would certainly have a word with her to clear up whatever misconceptions she had.

Levi also planned to address this issue with his team during their appraisal meeting on Monday. He was their boss and they had no reason to flout his or Ms. Preye's instructions for any other person.

Before he left for the kitchen, he locked the front entrance door to prevent anyone from ruining the carpet with muddy shoes. The last thing he needed was to add another task to his already packed To-Do list.

He hurried to the kitchen and met it bustling with activity. The first thing he noticed were more servers wearing white button-down shirts and navy pants like him. When he told the caterer he needed his servers to be dressed smartly and in uniform, he didn't think they would dress like him. But it was his fault for not making proper plans for his outfit.

Levi found the baker arranging the sweet treats and asked her to excuse him for a minute.

"Hi. So my team informed me that you said they shouldn't decorate the cake table until you are ready. Is that correct?"

"Yes. It is," the baker replied.

Levi bit his lip and nodded. He could feel his temper flaring and he needed to be careful with his words. "Why's that if I may ask?"

The baker apologized, saying she got carried away with wanting everything to go perfectly with the cake she had baked and decorated.

"That's fair but the bride's choice is final. Even if you don't agree with it, there's nothing you can do about it. I'm not pleased with what you did because it has added more stress to the situation."

"Once again, I apologize, Mr. Levi. I'll do my best to assist your team to set up the cake table just the way the bride wants it."

"It's fine and you don't have to worry about helping my staff. They've got it covered. Just set up the cake and fireworks in an hour."

"Okay. Thanks."

Levi nodded and turned to leave. He was glad he had been able to pass his message across firmly yet without sounding harsh. He went to meet the caterer, who was a first-time vendor of their company. He complimented the aroma of his food and asked him if the food for his team had been set aside. The caterer said he had kept the food himself and that Levi was welcome to grab a bite if he wanted. The offer was even more tempting now that the food was within his reach, but he still had a few things to do. He politely declined the offer and said he would come to the kitchen when he was ready to eat.

Then he went over to the wedding bar to confirm with the vendor that everything was set and ready to go. She offered Levi a mojito, but he declined by saying he didn't drink alcohol. Then she sweetly suggested he took a mocktail instead. Despite not having ample experience with women, if there was one thing Levi knew, it was when a woman flirted with him. He told her the mocktail would have to wait.

"You know where to find me when you're ready," she said, tucking her hair behind her ear.

Levi thanked her and turned away from her stiffly. He could imagine Josh telling him to maintain his steeze and composure if he were alive. Josh never had any problems flirting with girls which was one of the reasons he was popular in school. While for him, his relationship with girls was always a means for them to get close to his cousin. None of them ever liked him for who he was. Not even the church girls.

In spite of this, he still believed there was someone out there for him. Someone who would appreciate his love for God and value his commitment to wanting true love. Levi didn't know when or where he would find the love of his life because so far, working in the most-likely place where he could find *the one* was where he found it even more difficult to connect with anyone. But one thing was for sure. When he found her, he would know.

Chapter Six

Vivienne

When they got to the reception venue, a few cars were already packed with guests loitering around or taking pictures by the flex banner at the entrance. Vivienne wondered why people had such a terrible habit of skipping the church wedding ceremony to attend just the reception. The reason was simple. They cared more for the free food, drinks, and party favors than the couple.

It irritated her so much and she wished couples would stop including their reception venue on their wedding invitation cards. How wonderful would it be for a couple to have only people who loved them enough to be in church with them at their reception? Thankfully, she wouldn't ever be getting married, so she had nothing to worry about.

Vivienne took in her surroundings and she was left absolutely speechless. She had been to so many weddings, but none came close to what she saw. The decorations outside the hall screamed of excellence, and it made her wonder what inside the hall would look like if outside already looked so stunning.

During the ten-minute ride with the newlyweds from the church, the best man, whose name she later got to know was Connor, kept trying to engage her in small talk about his family's ranch in Pine Bluffs, Wyoming, and how his dad was the mayor of their town. The last thing she wanted was to give this foreigner the impression that she was interested in him. For all she cared, his father could be the president of the United States and she still wouldn't be interested in him.

While they waited in the car for the wedding coordinator to come get them, Vivienne told Amara that she wanted to get a few pictures and videos of the hall's entrance. Amara said it wasn't necessary, but Vivienne had insisted.

"Okay. But don't go too far. We are supposed to take pictures in the hall when the wedding coordinator comes to get us," Amara said.

Vivienne nodded. "I'll be quick."

When she got to the entrance of the hall, she asked the guests who were in her view to give her a minute to film the venue and take some pictures. They did as she asked without any questions asked.

Vivienne went on to film the entrance gate down to the driveway and flowerbeds, the lawn, and the fountains. She had even asked the driver to reverse and drive into the premises again so she could film it. He also obliged her without asking any questions, and neither Amara nor Brandon objected to her request. Vivienne was so pleased with the shots she had taken that she did an internal happy dance.

As she walked back to the car, a red Range Rover Sport sped into the compound. It caught everyone's attention, and she was also curious to see who was behind the wheels. A woman, looking and smelling like money, alighted the car and walked past her toward the back of the hall. Her hair bounced on her shoulders as she strutted elegantly and she spoke to someone on the phone, asking if the hall was ready for the couple to be photographed in it.

The wedding planner.

Vivienne couldn't help but watch her until she disappeared into the hall. She was in awe of this woman and how she carried herself. It wasn't hard for Vivienne to tell if someone was rich. She knew what to look for, and this woman ticked all her boxes. For her to be young, yet rich and successful, was more motivation for Vivienne to be successful. But *how*, was a story for another day. She had no job or business. In summary, she was as broke as a joke. Maybe her father was right. Maybe, after all, she was a waste.

Vivienne was so lost in her thoughts that she didn't realize Connor was talking to her until he tapped her lightly on her shoulder and asked if she was okay. She said she had a slight headache and needed to rest a bit. Then he asked if he could get her anything and she said he didn't have to. His concern for her made her feel bad for being unreceptive toward him the whole day. Then she noticed that the guests hanging around the entrance of the hall were filing into the lobby.

Shortly, the well-dressed woman she had seen earlier tapped on their car window and the driver wound it down.

"Hi, Mr. and Mrs. Langford, it's nice to meet you again," the woman said with such a brilliant smile and perfectly white teeth. She told them how amazing they both looked before reintroducing herself as Preye, the owner of the event planning company. The Langfords said they remember her, and the groom made a joke about his bank accounts remembering her even more, and they all laughed.

Even her voice sounds rich.

"Levi, who's been coordinating the logistics of your wedding and is supposed to take you in for your pictures, is busy right now entertaining your guests and keeping them occupied so you can be photographed in peace. This means I'll be in charge of your well-being for now. Please come with me to the hall. The videography and photography teams as well as your glam team are already there."

Vivienne couldn't help but steal glances at her while she talked to the newlyweds. A crazy idea crossed her mind about asking this woman for a job. She battled against that thought in her mind but eventually decided that it wouldn't hurt to try. Besides, getting a no was the worst that could happen. But then, what role would she be applying for, especially with a university degree in chemistry education and zero experience in the hospitality industry? Her father was right. She should have studied something else.

"Okay, guys. Let's go!" Ms. Preye said and opened the door for them.

Vivienne shook her head to clear away the negative energy fogging her mind. She lifted Amara's gown and veil as high as she could as they followed the wedding planner. Even though it had stopped raining, there were still puddles that could ruin her dress. When they got inside the hall, Vivienne was gobsmacked by how ethereal the place looked. She heard a few gasps and she wasn't sure if they had come from her or someone else. Vivienne looked at Ms. Preye, admiring how meticulous she was. She also thought whoever decorated the hall understood the brief.

Amara raved about how breathtaking the hall was. She talked about the cake, their attention to details with the decor and everything else she could see. Ms. Preye said she was glad Amara loved their work but that all the credit goes to Levi. Amara agreed and said that he was pleasant to work with.

This Levi must be good at his job.

While the glam team got Amara and Brandon ready for their photoshoot, Vivienne filmed them. She was thankful she had a phone with excellent camera quality and enough memory space. Otherwise, how else would she have been able to film this wedding? She was also thankful for the sacrifices she made back in school just so she could afford to buy the phone. Her motivation for buying the phone was simply to prove to her father that she didn't need him to get whatever she wanted. All those sleepless nights of doing assignments for her coursemates felt worth it the day she held the phone pack.

Till date, it made her ecstatic whenever she remembered how shocked and livid her father had been when he found out from her mother that she had bought the phone herself. She also remembered her mother telling him that if he had bought the phone for her when she begged him to, he wouldn't have had to worry about the means by which their daughter was able to afford buying the phone.

Soon, the first session of the shoot was over and they had to change into their reception outfits for the second photo session. Before Ms. Preye led the Langfords and their glam team to the bridal suite, Vivienne asked if she was needed, and Amara said she wasn't. So, she saw it as an opportunity to also take pictures of herself. Vivienne angled her phone for some selfies and while they came out great, she wasn't satisfied. She needed a full picture of herself. The photographers and videographers were busy and the only other person in the hall with her was Connor.

This rejected stone has become my only option.

"Hey, Connor, do you want me to take pictures of you?"

He spun around with his hand in mid-air. There was no denying the surprise on his face, and Vivienne couldn't blame him. He hesitated a bit before saying, "Sure! I need to show my folks something other than selfies."

When he gave her his phone, Vivienne raised a brow and nodded. It was the latest version of the iPhone.

Rich kid.

Vivienne asked him to pose in different styles as she clicked away. If she was being honest, Connor looked good. Not that she cared though. When she was done, she showed him the pictures, and he was thrilled.

"You're such a natural at taking pictures," Connor said, looking impressed. "Nobody has ever made me look this good in a picture before."

Vivienne laughed. "The pictures look great because you are a good model."

Connor chuckled and said, "I don't think so but I'll take your word for it. Do you want me to take pictures of you too?"

"Absolutely!"

Vivienne asked him for a few minutes to tidy up her hair which was slightly damp from when she got out of the car to film videos and snap pictures of the entrance. She no longer wanted to wear her hair in an afro so she settled for a messy bun and two tendrils in front. Thankfully, her hair was long enough to serve as a hair tie. She used her front camera as a mirror to style her hair, and when she was done, she gave Connor her phone.

Given the way she had treated Connor earlier, she knew the best way to ask him for a favor was to *offer* him a favor. That way, when she asked for his help, he would feel obligated to help because she had first done him a favor. It was manipulative, but it always worked, and in this case, she didn't even get to ask.

When she got her phone back from Connor, her smile turned into a smirk that only grew wider as she swiped to see each picture.

Hope these pictures don't disappoint you, Daddy dearest.

"I'm guessing you like them?" Connor asked.

"I love them, Connor. Thanks."

"You're welcome…" Connor continued to hold her gaze with a smile, then she realized he wanted to know her name.

"Vivienne."

"You have a beautiful name."

Vivienne smiled but didn't say anything else. She didn't like where this conversation was going, and she needed to get out of it fast.

"Connor, can we talk later? I have to film this hall before the Langfords get back for their second photo session."

"Uh, sure! But can I get a selfie with you first?"

Selfie ke? Why?

Although her internal alarms were blaring, she managed to stutter, "Yeah. Um, yes!"

Once Connor was done taking the selfies, Vivienne excused herself and got to work. She filmed different angles of everything in the hall. From the cake to the head table and its decorations, and down to the guest tables. Everything screamed luxury and wealth. It made Vivienne vow in her heart that she wouldn't remain the poor, struggling, and unloved girl that she was. She would work hard to make something of her life so that she can command the respect she deserves from everyone, including her father. Especially her father.

When Ms. Preye, the Langfords, and their glam team walked back into the hall, the Langfords had changed into their reception outfits, and even the bride's lipstick was a different color. They both looked so regal in their midnight blue outfits. The color of the dress against Amara's fair skin coupled with her popping red lips and sharp pixie cut made her look fierce and stunning. Vivienne caught herself smiling as she watched Amara and Brandon act lovey-dovey during their photoshoot. It reminded her of the days her dad would come home early, sneak behind her mom, and steal kisses from her when he thought she and Fisayo weren't looking.

At the end of the shoot, the photography and videography teams adjusted their equipment to make room for the reception. The DJ, a young eccentric-looking woman, was allowed into the hall to play some music to set the tone for the reception while the Langfords and their glam team went to the bridal suite to change back into their wedding dress and tux.

Ms. Preye called Levi again and told him to get ready to usher the guests in the lobby into the hall in ten minutes. She also told him to inform the ushers at the gate to send the guests to the hall instead of the lobby once the ten minutes were up.

Vivienne watched her speak to more people on the phone, asking if they had done what she'd asked of them or where they were with their tasks. Ms. Preye's tone was matter-of-fact, yet polite, and Vivienne wondered what it would be like working for such a woman.

I should just go ahead and ask her for a job now that we're both here. Right?

Ms. Preye ended her phone call and turned to Vivienne.

"Hi, maid of honor."

"Vivienne. My name's Vivienne." She smiled, putting out her hand for a handshake.

Time to put charming Vivienne to work.

"Right," Ms. Preye smiled and shook Vivienne's hand. "Vivienne, can I ask you for a favor?"

Vivienne was stunned but honored that Ms. Preye would ask her for a favor. Maybe this was even a good thing seeing that asking the woman for a job had already crossed her mind a few times since she got here.

"Yeah, sure! I'm happy to help," she said in a voice that sounded too high-pitched for her liking.

"Great! So, the Langfords will be out in a few minutes. When they get here, I want you to take them back to their car and wait with them there. But as soon as you hear the MC opening the ceremony, please gather the bridesmaids and groomsmen to the lobby." She paused, looking at Vivienne closely to be sure she understood everything she had said so far.

Vivienne nodded for her to go on and she continued.

"A few minutes before the bridal party will be asked to dance in, I'll come get you guys. That's all."

"Okay. It's fine. I can do this."

"Yeah?"

"Yeah! It's not a big deal." Vivienne shrugged.

"Uh, it is actually. But I think you can do this."

Vivienne nodded.

"Thanks a lot, Vivienne," Ms. Preye said and walked away.

The favor Ms. Preye had asked of her wasn't even a difficult one. Still, she was determined not to let her down. After all, this might just be her only shot at impressing the big boss enough to get hired.

Chapter Seven

Levi

The reception started at exactly 1:30 P.M. as scheduled. Levi was thankful he had been able to keep the guests entertained for an hour and a half. Some of them had even asked why they couldn't wait in the hall for the reception to start, and Levi said the hall wasn't ready for guests yet. He had encouraged them to enjoy some drinks and finger food while they waited.

Now, all the guests who had arrived earlier were seated in the hall and more were arriving by the minute. Levi wasn't worried about the seats not being enough or the guests not having enough to eat or drink because the attendance was strictly by invitation and anyone without a gate pass wasn't allowed in.

The MC asked a relative of the bride to lead the opening prayer, after which the parents of the bride and groom danced in with their wellwishers. Once the parents were seated at the head table, he announced that it was time for the bridal party to dance in. This was one of the parts Levi loved about wedding receptions. For someone who couldn't dance to save his life, he loved watching other people dance. This way he could live vicariously through them. He would often choreograph killer moves in his head that never translated the way he had imagined them. Levi chuckled, remembering how Josh used to mock him for not knowing how to dance.

"Guy, you are as stiff as dry concrete. Your parents know how to dance but you can't even dance to save your life. Are you sure you were not adopted?" he would say.

The bridal party was an equal number of four bridesmaids to four groomsmen. The first pair of bridesmaids and groomsmen danced into the hall to a trending TikTok sound. Many of the guests brought out their phones to film them, and it was nothing unusual to Levi. He just had to make sure none of them obstructed the videographers or photographers from doing their jobs. After the last pair of bridesmaids and groomsmen danced in, it was the maid of honor and best man's turn. The maid of honor also had bright orange hair like the lady he had seen earlier, but instead of a bouncy afro, hers was pulled up into a messy bun.

The DJ switched songs to the popular "Olufunmi" by Style Plus and the crowd went wild. That same song was Josh's favorite in their first year in university, and just like yesterday, he could remember his cousin singing it in the greatest off-key tone he'd ever heard. Levi's eyes watered and his chest tightened at the memory. He instinctively clutched his crucifix pendant as he took deep breaths.

Breathe. Just breathe.

He focused his teary vision back on the dancing duo. If he were alone, God knows he would have cried freely, but he wasn't. The last thing he needed was for someone to notice him crying on a job. He wiped his eyes with the back of his hands and blinked a few times. His vision was now clear but his heart still ached. The dancing pair looked stunning, especially the maid of honor. She was also such a good dancer it made it difficult for him to take his eyes off her. She sang along and danced while the best man tried his hardest to keep up with her dancing. Levi couldn't blame him. They were both cut from the same two-left-feet cloth.

As they got to the stage, the maid of honor lifted her dress to climb it, and Levi saw her shoes. They were the exact ones he had seen earlier. What were the odds that she would have the same color of hair and shoes as the lady who had dashed out of the car that blocked him? Unless…

Like puzzle pieces fitting together, he remembered how Cinderella had dashed out of the car toward the church. Although he hadn't seen her face, he was quite sure she had a blue dress on. Furthermore, the bride's maid of honor had been running late, and up until he was asked to leave the church, she hadn't arrived. So, it all made sense that Little Miss Gorgeous over there was the one who had destroyed his chances of witnessing the wedding ceremony of the first wedding he ever planned.

"Wow!" Levi snorted and left the hall. He didn't even have the time to process how he felt because he had a job to do, and he wouldn't give this woman any more opportunities to ruin his hard work.

"Ladies and gentlemen," the MC said, stretching each word and making it longer than their combined six syllables. "The reason we are gathered here today… The moment we have all been waiting for is finally here!"

Then he introduced the newlyweds with enthusiasm, which made the guests anticipate their arrival even more. By this time, all the guests had their eyes on the entrance door, which Levi had shut. He asked everyone to honor them by standing up, and the DJ started playing the upbeat "Uptown Funk" by Mark Ronson featuring Bruno Mars. Guests who knew the song whooped as the intro beat blasted through the speakers.

"Introducing, for the first time in this hall, Mr. and Mrs. Brandon Langford!" the MC said, and the doors flung wide open to reveal the Langfords wearing the coolest party glasses Levi had ever seen. They stood facing each other, and as soon as the first lyric of the song started, the couple started their choreography. The guests went wild with cheering, whooping, clapping, and whistling.

For a minute, Levi forgot he was mad at the maid of honor as he reveled in the sight of the happy couple. He smiled wistfully while silently praying that someday he would get to experience such happiness from finding *his* person. The fireworks were now lit and the slight fog in the air made the hall look dreamy. Levi couldn't be happier with how beautifully everything had turned out. But when he saw the maid of honor again, his smile vanished. She looked so diligent helping the bride fluff out her train, when she wasn't filming the couple.

If she had been just as diligent with her time this morning, I wouldn't have ranted to Ms. Preye about her tardiness, and I wouldn't have been kicked out of the wedding ceremony.

Levi rolled his eyes and looked away. He knew he had to let go of his anger, but it was an internal battle with his conscience as he tried to justify it. He also didn't want to acknowledge that he was angry so he called it *a little* frustration.

"Oga, this wedding sweet o," Bayo said behind him, making Levi almost jump out of his skin.

"Bayo, why you appear for my back like ghost? See how you make me fear."

Bayo chuckled and said, *"No vex."*

Then he continued talking about how opulent the wedding was. Levi was fed up with hearing the same thing from Bayo every other weekend. Their company worked with HNIs, and by now, he expected Bayo to be used to seeing lavishly funded events and wealthy guests.

"Bayo, you don chop?" Levi asked, cutting him off.

"No, sir. Na wetin make me come find you sef."

Levi chuckled. He believed Bayo wasn't hungry enough because if he was, he would have gone straight to asking about his meal instead of talking about their clients.

"Okay. Make you, Chuks, and one other person go meet the caterer for kitchen. Tell am to give una food. Sharp sharp o! Make una no go there dey gist. Work still dey," Levi said.

"Yes, sir. But you nko? When you go chop?"

"No worry about me, Bayo. I go chop later. I dey busy now."

"But Oga Levi, work no dey now. Come chop, your bele don dey ring since morning."

Levi's eyes widened. He didn't think any other person heard his rumbling stomach. However, Bayo telling him that wasn't the case made him wonder how many others had heard it too. Still, he was appreciative of Bayo for always looking out for him.

Levi laughed. *"I no know say my bele been loud o. But no worry, I go chop during the after-party."*

Bayo began to protest Levi's decision, saying how far away the after-party was and that Levi would have probably fainted by then.

"Bayo!"

Levi knew if he didn't stop Bayo, they would stay there going back and forth, wasting precious time.

"Oya, no vex. I dey go now."

"Once una three chop finish, tell the others to go chop. Give dem time if not dem go stay that kitchen dey gist till night."

"Na true," Bayo laughed. Then he left for the kitchen.

The rest of the reception went on smoothly. Levi would occasionally find the maid of honor filming the reception when she could. At first he thought it was a one-time thing during the couple's intro dance. But when he saw her filming the father-daughter dance and cake cutting session, he knew it wasn't. She obviously loved filming.

Soon, it was time for the bride to throw her bouquet. All the bridesmaids and single ladies in the hall rushed to the front, except the maid of honor. She stood at a corner, filming the whole thing, and Levi found it strange. Levi watched the best man talk to her, but she shook her head and pointed to her phone. He said something to her and she laughed. Then he walked away.

The bride looked at the small crowd of excited ladies in front of her, but her eyes kept searching for someone. Levi wondered who it was until he saw her eyes light up. The bride waved her maid of honor over to join the women in front, but she declined, pointing to her phone again. This was the first time he would see a woman so uninterested in catching the bride's bouquet.

Despite being annoyed at her, Levi watched the maid of honor as she filmed. He thought she was beautiful and the color of her hair matched her skin tone and even made it glow. Her form-fitting dress was also just the perfect color shade and style for her petite frame. He wasn't one to be moved by a woman's beauty, but there was something different about her. He concluded that he was just intrigued by her, nothing more.

A few events later and it was time for the couple to give their vote of thanks. They thanked everyone for coming to celebrate with them and for making their day special. They also thanked his boss for a job well done and then wished their guests safe travels back home. The reception came to an end, and it was time for the after-party. Elderly guests and parents with kids began to leave.

Levi signaled for Chuks to come. He first asked if he had eaten, and Chuks said that he had. Then Levi told him to round up the others so they could start packing up the things that were no longer in use into the company van.

"Great work, Levi. Everything looked and went amazingly well," Ms. Preye said.

"Oh!" Levi turned sharply to his boss. "Thank you, ma'am," he said, smiling broadly.

It had been satisfying seeing her reaction to the decor when she entered the hall for the first time earlier that day. He had even asked Chuks to help him film her reaction. That video would be his morale booster whenever he had doubts about his abilities.

"See you at the office on Monday. I have somewhere to be now."

Is it just me or is that excitement I hear in Ms. Preye's voice?

"All right, ma'am. Drive safe."

"You too, Levi. Take care of yourself." She paused and looked him in the eye. "I mean it."

Levi playfully saluted her and said, "Yes, ma'am!" She laughed and walked away.

The DJ had already charged up the atmosphere with Afrobeat party bangers. Jackets were strewn carelessly across chairs, ladies's shoes were littered on the stage, and the guests wore their LED shutter glasses and held light-up foam sticks. Levi watched as people paired up in twos, grabbing whoever caught their eye.

While a few of them danced decently with their partners, the others dirty danced with each other. This was the aspect of weddings Levi didn't like. He had often tried to comprehend how weddings could go from cute and sweet to vulgar because of after-parties. Each time, he came to the conclusion that the type of songs played at after-parties had everything to do with the lewd behavior displayed there. If he didn't have a job to finish, he would have left this place already.

Watching the dancing crowd made Levi reaffirm that an after-party was definitely something he wouldn't have at his wedding. But if his bride wanted it, then they would play only gospel Afrobeat to keep the atmosphere clean.

Bride.

Levi chuckled at how he was already thinking of his wedding when he didn't even have a love interest. Just then, an odd scenario in the middle of the dancing crowd caught his eye. It was the maid of honor heading to the bar. The way she had danced at the reception was enough to convince Levi that her reason for escaping the dancefloor wasn't because she didn't know how to dance. There was just something about this mysterious woman that made her avoid activities that involved many people.

First, it was the tossing of the bridal bouquet and now dancing with others. He couldn't blame her though—even he wouldn't dance with people this way. Before she could reach the bar, the best man caught up with her. The top two buttons of his shirt were undone, his LED shutter glasses were lopsided, and he was sweating profusely with his shirt sticking to his back. He took a staggering step toward her and the drink in his hand splashed out of the cup.

The maid of honor's first reaction was to take a step back, but the man lurched forward again. He said something to her and she put out her hand to stop him while shaking her head at the same time. The man grabbed her hand as she turned to leave, and she yanked it away. She waggled her right index finger in front of him and walked away to the bar, leaving the drunk man looking confused.

A young woman who looked like she had been waiting for the right opportunity to be with the best man leaped in immediately. Levi couldn't hear their conversation but he certainly saw the woman rub the drunk best man's open chest, which made him shift his attention from the maid of honor to the woman in his arms. He also had a sheepish grin on his face as she led him back to the dancefloor.

Levi was done watching the drama. What he needed to do was get his food from the kitchen before the caterer left. He jogged to the kitchen and found the caterer packing up the last of his things. The man said he was about leaving and that if Levi had been even a minute late, he would have missed him. He gave Levi his food as a takeout, and Levi thanked him. Once the kitchen had cleared out, Levi sat on a chair. He contemplated eating now or taking the food home to eat where he would be relaxed. He decided taking it home was the best. So, he went to his car and kept the food in the front passenger seat.

Before going back into the hall, Levi stayed outside to receive some fresh air. It was a welcome change from the arid smell of perfumes, sweat, and alcohol. The couple still had about an hour left on their reservation for the hall. Which consequently meant an hour left of partying. Levi sent a text to the DJ asking her to announce that the party would be ending in an hour. That way people wouldn't think it was an all-nighter. He leaned on his car and waited to hear the announcement before going in. As he walked back into the hall, Levi braced himself mentally to power through this remaining one-hour shift.

"Once this after-party ends, I'll organize a ride for the Langford's back to their hotel. Then I can go home and rest," he said under his breath.

Levi was parched and needed to drink something urgently. His plan was to head straight for the bar, but thankfully, a waiter holding a tray of drinks walked past him. Levi took the only glass of water on the tray and gulped it. The cold water in his throat felt like pouring water on dry, hot ground. By the time he stopped drinking, his glass was half-empty and he needed another one. More so, the only place with a seat in the entire hall was the bar so he might as well go sit down there and enjoy his water.

Levi's eyes were so fixed on the bar as he walked that he didn't see when someone turned and bumped into him. It was the cold drink running from his chest down to his stomach that stopped him in his tracks. He expected whoever it was to have offered an apology by now for bumping into him and spilling his drink on him. That was the normal sensible thing to do. But apparently, nothing was normal with this person because they didn't utter a word, much more an apology.

Just great!

He took a step back to see who the offender was. It was *the* mysterious maid of honor, who had cost him his attendance at the wedding ceremony. Levi's nostrils flared and the *little frustration* he thought was out the door came rushing back.

Chapter Eight

Vivienne

Vivienne sat by the bar watching people grind on each other as she sipped her cocktail. The after-party had turned to a full-blown night club and both the DJ and bar were the ones to blame. She had been to a couple of wedding after-parties, but none was like this. She watched in shock as the sweet-looking Amara got her freak on. Though she already had clips from the after-party, she opened her camera to film what she saw for Oluchi. She sent the clip to Oluchi on WhatsApp and added, *"See your cousin,"* with the fire emoji attached.

At least Amara and Brandon were pleasant to watch, but she couldn't say the same about Connor, who was sweating and dancing like a pig with the girl he left with at the bar. Vivienne rolled her eyes and took another sip of her drink. She couldn't care less about what Connor did and whoever he did whatever with as long as he stayed far away from her. Not that she had been interested in him or anything, but it was funny how he quickly went with the strange woman he had never met simply because she had refused to dance with him.

This was one of the reasons she agreed with the *men-will-stain-your-white* propaganda. When it came to relationships, she knew men would always put their needs first, not minding who got screwed over. She had seen this happen with her parents countless times and it was enough conviction for her to stay away from love or even marriage. After all, the easiest way to succeed in life was to learn from other people's mistakes. Her mother's mistakes were enough lessons for her.

Vivienne looked around, hoping to catch Ms. Preye, but she was nowhere in sight. She had even asked one of her staff members if he knew where she was, and he said he hadn't seen her in a while. She had been hoping to catch her at an opportune time and pitch herself for a job. But each time she had seen her during the reception, the woman was either busy doing something or talking to someone. So, she had decided that she would look for her once the reception was over, but maybe she was already too late.

The last time Vivienne had seen Ms. Preye was when she was talking to a man in a white button-down shirt and navy blue pants. She hadn't seen his face because he had his back to her, so she assumed he was one of the waiters. That was probably when she should have approached Ms. Preye, but she couldn't because that was also when Amara had her in a tight embrace, thanking her for the picture frame she had gotten for them.

Vivienne finished her drink and told the bartender to keep another glass of piña colada for her, saying she would be back. She also left her gift bag on her seat to begin her mission of finding Ms. Preye. When she didn't find her anywhere in the hall, she checked the bridal suite and kitchen, but both places were empty. In fact, only a handful of her staff members were still around, and they were busy moving their things to their company van.

Disappointed, she walked back into the hall to get her final glass of piña colada for the evening before heading home. It was already getting late and she had no intention of being outside her home by 8 P.M. As she walked on the aisle runner, she remembered feeling sorry for Connor during their entry dance. The man had tried his best to keep up with her dancing but he just couldn't, not especially when the DJ played all her favorite songs. If she had her way, she would have carried on dancing without him as it was one of the few things that made her happy. But she had to be considerate since they were a pair.

Vivienne got back to her seat and the bartender gave her a glass of mojito saying there was no more piña colada and that he had saved the very last glass of cocktail for her. Vivienne thanked him with a smile and tipped him a thousand naira. She chuckled, wondering if the bartender thought she was rich with his repeated, "Thank you, ma'am."

If only he knew how that money came to be.

She mentally calculated how much she should have left in her purse, including what was now nineteen thousand from the twenty thousand naira she had won earlier. The universe had certainly made up for her crappy morning because she had won both the twenty thousand naira cash prize for the bridal party dance off and the scavenger hunt prize of a free spa session. The MC even joked that she shouldn't participate in any more games so she wouldn't take all the prizes home.

Vivienne had such a nice time at the reception that she forgot she hadn't felt up to attending the wedding when she woke up that morning. Not excluding the ordeal she had passed through to make it down to the church just in time for the wedding. But she was glad she'd powered through all the setbacks to be present for both Oluchi and Amara. The time was already 6:45 P.M. She needed to finish her drink quickly so she could book a cab home before it got too late and the price doubled.

Ten more minutes and I'll be out of here.

She smiled, happy that she didn't have to board public transport to TBS or Obalende to save cost. All thanks to her win, she would ride straight home in a cab no matter the cost. Vivienne opened her photo gallery and scrolled through all the clips she had filmed that day. Her finger paused on Amara and her dad's father-daughter dance clip, and she played it without the audio.

Even though the video played without sound, Vivienne remembered how she had felt when filming the duo. Her dad's conversation with her mom resurfaced in her head and it filled her mouth with bile. She took a sip of her mojito to wash off the bitter taste on her tongue, but the taste was still there. Vivienne swiped left, and the next clip was the one from the bridal bouquet tossing. She played it and it showed Connor asking why she wasn't in line to catch the bride's bouquet. She had told him she would rather stand aside filming than to get eaten alive by a bunch of desperate women. To which he replied that if the groom decided to throw anything to the men, he would be the first one in line. She shook her head at the irony and laughed quietly. She stopped scrolling when the volume of the music went low.

Vivienne looked up from her phone to where the DJ was to see what was happening. The DJ picked up her microphone and said, "Okay, ladies and gentlemen, I'm sure y'all having a nice time, right?"

The guests echoed, "Yeah!" with whistling and hooting following.

"All right! This party will be shutting down in an hour so make the most of the time you have left," she added.

Vivienne looked at her phone.

7:00 P.M.

"My cue to leave," she said.

She sucked hard on the straw, pulling up a large gulp in an attempt to finish the drink but she couldn't. The cocktail was just too sweet. She felt bad she was wasting almost half a glass, but there was nothing she could do about it. Vivienne thanked the bartender and grabbed her purse. She also needed to let Amara know that she was leaving already.

She stood up, picked the hem of her dress and tucked it between her left elbow and hip. She hadn't walked more than a few steps to where the newlyweds were dancing when the bartender called her. He pointed at her gift bag on the counter and her free hand flew to her mouth. There wasn't anything important in the bag except for her slippers, which she would change into when she got into the cab. She took the bag and walked backwards, thanking the bartender.

When she turned, nothing could prepare her for what followed. Vivienne felt the hit from a man's woodsy oriental cologne before the toned chest he had bumped into her with. The drink in his hand splashed on her chest and dripped into her brassiere. The cold from the drink sent her into instant shock mode. Her eyes were wide open, and she just stared at his chest blankly. The only thing her brain could process amid the chaos was the wet dangling crucifix pendant in between the top buttons on the chest of the man who had just bumped into her.

"Seriously?!" Vivienne blurted out.

The man who had just bumped into her laughed incredulously and said, "Wait a minute. *You* are the one at fault here!"

His statement snapped her out of her shocked state. She pulled her eyes away from the dangling crucifix pendant on his neck and planted them on his face. On a normal day, she would have easily considered him handsome and forgiven him if he was polite and because he also smelled nice. But right now, his critical tone made him extremely unattractive.

For someone who wasn't watching where he was going, he sure has the nerve to raise his voice at me. And if he thinks he is the only one who can raise his voice, he has another thing coming.

Vivienne let go of the hem of her dress and crossed her arms in front of her chest. "How am I the one at fault? You were obviously walking on autopilot instead of paying attention to who or what's in front of you!"

He scoffed and said, "Really? That's your apology for spilling a drink on me?"

Vivienne huffed and cocked her head to the side. If this man wanted to remain obnoxious, then she would match his energy. "Look, mister. I don't know what you want from me. In case you haven't noticed, *I* am also wet," Vivienne said, waving her free hand around her chest. "Yet you don't see me fishing for an apology. Do you?"

She watched the man avert his eyes from her chest as though he had just seen something he wasn't supposed to. His voice took on a more defensive tone when he said, "Well, what can I expect from someone who knows nothing else than to ruin things for others?"

"Excuse me?" Dumbfounded, she wondered if he knew her enough to say what he'd just said about her.

Her father, her biggest critic, had already made it his life's mission to make her feel incompetent. The last thing she needed was for a stranger, who she was sure knew absolutely nothing about her, to criticize her, too. "What makes you think you can speak to me in this manner?!"

Vivienne couldn't believe her ears. Who did this waiter think he was to speak to her rudely? As far as she knew, they had never met before, not to talk of her ruining anything for him. The man opened his mouth to say something but didn't. She watched him as her nostrils flared with each hot breath and the loud music faded away to the background.

All she could hear was her father saying, *"She never does anything right… What a waste!"*

"You know what? Just leave!" The man sneered.

Her eyes narrowed into slits. If anyone had the right to be angry, it was her.

Before she could respond, he continued. "Reasoning with you is a waste of my time, and I have a job to get back to. Besides, the only thing you seem to be good at is frustrating others."

The reality of Vivienne's joblessness had never hit her as hard as it did now, and her vision blurred with rage and tears. Her lack of a job was the only reason she was at this wedding in the first place, which her dad clearly considered a waste of her life. Now, this man who knew nothing about her just made her feel even more useless. It took everything within her to hold back the tears that threatened to spill. Even if it was the last thing she did, she was determined to not give this uncouth waiter the satisfaction of seeing her cry.

Vivienne bit her trembling bottom lip so hard that she tasted blood. Just as he was about to walk away, she snatched the glass from his hand, doused him in the face with whatever was left in the glass and dropped it on the floor.

"There goes your apology, jerk!" she said before stomping away.

Vivienne didn't know if it was the shattering glass or the cold drink in the man's face that was responsible for his shock. She didn't care either, and even though it wasn't enough to placate her, it was certainly enough to show him that she wasn't one to be messed with. Her heartbeat had doubled, and all she wanted to do was scream at the mannerless man that she wasn't useless or incompetent at anything. Amara had even thanked her for helping her out, so that should count for something. Or didn't it?

Vivienne let her tears flow freely as she left the premises to book a ride home.

Chapter Nine

Levi

"Levi, let your speech always be gracious…"

Levi gritted his teeth as he remembered how the Holy Spirit had warned him a few times to keep his emotions in check and watch his words. But he had disobeyed. Now he couldn't forget the look on the maid of honor's face as he had not only called her incompetent but also a frustrator. In a split second, the shock on her face had turned to deep hurt. He gripped the steering wheel tighter until the skin under his knuckles stretched and the bones beneath it showed.

Gosh! I was so stupid! Why didn't I listen?

He couldn't even believe that what could have been the beginning of a potential happily ever after had turned into an altercation. Wasn't that the way it happened in novels and movies? A guy bumps into a girl, or vice-versa, their eyes meet, and they form a connection that lasts a lifetime. Wasn't it supposed to go this way? Or did the writers of those romance movies and books lie?

"If you had just apologized to her, things would have played out differently."

Levi slammed his fist on the steering wheel and honked incessantly at a *danfo* in front of him. "Move *now!*" he said, waving his hand in a sharp arc. This was a failed attempt at blocking out what the Lord had just said to him.

The aftermath of his run-in with the maid of honor had left him feeling both sour and ashamed. Now, every little thing irked him. He couldn't believe how very unchristian-like he had behaved when he let his emotions get the best of him, and if he was being honest, he was still acting very unchristian-like. Maybe his behavior would have been excusable if he was a baby Christian, but he wasn't. Which made it even more disappointing to him that he heard the Lord's warnings and still ignored Him.

You are right. I screwed up and I am so sorry.

Levi took a deep breath and held it for a few seconds. As he let it out, he asked the Lord to take charge of his emotions and teach him how to manage them better, especially in unpleasant situations. His stomach growled and he looked at the takeout beside him, but the last thing on his mind was food. He had to right this wrong, but he didn't know how. Even though he regretted his words as soon as they left his mouth, it was already too late. The damage had been done. He also couldn't fathom how he had gone from being attracted to her to being hostile to her. It made him question if he was even emotionally ready for a romantic relationship.

Like a crack of thunder, the thought that she might have seen his crucifix necklace hit him suddenly. Levi felt horrible about the kind of impression he must have made on her as a Christian. What made him feel worse was that he was a campaigner for Christians living by Christ's example and not declarations. He hoped by some miracle that she hadn't seen the necklace.

"Lord, how do I find this girl so I can apologize to her and make things right?"

The thought of calling Ms. Preye to ask if she knew the girl or could reach her crossed his mind, but it was way past her working hours. Besides, he could ask her when he saw her at work on Monday. Still, how he would survive the next thirty-four hours with a guilty conscience was something he had no answers to. Throughout the drive, Levi plotted different ways of finding the maid of honor's contact in case his boss didn't have it, one of which included contacting Mrs. Langford.

If only I knew her name.

He must have gotten home by muscle memory because the drive was a blur to him. Levi took a cold shower, hoping it would help to clear his head, but it didn't. Although his body was exhausted, his mind kept working overtime. He replayed the run-in over and again until he started to find reasons why his reaction was justified. He convinced himself that if only she had apologized and not spoken to him rudely from the outset, they wouldn't have argued. But the Lord cautioned him with 1st Peter 3:9 and he knew he couldn't argue his way out of that.

The microwave timer dragged Levi out of his thoughts. He stared at the steaming meal before him with no appetite. So he downed a glass of water instead. He tapped his phone screen to check the time—11:00 P.M.

Less than thirty-four hours until the end of this torture.

Levi downed another glass of water and put the heated takeout in the fridge. At least making sure the only cooked meal in his apartment didn't go bad was something he could tackle immediately. He thought of what he would say to the maid of honor if he found a way to reach her.

"Okay, let's say I find her and ask for her forgiveness. What if she rejects my apology?" Levi muttered.

Thinking about it made him cringe. For as long as he could remember, he didn't handle rejection well, and since Josh died, it was one of the things that triggered his anxiety.

Levi switched off the lights and walked out of the kitchen, contemplating whether to go ahead and look for the maid of honor's contact and apologize to her while risking getting rejected or pray his guilt away and stay determined to watch his mouth going forward while keeping his dignity intact. The latter appealed to him more because Lagos was big enough to minimize the chances of coincidental meetups to almost zero percent. Yet deep down, that option made him restless.

As he turned the corner to his room, he saw the wet shirt he had hung out to dry and the events of the night came rushing back. He also remembered how embarrassed he had felt for staring at her bosom longer than he should have. If he was being honest, the last thing he said to her was an attempt to hide his embarrassment because he was sure she had noticed him staring.

Levi also couldn't seem to get the word *jerk* out of his mind as he got underneath his comforter. He was hoping to fall asleep from exhaustion, but he kept counting sheep as the maid of honor's last words to him taunted him. He tossed and turned countless times as sleep wasn't forthcoming. She was right. He had acted like a jerk, and it was enough reason for her not to forgive him for hurting her.

So right there, Levi made his choice. He would make peace with his bad behavior and not reach out to her. With time, he would forget this ever happened, especially since he wouldn't be running into her ever again.

Chapter Ten

Vivienne

It was 8:15 P.M. when Vivienne entered the house. She had hoped nobody would be awake when she got home, but her mom was in the living room reading her Bible. Her mom turned when she heard the door, and Vivienne greeted her.

"Buks Buks!" her mom said cheerfully.

She closed her Bible and kept it beside the prayer journal Vivienne had seen earlier, giving her daughter her full attention, which wasn't what Vivienne needed now.

"How was the wedding? Did you enjoy yourself?" her mom asked.

"It was fine, Mommy. Goodnight." She avoided eye contact before proceeding to walk to the room she shared with Fisayo.

Her mom removed her reading glasses. "Buks, you don't sound okay. What is the problem? Did anything happen to you? Do you want to talk about it?"

Vivienne paused and shook her head. Lying to her mother that nothing happened would only invite more probing and she wasn't in the mood to talk. "Not now, Mommy. Maybe tomorrow," she said in a shaky voice, still avoiding eye contact.

Her mom sighed. "Okay. We *will* talk about this tomorrow but know I'm always here when you need me, Buks. I'll pray for you too."

"Thanks, Mommy. Goodnight," she said and walked away to her room.

Vivienne leaned on the door and just stared at her ceiling. She counted each box as she had done many times over the years. When she got to the last one, she started again.

19, 20, 21, 22…. 1, 2, 3…

On her tenth count, she heard her mom praying. The words were unintelligible, and she knew her mom was praying in tongues. That was what Fisayo had told her when she had asked one day. She had heard both her mom and Fisayo pray many times, and both of them spoke different forms of this "tongues" each time. It baffled her how God would understand such inconsistent and incoherent language. Her mind wandered away to different thoughts about church and how much faith in God her sister and mom had. It was the one thing she didn't have in common with them. Sometimes she wished things were different, but she just couldn't bring herself to trust a God that made His followers suffer just to please Him.

She took off her dress and smelled it. Surprisingly, it smelled of nothing but her perfume and she began to suspect the drink that had spilled on her was water. But to be on a safe side, she took the dress and rinsed it with cold water in the bathroom sink. The last thing she wanted was to ruin an expensive dress she had worn just once. There was no color in the running water from the dress, and it made her feel better. She also hoped there would be no stains when it dried.

As Vivienne took off her makeup, her mind wandered back to her dispute with the waiter, and she remembered the crucifix on his neck. She couldn't believe a Christian would behave so crassly toward her. If she didn't know any better, she would have said Christians were unlikeable people, just like their God. But living with her sister and witnessing her mom handle aggravating situations with both her dad and strangers was enough proof for her to conclude that the waiter was just a badly behaved Christian or someone who wore the crucifix for fancy.

Vivienne hissed loudly in irritation as she imagined several hurtful things she should have said or done to him. She tapped her sister, who was sprawled out on the bed, to make room for her. After much difficulty with getting Fisayo to make room for her, she finally settled in. Since sleep wasn't forthcoming, she began to edit the pictures and videos she had captured at the wedding.

She started with her pictures, and when she finished, she uploaded them to Instagram. She also made sure to post one of the selfies she took with Connor for effect. One thing was for sure—her dad would see the pictures with his anonymous account since he was stalking her every move. Maybe these ones would finally tame his mouth and keep him off her business.

I hope you feel as miserable as I do right now when you see these pictures.

Then she went on to edit the videos from the reception. Watching the video clips made her feel less crappy about her performance as a maid of honor. They were even enough to make her smile a few times, forgetting the waiter's hurtful words that had been ringing in her head. Three hours later and she was adding finishing touches to the last video when Oluchi's message came in. Oluchi praised her for a job well done and thanked her for sending the video of Amara at the after-party. She also said Amara spoke highly of her and was pleased with how Vivienne helped her throughout the day. Then she asked if there were more videos from the wedding and Vivienne said she was putting finishing touches on them.

"There are ten videos altogether. I should be done in an hour."

"Vee babe, you are too much! Ten videos? I cut cap for you, abeg."

Oluchi and flattery were two peas in a pod.

Vivienne thanked her and asked how she was feeling.

"I am one hundred percent fine now that I know you have video clips from the wedding," Oluchi replied, and Vivienne laughed.

"Once again, thank you so much for helping me out today and for capturing those precious moments. Watching the one you sent made me feel like I was at the wedding. I can only imagine how I'll feel when you send the rest."

Vivienne chuckled and typed, *"You are welcome."*

"Please don't forget to tag me when you upload all the videos. I'll also send Amara and Brandon's Instagram handles to you so you can tag them too."

"Okay, fine. While you are at it, also send the handle of the event planning company and every single vendor. Thanks!"

"That's not a problem. You will get them in the next thirty minutes,"

"Okay. Talk soon," Vivienne responded.

"Vee babe, please hurry up and upload the videos. I can't wait to see the rest."

"You will wake up to them tomorrow morning. Don't worry," Vivienne replied.

"All right. Bye! By the way, Amara said she has something to tell you. So, she will be reaching out. Goodnight."

Vivienne's heart skipped a beat and she wondered if she had done anything wrong. She racked her brain for what could be the issue, and the only thing that came to mind was her leaving the after-party without informing Amara.

It was 11:30 P.M. when Vivienne finished editing the last video. Though her mind was still restless from knowing that Amara had a message for her, it was still a lot easier to fall asleep because Oluchi had said Amara was pleased with her work. She must have slept only a wink when her phone chimed. With groggy eyes, she picked it up. It was a WhatsApp message from Amara.

She rubbed her eyes to make sure she wasn't imagining things. Another message came in, and Vivienne was sure she wasn't imagining things. A part of her was hesitant to read the messages because she wondered why Amara couldn't wait until morning to talk to her. Not wanting to stay in the misery of doubt, she tapped on the notification bar to open her chat with Amara.

"Hey, Vivienne. Sorry to bother you so late at night but I wanted to send this message now because I will be traveling to Tuscany for my honeymoon tomorrow and may not remember to text you."

See? You were just worried for nothing.

"Thank you so much for your hard work today and your gift to Brandon and I. You came through for me in so many ways and I am deeply grateful. Thank you! Oluchi also said you have videos from my reception and after-party. I cannot wait to see them!" She inserted the excited emoji at the end of the text.

Vivienne was relieved that Amara wasn't angry at her for leaving the after-party, but she would still apologize for it. She started typing her reply when the chat bar showed that Amara was typing. Vivienne waited for her to finish typing, but it didn't seem like it was a short message so she sent her reply.

"You're welcome, Amara. Thank you too for being so accommodating and understanding. It meant a lot to me. And I am still sorry for coming late to church and making you worry, and for also leaving the after-party without letting you know. Something came up and I had to leave in a rush."

A minute later, the message Amara had been typing came in. *"I have a proposition for you. How would you like to get paid to attend two weddings as a professional maid of honor and bridesmaid respectively?"*

Vivienne couldn't believe what she had just read, so she reread the message. While she was still reading it, Amara used the heart emoji to react to Vivienne's apology message. Then she sent her final message for the night.

"I'm not expecting an answer from you immediately. However, I would like to know your decision by Monday. Even if I am not online, just leave a message for me. Vivienne, I am hoping that you will accept my offer, and in case you do, here are my friends' numbers. Reach out to them and say you are the professional maid of honor Amara talked about. Ciao, bella!"

Professional bridesmaid?!

Amara had just offered her a job. No, two jobs with two of her friends getting married the following month. The first one, Funke, needed a maid of honor and the second one, Mariam, needed a bridesmaid to replace a cousin who wouldn't be available. She sat up straight and read the message a third time. They were going to pay for her dress, shoes, hairstyling, makeup and transportation to the wedding venue. But what made it surreal was them paying extra for her time and services.

She fist-pumped the air and did a little happy dance. Maybe she wasn't so useless after all if helping Amara out today had provided more job opportunities for her. Speaking of jobs, this could even be the end of her joblessness. Vivienne was about to type her response agreeing to take the job offer when the waiter's words hit her unexpectedly like a truck with no brakes.

What can I expect from someone who knows nothing else than to ruin things for others?

Vivienne dropped her phone and buried her head in her hands. Flashes of everything that could go wrong if she accepted Amara's offer flooded her mind. It didn't even matter anymore that Oluchi had praised her earlier or that Amara was pleased with her work enough to recommend her and even broker a service charge for her. She could either accept the offer and risk failing at her job or decline it and stay penniless. It was the proverbial caught between the devil and the Red Sea.

She didn't need to wait until Monday. Her mind was made up, and whatever the consequence of her choice was, she would face it when the time came.

Vivienne picked up her phone and typed, *"Hi, Amara. About your offer, here's what I've decided…"*

Chapter Eleven

Levi

It was a custom to hold a yearly memorial service for Joshua and his dad in their two-acre family residence in Abuja. Although their death anniversaries were two months apart, Levi's aunt felt it was best to hold the service for the both of them at once.

So after Monday's review of the Langfords' wedding at work, Levi had reminded Ms. Preye that his one-week leave off work was effective from that day and that he would be traveling to Abuja.

"Hope everything is okay."

"Yes, ma'am. I just need to travel for my cousin and uncle's memorial service."

"Oh, uh. Sorry about that and I hope you have a safe trip," his boss said awkwardly.

"Thank you, ma'am."

"Levi, you can take an extra week off if you need it," she said.

"That wouldn't be necessary, but thank you."

Levi was the last person in his family to arrive at the Adams' residence. His mom had traveled with his aunt two days earlier to prepare for the service. His dad was supposed to join them the next day, but he called to say his trip had been extended impromptu so he couldn't physically make it to the memorial service. Each year they held the memorial service, Levi couldn't help but feel awful that what should have been their annual Easter family vacation had become a memorial service all because of one wrong decision.

Levi, his mom, and his aunt stood, arms linked, in front of Josh's and his dad's gravestones at one end of their property beside the orchard. His aunt had specifically chosen that spot because she didn't want them abandoned somewhere in the compound without any sign of life or love around them.

Levi's dad and Josh's younger sister, Jemima, who was away in Canada, joined the service through livestream. The air was thick with the scent of fresh flowers and fruits mingled with the earthy aroma of the soil. The sky was a somber gray, with the clouds casting soft shadows over them. At almost noon and no sign of rain, the air was surprisingly chilly.

Levi looked at his aunt beside him. She stood tall and graceful with her shawl wrapped around her while his mom bawled uncontrollably. His aunt pulled her in and hugged her tightly, telling her it was okay. Levi clenched his jaw and blinked rapidly, holding back the veil of tears that had formed in his eyes from spilling. He clenched and unclenched his fists as the pastor read the concluding verse of 1st Thessalonians 4. When he was done, he prayed for the family, asking God to continue to strengthen them and keep their faith intact despite their losses.

"Amen," the five of them chorused at the end of the prayer.

His aunt touched his arm and asked if he was okay. This time, he didn't try to hold back his tears. He shook his head and she drew him close for a hug too. Four years had gone by since his cousin passed away but it still felt like yesterday. How his aunt managed to hold it all together—even after losing her husband and son in the space of two years—and still have the strength to comfort him and his mom was something he would never understand.

The service ended and they bade the pastor farewell. His aunt walked him to the gate, thanked him for coming, and gave him a basket of fruits to go. When she joined her family again, she met them talking about what each person was up to and how they were faring. She and Jemima talked about school, how she was enjoying the weather change, and life in general. It was a sweet mother-daughter bonding time, and Levi was honored to share in the moment as he had many times before.

Growing up and having his mom's twin sister and her family nearby had given him a vision of the kind of family he wanted for himself. He and Josh were practically twins, and their moms did everything together. Though he didn't have any siblings, he had enjoyed the love of having a large family around, especially when they lived just a few houses away from each other.

The wind had picked up and his aunt said it was time for them to head back in.

"Bye, Mama. I'll talk to you later. I love you!" Jemima said, blowing her mom kisses.

"Bye, baby. I love you too. Call me when you are free," Levi's aunt said and waved at her daughter, teary-eyed.

Since the memorial service, it was the first time Levi saw his aunt being emotional. This time it was his mom who hugged her.

"Bye, Auntie. Bye Uncle," she said to Levi's parents, and they both waved at her.

"Bye, Leafy," Jemima said to Levi.

Leafy was what she called him when they were kids. She said his name was too difficult to pronounce properly, and her two missing front teeth didn't help either. Since then, the name stuck and it became his nickname in the family whenever anyone wanted to tease him. It also didn't help that he hated leafy vegetables as a kid.

"Jems, when will you stop calling me Leafy? You don't have missing front teeth anymore."

Jemima stuck out her tongue at him, and everyone laughed. It was the first joke anyone had shared since the memorial service ended and it felt good to hear something other than sniffles and sobs.

"Jem Jem, how are you? Hope school is fine?" Levi's dad asked.

Leave it to my dad to start a conversation when someone clearly has to go.

"I'm fine, Uncle. School is fine too," she said, smiling.

"*Ehen*, Jems," Levi's mom said and cleared her throat. "I sent some stuff to you. *Ankara* summer clothes, foodstuff, local snacks, and hair care products. You should get them this week."

Jemima squealed with delight. "Thank you so much, Auntie."

Her mom teased her for liking free stuff too much, and Levi's mom said, "The apple doesn't fall far from the tree."

Levi's dad and aunt had a little chat after which he spoke to Levi and his mom. When he logged out, only Jemima was left online.

"I'll chat with you on IG. I have something to ask you," Jemima said to Levi.

"All right. I'll be waiting," Levi replied.

"Bye!" Jemima said in a sing-song voice as she waved and they all waved back.

When she logged out, her mom sighed and said, "Let's finish up here and go get something to eat."

They took turns, placing single flowers on each gravestone. A soft breeze rustled the leaves of the nearby trees, highlighting the gloom of the moment. When Levi got to Josh's gravestone, he lingered for a bit. He shook as he read the words that would forever be etched into his memory.

In loving memory of Joshua Diepreye Adams
February 16, 1998 - April 10, 2020
Our beloved son, brother and friend, who is gone too soon but forever in
our hearts. Your light shines on in our memories, and your love remains our
guide. Forever cherished; never forgotten.

His mom tapped him on the shoulder and said it was time to go. She took his hand and led him to the house while his aunt stayed back. When he asked her why his aunt wasn't going in with them, his mom said, "Let's give her some time alone with them. Maybe this is the only way she can stop being strong for everyone."

Levi nodded, letting his tears flow freely, and his mom hugged him as her body wracked with sobs. They walked into the house, holding each other, and sat in silence.

A few minutes later, his aunt entered the house, loudly announcing her presence as she stamped the dust off her feet on the doormat.

"Why is it so quiet in here? I thought you guys would be eating by now," his aunt said in a raspy voice, and Levi could tell she had been crying.

Levi and his mom exchanged looks as they watched her clatter through dishes. "We were waiting for you to come back, Jessica," Levi's mom said.

His aunt stopped what she was doing and turned to them. "Why?" she asked.

Levi and his mom looked at each other again and back at his aunt. His mom threw her hands in the air and told Levi to answer his aunt while she took the dishes her sister had brought out and served their food. His aunt looked at him with raised brows, clearly expecting an answer. He had none for her. She shrugged and helped her sister set the table. They ate lunch in silence, the only sound in the house being the buzzing refrigerator and the clinking of their cutlery against the plates. His aunt dropped her cutlery loudly, shocking Levi and his mom.

They turned to her sharply, and his mom said, "Jessica are you okay?"

"I'm fine. This silence, however, isn't fine. We are not mourning anybody."

"Huh?' Levi asked.

His mom didn't waste any time touching her sister's neck with the back of her palm. His aunt chuckled and removed her twin sister's hand. "Don't be dramatic, Jasmine. I said I am fine."

"I shouldn't be dramatic, *ke?* Levi, is your auntie okay like this? Because I don't think so," she said, clicking her tongue.

Why are you asking me?!

Levi's eyes went wide, and he wondered why his mom always had to put him on the spot. Truthfully, he thought his aunt was having a mental breakdown. They were clearly mourning, plus she had obviously been crying, and now she said they weren't mourning.

Make it make sense!

"I'm serious. Look, guys, the past year has been a revolutionary one that has changed my mindset about certain things, including death. I know I sound crazy but like I said, we are not mourning."

Sorry, Auntie, but you sound crazy.

"You have no idea how much I miss Josh and Luke. Sometimes it hurts so much that I can barely breathe. When this happens, I scream my lungs out and cry myself to sleep," his aunt continued, wiping away tears from the corner of her eyes. Levi's mom patted her sister on the shoulder and wiped away a few tears of her own.

"But guys, we can't keep mourning twenty-four-seven. Why do you think I specifically said nobody should wear black or any dark clothing today?" She paused. "I want us to fill our days with happiness, even if we don't know what tomorrow holds but because we know who holds tomorrow. If anyone had told me I would survive losing my husband and son in the span of two years, I wouldn't have believed it."

"You are so brave, Jessy," Levi's mom said, rubbing her sister's hands.

"I'm not brave, Jasmine. I have just learned to trust God and remember my family with love while they were alive rather than the sorrows of their deaths. This is why I want us to fling any gloom out the window and talk about the fond memories we have of Josh and Luke instead of mourning them."

Levi stared at his aunt in awe. He needed to know what she had learned about losing a loved one that made her so brave and how she survived after losing two-thirds of her immediate family. He made a mental note to ask her before he left for Lagos in two days. Because of his aunt's request, the atmosphere around the dinner table became lighter as they shared jokes and memories from Levi and Josh's childhood. His mom also talked about what growing up with an identical twin was like and all the shenanigans they pulled off. Surprisingly, his aunt was the troublemaker, not his mom as he had presumed. Who would have thought? Especially not when his mom was the spunky one and his aunt, a tad more reserved. After lunch, Levi's mom said she had a headache and needed to go to bed.

"But Jasmine, you promised to spend time with me."

"Yes, I did. And I intend to keep my promise."

"Okay. So we were supposed to spend some time picking ripe fruits together," his aunt said.

"Jessica, why is it that spending time with you always involves some form of hard work?" Levi's mom asked, putting her hands on her waist.

Levi chuckled as he watched the exchange. Experience had taught him never to get involved in the twins' exchanges.

"Jasmine! Picking low-hanging fruits isn't hard work *now*. Consider it bonding time," his aunt said, smiling broadly.

"Whether they are low-hanging or high-flying, I am not cut out for hard work in any manner, form or size. We can spend time together bonding over movies or meal prep. As for this one, please count me out," she said and did the peace sign. Levi laughed, surprised his mom just did that.

"Jasmine!" his aunt said in disbelief.

"*Wo,* Jessica, take Levi with you." His mom shooed them away before heading upstairs to her room.

Levi's aunt sighed and shook her head. Then she turned to him and said, "Levi?" in a sing-song voice.

Levi laughed. "I'll go with you, Auntie. Besides, I have something to ask you."

"Awesome. Walk with me?" She gave him the basket she was holding.

They picked some oranges and lemons, which his aunt said she would use to make lemonade and orange juice later. Levi offered to climb the tree to get the ripe oranges at the top, but she declined, saying the security man would get them. When they got to the bananas and mangoes, they were disappointed as they still had at least two more weeks until they were ripe enough to be harvested.

"I'll tell Usman to harvest and send them to me. When they arrive, I'll bring some over to your house."

"Thanks, Auntie."

"Anything for you, Levi," she said and tenderly touched the side of his face.

Levi watched as her eyes fell on the crucifix pendant on his neck and misted over. She looked up at Levi and smiled wistfully.

"I remember how Josh begged his dad for this necklace but Luke wouldn't give him. He said Josh just wanted it because it looked pretty, not because it meant anything to him."

They walked beside each other in silence for a few minutes, looking for more ripe fruits. Then Levi's aunt told him they needed to head back in since there was nothing more to harvest. When they got to the verandah, instead of going inside, she sat on the bench and asked Levi to join her. They listened to the sounds of nature around them. Birds chirping, leaves rustling, wind whistling, and dogs barking in the distance.

"You know, Luke was right," Levi's aunt said.

She paused for a while as though she was thinking of what to say next.

"It was only after he passed away that Josh found a deeper meaning with the necklace. So I let him have it. But right now, I have no doubt Josh would have wanted you to have his necklace," she continued.

"I miss him so much, Auntie," Levi said, tearing up.

"I know, dear. I know." She patted his clenched hands.

Levi raised his head and took a deep, shuddering breath. "Sometimes I wish Josh had been more forceful that day and not given in to what I wanted. Maybe he would still be alive," Levi said and completely broke down.

His aunt held him as he cried, and a few drops of her tears landed on his shoulder. She continued to hold him, even after he stopped crying.

"Levi, you and I know Josh wasn't someone to be easily talked out of or into anything. As much as you take the blame for what happened that day, Josh also had a part to play." She paused. "Yes, I wish things had turned out differently but they didn't, and I have made peace with it. The silver lining in all of this is that at least I didn't lose two sons."

Levi's breath caught in his throat as he tried to speak. His aunt patted his back and waited for him to continue. When he didn't, she said, "Many times, as difficult as it is, I thank God it wasn't you who died that night. I don't think your mom would have survived it."

Levi remembered how distraught his mom had been after Joshua's death. She had even refused to speak to him for days, only speaking to him when she needed to give him his medication or change his wound's dressing. One night he overheard his parents arguing about him. His dad had said he wasn't happy that his wife wasn't talking to their son, who had narrowly escaped a fatal accident. His mom had replied that her anger was because Levi hadn't thought about what would have become of her if he—her only child—had died.

"He's my only child too! What do you think would have happened to me if he had died?" That was the only time Levi ever heard his parents raise their voices at each other.

"He could have died, Aaron," his mom said and started crying.

"But he didn't. And you have to forgive him so that you can be fully present for Jessica. She needs you now much more than you need to hold on to any anger you feel. Levi already has survivor's guilt. Don't allow your anger to drive him into doing something drastic like killing himself."

After that conversation, his mom apologized and asked Levi to forgive her for treating him harshly. She had also said she couldn't even look her sister in the eye without feeling like she'd cheated her out of something.

"I don't think so either," Levi said and raised his head. He looked at his aunt's red-rimmed eyes deeply and asked her, "Auntie, but how did you survive it? How do you survive?"

His aunt said her pastor had asked her to consider therapy a year after her husband died, but she had declined. It wasn't until Joshua died and Levi left her house and went back to his parents' that she realized she wasn't coping well. So she enrolled in counseling and group grief therapy.

"Being around people who have also lost so much, yet live with joy, was all the encouragement I needed. There's a woman in my grief therapy group who has had five miscarriages and two stillbirths. The worst part is that her husband is also threatening to leave her if her current pregnancy doesn't yield any positive result. Yet, every day she comes with a warm smile and worships God with reckless abandon."

Levi's eyes went wide open in shock. He could only imagine the amount of pain the woman was going through and yet the one person who should comfort and encourage her was the same person making life even more difficult for her. He wished he knew the woman's husband so he could punch some sense into him as he clearly had none.

"Levi, tell me, how can I even stay angry at God after meeting that woman? Yes, we grieve differently, but how can I wallow in grief when I see how much that woman still loves and trusts God despite her terrible losses? At least I got to enjoy twenty-three years with my child and I had a happy marriage of twenty-five years before I lost my husband. This woman who has never heard the cry of her babies or held any alive still radiates joy to everyone around."

Levi's aunt also explained her new-found perspective on death as a believer. She said God is more interested in our eternity than our time on earth, which is why He sent Jesus to die for us so we can be with Him for eternity.

"God can raise the dead back to life, and He has. The proof is the replete examples in the Bible and even in today's world. However, there are people who prayed for their loved ones to get well or come back to life and they didn't. Does that mean God was unkind to them?"

"I don't know, Auntie. I have also wondered why we pray for some sick people to recover yet they die," Levi said.

"When my husband, Luke, died after being sick for a while, I thought God didn't love me or care for my prayers. It wasn't until after Josh's death that I saw the blessing in it."

"How's that?" Levi asked, genuinely confused.

"Let me tell you exactly what I told Josh a few weeks before he died. He had asked me why I still went to church and served God when He couldn't heal his dad. I had told him that my love for God wasn't based on what He could do for me. I also said I may not know why his dad died but I know that God remains a good God regardless of what happens."

Levi remembered how his cousin had struggled with his faith after his dad passed away. He had stopped going to church and their campus fellowship. Josh had also asked him why the Bible said believers will lay hands on the sick and they shall recover yet he had prayed many times for his dad to recover, but he didn't. He hadn't given Josh an answer because he didn't have one. Even now, he still didn't have an answer.

"You know, there are many people in the Bible who Jesus didn't raise from the dead. Or did you think the only people who died throughout Jesus's time on earth were the ones the Bible recorded?" She paused and continued. "We may not find answers to all the questions we have in this lifetime, but one thing we can hold firmly to is our faith. I believe that the blessing in my loss is that I can comfort others who are going through the same thing because I, too, have been comforted."

Levi sat quietly as he tried to digest all his aunt just said. This was probably a cue for him to study his Bible more and pray for answers to difficult questions. Who knows, someone else, maybe an unbeliever or a struggling Christian, might ask a similar question one day and his answer could be the difference between their accepting Jesus or staying far away.

"On to happier topics, shall we?" she asked, smiling broadly.

"Okay?" Levi was skeptical.

"Levi, how long do I have to wait to see my grandbabies?"

Levi gasped and dramatically placed his hand on his chest. "Auntie, have you and my mom been talking?"

"Ever heard of twin telepathy?"

Levi chuckled and playfully shoved his aunt. She laughed and looked at him seriously.

"Jokes apart, Levi. Are you seeing someone or are you at least interested in anyone?"

Levi shook his head. "No to both questions. At least not yet. Besides, I don't think I am emotionally mature to handle a relationship."

"What do you mean?" his aunt asked, paying keen attention.

He went on to explain his encounter with Vivienne and how poorly he handled the situation.

His aunt sighed. "Did you apologize to her?"

"I didn't. She was the maid of honor at the wedding I coordinated last weekend, and she stormed off before I could apologize, after dousing me with the remaining water left in my cup, if I might add."

"You sound like you are still bitter about it. Were you even going to apologize to her?"

"I'm not bitter about it, Auntie. That's just the emphasis you hear in my voice, nothing more. To answer your question…" Levi paused and considered his answer carefully before speaking again. "Honestly? I wasn't going to apologize to her in the heat of the moment. But on my way home, the Lord reprimanded me, and I felt bad about the things I had said to her. Auntie, you should have seen her face when I called her a frustrator. She looked so broken."

His aunt sighed and thought for a moment before speaking. "Levi, you have to forgive yourself and move on, determined to not repeat this in the future. It's not a good look for a child of God, which I believe you are aware of."

Levi nodded. He also had more to say, and now was the time to get this weight completely off his chest.

"Auntie, but here's the thing. I could have made an effort to find her contact to apologize to her but I didn't."

"Interesting," his aunt said before asking, "And why was that?"

"I didn't want to get rejected. Auntie, I saw the look in her eyes before she walked away. There is no way she would have accepted my apology. So, I just saved myself the embarrassment."

"Oh, Levi." Her voice was soft and compassionate. "But you don't actually know that she won't forgive you. Also, vulnerability is an attractive trait to have. When I met Luke, his vulnerability was what made me attracted to him. He wasn't afraid to show and say that he wanted to be with me even when he wasn't sure how I felt about him."

"Really?" Levi asked and his aunt nodded.

"It is one of the things that show a person's emotional maturity. I think that until you learn to be vulnerable despite your fear of getting rejected, you won't find true love. And even if someone dates you, they will eventually get tired of not seeing the real you because you refused to be vulnerable. They will always keep wondering if what you feel for them is true," she said.

Levi couldn't argue. His aunt was right and he knew it.

"If you want to work on being emotionally mature, learn to risk rejection and genuinely put yourself out there. It's the only way you can figure out who you are meant to be with. Someone who genuinely loves you will appreciate your vulnerability and reciprocate it," she said.

"Thanks for your advice, Auntie. As for the maid of honor I offended, I know I won't be seeing her again so I guess I am good. Still, I will work on myself for future sake."

His aunt chuckled. "Good, but you'd be surprised, my dear. This world is a small place."

Chapter Twelve

Vivienne

Getting paid to attend a wedding was certainly a great way to start a new month even though this bride was the dictionary definition of a bridezilla. From Vivienne's first call with Funke, Amara's friend, she already knew the bride would be difficult to work with. If not that she had collected payment for her service and given her word that she would be the maid of honor, Vivienne swore she would have backed out already.

The first indication that Funke wasn't only sassy but also a pain in the neck was when she said Vivienne couldn't wear her natural hair because it was too bright for her chartreuse green maid of honor dress, plus it would make her stand out awkwardly from her bridesmaids who had dark hair. Vivienne saw reason with her and asked if she could braid her hair instead. Funke had vehemently refused saying that Vivienne's hair would look different from the bridesmaids so she had to use a full frontal wig.

For Vivienne, wearing the wig wasn't even an issue. The issue was that she didn't have any because wigs were expensive, especially the full frontal ones. She also explained to the bride that she didn't have wigs and couldn't afford to buy the kind Funke wanted with the budget she'd provided for her hair. After much deliberation, a day before the wedding, Funke eventually agreed for Vivienne to braid her hair. Vivienne also had to use temporary black dye on her hair so the braids wouldn't have hot roots.

Unlike Amara's wedding, Funke had asked Vivienne to spend the wedding eve at the hotel with other bridesmaids. So after getting her braids done, she packed an overnight bag and went to the hotel. When she saw Funke, she complimented her dreadlocks and said they were almost twins. Funke grumbled a response she couldn't figure out but Vivienne wasn't surprised by it. Over the next few hours, she thought Funke was being cold to just her. Until she saw her speak rudely to two of her bridesmaids, one of whom was her younger sister. It then made sense why she would ask a stranger to be her maid of honor.

If I were her sister, I wouldn't want to be her maid of honor either. I just feel sorry for whoever has the misfortune of marrying this ill-mannered woman.

Vivienne was alone in the hotel room she shared with one other bridesmaid who was the bride's high-school BFF. The other three bridesmaids had gone for Funke's bachelorette party while she stayed behind. She had declined the invite majorly because she didn't want to spend unnecessary time around Funke, not because of the headache she had used as an excuse even though she hadn't lied about it. Getting braids was always painful for her because she had a tender scalp, but given how much she had spent on this hair, she would certainly be getting her money's worth out of it.

She had nothing else to do after trying on her dress and shoes. So far, those were the only positive aspects of being Funke's maid of honor. Funke had bought the dress and shoes herself, and if she was being honest, the woman had a great taste. It was a form-fitting mono-strap chiffon dress with a knee-high slit in front, and the shoes were sparkly four-inch gold slingbacks.

To while away time, Vivienne checked the internet for eye makeup inspiration. She finally settled for a sparkly eye look, the same color as her dress, and her lips would be her signature red color but matte this time around. With nothing further to do, she decided to check her business pages to see if she had any messages from any potential clients. She also made it a point of duty to check her spam email at least three times daily. There were no messages from anyone, and she felt a little disappointed.

When she decided to accept Amara's offer and start a professional bridesmaid business, she had hoped it would be successful. But who was she kidding? Her business was an extremely niched one that wasn't only unheard of but would most likely not be embraced.

She also remembered asking her sister many times if it was a good idea. Fisayo had said the business was a weird one, but even the most successful businesses in the world seemed strange at first until people learned to embrace them. Now they were a part of people's everyday lives.

"Good things take time. So be patient and keep putting your best work out there. With time you'll be overbooked and busy."

"Fifi, are you sure?"

"Yes, Buks. It'll work out fine, you'll see."

I hope so. I really do. Because if this doesn't work…

Vivienne shook her head vigorously to clear away the negative thoughts. This wasn't the time to be negative, especially not after the work she had put into making sure her business started on the right foot. One of which was coming up with a name for her business. After many torn papers and rejected ideas, Fisayo thought *Best Girl for a Day* was the perfect name.

"Buks, the name isn't only catchy but unique and practical. Lest I forget, the acronym also sounds like an actual word."

"How does B-G-F-A-D sound like an actual word?" Vivienne asked, her top lip curled to the left.

Fisayo sighed. "Buks, kick your imagination into gear."

"The only thing I would be kicking here is you."

Fisayo giggled and clapped her hands. "You want to kick your helper?"

Vivienne gave her a dirty look and she said, "Okay, okay. *No vex.* It is pronounced *BIGFAD.* Just add an *i* in between b and g. Viola!"

"Hmm. It actually makes sense!" Vivienne said after considering it for a minute. "Fifi, the business consultant." She hailed her sister who flipped her hair left and right.

"*Oya,* let us work on creating social media accounts for *BIGFAD,* please."

"I can also help you get it registered. Why am I studying to become a lawyer? But you will pay *o.*"

Vivienne laughed. "I'll pay you when I see the registration certificate." She grinned, and Fisayo feigned shock.

Together, they set up Instagram and TikTok accounts for BGFAD and uploaded the videos from Amara and Brandon's wedding. Those ten videos were enough to get her a thousand followers on both accounts within a week.

After refreshing her email and not seeing any new messages, Vivienne made a list of video ideas to shoot at Funke's wedding the next day before retiring for the night.

The next day started bright and sunny—perfect for all the video ideas she had. She got dressed, styled her braids into a side-part chignon and wore her makeup.

Before leaving her room for the bride's, she asked her roommate to snap her a few pictures. When Vivienne got to the bridal suite, it was already bustling with activity. She managed to squeeze her way into the room and she couldn't believe how many people were in it.

"Hi, Funke. You look stunning," she said, meaning every word.

Funke smiled and thanked her, which surprised her a little given the bride's compounding nasty attitude. Vivienne filmed as many videos as she could and moved on to helping the bride pack what she needed for the day into the waiting car.

The church wedding had gone smoothly, as she had expected, but she still thought vows were corny. At the end of the ceremony, they took pictures and she used her free time to film videos of the photo session and church decor. As they drove into the reception hall, she saw the van of the wedding's event planning company in the parking lot.

Preye's Elite Parties… Where have I seen that name?

For some reason, the name on the van felt oddly familiar, but she couldn't put her finger on it. Just like she did at Amara's wedding, she filmed and took pictures of the reception hall's entrance and the couple as they alighted from their car. In the middle of her shoot, Funke gave Vivienne some instructions on how to coordinate the bridesmaids for the reception. When Vivienne asked if she could assist her with getting ready for her shoot in the reception hall, Funke replied curtly, "That's the reason I hired a stylist. Just do what I asked."

They exchanged a look that said a thousand words before Funke left with her stylist, makeup artist, and photography crew. Vivienne was holding on to the last bit of patience she had and she hoped she wouldn't run out before the day was over. She told herself that in a few hours, all these would be over and she never had to see Funke or put up with her nasty attitude again. Her experience with Funke also made her determined to properly vet the next bride, Mariam, before committing herself to the job.

Vivienne made up her mind to still go into the reception hall and get as many videos and pictures as she could. Come what may, there was nothing Funke or her ill manners would do to stop her from creating content for her business. On her way to deliver the bride's instructions to the bridesmaids, she saw Ms. Preye speaking to the bouncers at the gate.

It's her! No wonder the name on the van seemed so familiar.

Funke being friends with Amara made sense that Ms. Preye would also plan her wedding. It should have dawned on her when she first saw the bus in the parking lot. The last time she saw Ms. Preye, she didn't get the opportunity to ask her for a job. Now that she had another opportunity to meet her, Vivienne didn't think she needed a job anymore. She already had a business and needed to focus on it.

As she walked to the lounge to meet the bridesmaids, remembering how she had stormed out of this same hall the previous weekend because of the rude waiter who left a bitter taste in her mouth. A part of her wanted to see the waiter and treat him like he deserved while another part thought he wasn't worth her energy. She found the bridesmaids and delivered Funke's message. It elicited a few murmurings, but that wasn't her problem.

Vivienne made her way back to the hall and got right into taking pictures and videos for her business. As much as she disliked Funke, she couldn't deny that the woman looked stunning. She and her husband looked like they were fresh off a magazine cover. Once Vivienne was done filming and taking pictures, she left the hall and went to join the bridesmaids in the lounge.

A few drinks and snacks later, it was time for the reception. Unlike Amara's wedding, Vivienne wasn't too keen on dancing. Luckily, the best man was a great dancer and she let him take the spotlight. The reception continued smoothly but Vivienne didn't participate in any of the games because she was busy serving the bride, even down to things she could do herself like adjusting the tiara on her head.

Hours later, the reception ended and it was time for the after-party. Vivienne thought of sneaking away to the bar to take a break but each attempt was met with Funke sending her on an errand. Something that also didn't make sense to her was how her heart would skip a beat each time she saw a waiter. She just couldn't wait to leave the venue so she could feel like herself again.

Thankfully, the DJ announced that they had thirty more minutes until the after-party was over. It was now or never for her. Instead of going to the bar as she had intended, Vivienne decided to go home. But she wouldn't tell Funke that. She told Funke that she would be at the bar grabbing a glass of water if she needed her. It was the only way she could go home without Funke making a fuss, especially since the after-party hadn't ended. More so, she didn't think Funke would need her for anything in the time they had left.

"Get me a glass, too, while you're at it," Funke said to her and continued dancing with her husband.

Unfortunately for Funke, she had run out of patience and she didn't care if she had only five minutes left on the job. She was ready to snap. Vivienne scoffed and tapped Funke on the shoulder.

"Ask nicely."

"Sorry?" Funke asked, looking stunned.

"You heard me!" Vivienne said and folded her arms. She'd had enough of Funke's nonsense, and now it was time to pull the plug.

"You don't get to talk to me like I am your slave! Funke, I have put up with your nasty attitude for days just because I committed to being your maid of honor. Oh, lest I forget, something even your own sister didn't want to do!"

Funke stared at Vivienne in shock. Vivienne's voice must have been loud enough for Funke's husband's to hear despite the loud music because he turned to ask his wife what was going on, but she ignored him.

Vivienne let out a deep breath as she tried to control the emotions coursing through her.

"When you want someone to do something for you, be respectful and learn to ask nicely. If you want me to get a glass of water for you, say please. Otherwise, I didn't hear you say a thing," Vivienne said.

Funke and her husband froze. She tried to talk but no words came out while her husband fidgeted with the lapel of his jacket. Vivienne didn't care. She would be out of her mind if she let Funke walk all over her one more time. It still pained her that she hadn't been able to stand up for herself more during her encounter with the waiter. But not this time. Being treated like she was nobody by her father was already enough of an insult. Nobody would be doing that to her ever again.

"You know what? I'm out of here. Get your water yourself," Vivienne said and walked out of the hall.

Unlike her last encounter in this same hall with the waiter, she felt victorious. She could feel Funke and her husband's stares boring holes into the back of her head, but that was the least of her problems.

This hall must be cursed with ill-mannered people.

When Vivienne got to the parking lot, Ms. Preye's company's van was open and it looked like someone was arranging stuff into it. She booked a ride to the hotel first so she could pick up her overnight bag, after which she would head home.

Vivienne told the cab driver to wait for her in front of the entrance gate. He said cars were not allowed to park outside the gate and he didn't want to be fined. So she told him to drive inside and that she would be beside a black event planning company van waiting for him.

"Please excuse me," one of Ms. Preye's staff, carrying some boxes, said to Vivienne.

Vivienne got out of her way and said, "Sorry about that. Good evening."

The girl smiled at her and kept the boxes in the van. She was about to leave when she paused and said, "Are you looking for Mr. Levi?"

What?

Vivienne's brows furrowed and she shook her head. "No. I'm waiting for my ride to get here."

"Oh. Okay then," the girl said and laughed nervously, making Vivienne wonder what she had been thinking.

She checked her phone and saw that the driver was five minutes away. That was enough time for her to use the restroom and come back. She walked as fast as her legs could carry her to the restroom in the lounge. At that moment, she wished she had a pair of slippers to change into as her feet were killing her. Vivienne got out of the restroom in exactly five minutes, expecting to see that the driver had arrived. Instead, it showed he was now ten minutes away.

"What is wrong with these people?" she murmured through gritted teeth.

This was one of the reasons she disliked using ride-hailing companies. She texted the driver through the app to ask where he was, but there was no response so she called him. He explained that he had taken a wrong turn and would be there in ten minutes. Vivienne hung up and walked back to her waiting point, Ms. Preye's company van. Shortly, she saw Ms. Preye walking toward the van with the girl she had seen earlier.

When Ms. Preye saw her, she gasped and said, "Just exactly who I was looking for! Hello, Vivienne."

Vivienne raised her brows, wondering why Ms. Preye would be looking for her. "Good evening, ma'am. You actually remember me?"

Ms. Preye chuckled. "How can I forget that ginger-colored afro of yours, even though you look different today?"

Vivienne smiled and checked that she wasn't in their way. Ms. Preye told Vivienne to give her a minute to finish with her staff. She went over a list of items the girl should have kept in the van and she ticked them off her list when she saw each item. Vivienne was impressed with how much effort it took for someone to be that meticulous.

Once they were done and the girl had left, Ms. Preye turned to Vivienne. "You know, it's a good thing we ran into each other. I've been meaning to reach out to you after I saw the videos you posted from the Langford's wedding, but I've been so busy with organizing this one."

Uh… Did she not like that I tagged her company in the posts? Are the videos that bad?

"Walk with me, please," Ms. Preye said, and Vivienne nodded, apprehensive.

They walked in silence, and when they got to her car, she stopped. "The videos are really good, Vivienne."

"Oh!" Vivienne let out a nervous laugh. "Thank you, ma'am." It felt good knowing her concerns were null and that someone valued her work.

"I don't want to assume anything, but you filmed and edited those videos yourself, right?"

"Yes, ma'am. I even filmed today as well. I can show you the clips," Vivienne said.

"That's fine, Vivienne. I just needed to be sure because I have a job offer for you."

Wow! Is this really happening? She thinks I'm good enough to be hired at her company?

Many thoughts ran through Vivienne's mind as she tried to process what was going on. If this job offer had come before she started BGFAD, she wouldn't feel this hesitant. But now, she didn't think she needed a job since she already started a business that needed her full attention. The only advantage having a job offered her was the consistent salary because with her business, it was possible she could go months without getting even one client.

"Uh," Vivienne exhaled slowly. "What kind of job is it?"

"Social media manager and video content creator for my company," Ms. Preye said, opening the front passenger door of her car and keeping her purse on the seat.

Vivienne knew what a social media manager did but she wasn't sure what she would do as a video content creator. So she said, "I'm not sure I know what a video content creator does."

Ms. Preye chuckled. "Vivienne, those video highlights you create from weddings is exactly what a video content creator does. And whenever there are viral wedding trends, you try to recreate them with the couple.”

“Oh. I get it now,” Vivienne said.

Ms. Preye looked at her watch and clicked her tongue. “So, what do you say? Will you like to work with me?”

Vivienne weighed the pros and cons of accepting or declining Ms. Preye’s offer, but she couldn’t decide. Either accepting or declining the offer came at a cost, one that she needed to think about carefully before giving an answer.

“I’ll have to think about it. I just started a business and I wouldn’t want it to clash with my job at your company at any point.”

“Yeah, I figured you’d say this. I already looked at your business pages and I must confess that you have something good going on. I wouldn’t want to disturb that, which is why you will be free to go for your gigs whenever you need to. I just need you to do your job well when you’re at the office.”

Vivienne nodded but said nothing. Ms. Preye reached for her purse and pulled out her business card.

“Your salary offer is two hundred thousand naira a month, subject to review after your three-month probation,” Ms. Preye said.

Vivienne couldn’t believe her ears. This was too good to be true and she was tempted to accept on the spot, but she remembered her mom’s advice of not making hasty decisions, especially when scared or excited. So she said, “Can I think about it and get back to you on Monday?”

“Sure. Take my card,” Ms. Preye said, handing Vivienne the business card. “Come see me on Monday no matter what your decision is.”

“I will. Thank you so much for the offer, ma’am. It means a lot to me.”

"I'll accept your thanks if you agree to work with me," Ms. Preye said. "Okay, I have to run now. See you on Monday?"

Vivienne nodded, and Ms. Preye got into her car. She stood, watching her as she drove off. A smile crept up her face, and as soon as Ms. Preye's car was out of sight, she did a little happy dance. She couldn't wait to get home and tell her mom the good news. Too bad Fisayo had gone back to school and wouldn't hear it in person.

Her ride home was uncomfortable as the car smelled musty, like an animal had died in it. Thankfully, it wasn't raining so she wound down the windows to allow fresh air in. Vivienne thought about Ms. Preye's offer. Though she was ecstatic about it, she still felt a little hesitant to accept it. She had never been a social media manager before, and even the video content she had created from Amara's wedding was initially because she needed something to spite her dad. Vivienne couldn't help but think about what would happen if she accepted the job and failed miserably. So it was probably best to decline and focus on her business. That way the only person she would be disappointing would be herself.

Once Vivienne opened the gate to her compound, she could have sworn that the car parked in front of their door was her dad's, but there was no way that could be the case. She opened the door to the living room, and nothing could have prepared her for the sight she met at home. Her dad was in their house. The last time he had set foot in their house was over a year ago. Her parents were obviously talking about her because as soon as they saw her, they became quiet.

"Good evening, Mommy," she said, hugging her mom.

"*Pele,* my dear. How was the wedding?" her mom asked.

"It was fine, Mommy. I have good news, too, but I'll tell you later," Vivienne said excitedly.

"So you will say you didn't see me *abi*?" her father interjected.

"I was going to greet you after speaking to my mom. Good evening, sir," Vivienne said coldly.

"Keep your greeting to yourself! Mannerless girl! And where are you coming from at this time of the night all dressed up?" her father asked.

Here we go again.

Vivienne looked at her dad, unsure of what to say to him. It was only 7:30 P.M. yet he was acting like she had snuck into the house at midnight. No matter the resentment she had for her dad, her mom was against her disrespecting him, so she needed to watch her tone. "I went out for a maid of honor job."

Her father scoffed. "Maid of honor job? Since when? How? Do you take me for a fool, Bukunmi?"

Vivienne swallowed hard and heaved a sigh. She knew her father. He wanted to get under her skin but she wouldn't let him. "Yes, sir. It's the business I started. Mommy will explain it to you. Goodnight, sir."

She hugged her mom again and whispered, "Goodnight, Mommy." Then she walked to her room and shut the door. She wished Fisayo was home so that her dad would have someone else to focus on.

As she changed out of her clothes and took off her makeup, she could hear her dad saying all sorts of things about her pictures and the videos from Amara's wedding. Vivienne chuckled, thinking about how high his blood pressure would be that month since she still had at least one wedding to attend. She was about to tuck herself in to sleep when she heard her father say,

"Vicky, are you sure that daughter of yours went for a wedding? Did you see the way she was dressed? How are you sure she isn't whoring herself all over Lagos seeing that she has no job?"

Vivienne gasped. She couldn't remember the last time he had anything good to say to or about her, but calling her a whore? That was too much, and she wouldn't stand for the disrespect anymore. She wore a robe over her sleepwear and headed to the living room.

"Adekunle!" Vivienne saw her father flinch when her mom yelled his name.

Surprised, huh? This is just the appetizer.

"All these years you have said so much nonsense about Bukunmi and I have kept quiet because I was so stupid to put your feelings above my children's feelings. But not anymore. I will also not watch you call *our* daughter derogatory names ever again!"

Her mother's hands shook while her dad continued to stare at her in disbelief. Vivienne made sure her mom had finished speaking before she walked toward them clapping her hands. Her dad's brows drew close together in a slight furrow and he squinted as though he had an eye defect. Her mom wiped away tears from the corner of her eyes. Vivienne stopped clapping and shot daggers at her dad.

"For someone who said he doesn't care about what I do with my life, you are certainly obsessed about my life. First, you have an anonymous account with which you monitor me on Instagram because you know every party I attend even after I blocked you. Then you keep asking my mom if I have a job or what it is I am up to. Your behavior is giving stalker, *Dad,*" Vivienne said.

For the first time ever, her dad was tongue-tied, and it surprised her. It was time to go in for the kill, and she didn't waste a second. "Why don't you leave me alone and worry about your golden child or even your legitimate children? After all, you said I am a waste. So what are you doing hovering around a waste?" Vivienne paused, pretending to be deep in thought, then smirked. "Unless you are now a waste collector."

"Bukunmi!" Her parents said in unison, but she ignored them.

All these years, her father had said mean things to her and not even once had she talked back at him, but that was in the past. Vivienne was thankful her mom finally stood up to her dad the way she had expected her to all these years. She would apologize to her later, but right now, she needed to close this chapter of abuse.

"Not that it is any of your business, Daddy Dearest, but I have a job now. And I will advise you to keep taking your blood pressure medicine because this Lagos whore will keep you heated on social media," she said and walked away.

"Did you hear what she said to me, Vicky?"

"I did, and you know what? I don't blame her. You kept poking and prodding her, now she has struck back. I don't support her behavior, but you deserve it. I will suggest that you leave and stay away like you have done all these years," Vivienne's mother said and opened the door.

From her room, Vivienne could still hear arguments, but she decided to drown it by listening to music. She set the volume at the highest and let the sound wash over her as tears flowed from her eyes.

Chapter Thirteen

Levi

Driving to work the following Monday made Levi miss Abuja's serenity and traffic-free roads. A part of him regretted not extending his leave as his boss had suggested. But at the same time, he missed his job and wanted to get back to creating beautiful memories for his clients. When he got to work, the first item on his agenda was to attend the review meeting for the wedding he had missed the previous Saturday.

Ms. Preye commended their effort and told them the areas they needed to improve. Then she briefed them about their next wedding, which was in May. It would be a high-profile wedding, and their deliverables for the couple were twice their usual. To Levi's surprise, Ms. Preye put him in charge and said she would be assisting him. He was honored that she trusted him with yet another wedding.

After the meeting, Ms. Preye pulled him outside for a brief chat. First, she showed him the videos from the Langfords' wedding on their Instagram page and the analytics. Not only were the videos good, they also had the highest views and engagement of all their videos.

"Wow! These videos are really good," Levi said.

"I know right? I talked to the creator about doubling as our social media manager and video content creator. She'll be coming over this morning at ten to let me know if she wants to work with us or not," Ms. Preye said.

"How did you find the creator?" Levi asked.

"You know she added us as a collaborator to the uploads. That's why they also appear on our page. Anyway, I clicked on her profile and discovered she was the maid of honor at the Langfords' wedding. I thought of reaching out to her but got so busy planning and coordinating the Ladipos' wedding. Then, coincidentally, I met her again at their wedding last weekend."

Oh my goodness. My aunt was right. Oh my goodness!

Levi blinked a few times as though to be sure he had heard Ms. Preye correctly.

"Did you say she was Ms. Amara's maid of honor?"

"Uh huh," Ms. Preye nodded.

Before she could continue speaking, Levi interjected.

"And you said she will be here at ten?"

"Yes, Levi. Pay attention," Ms. Preye said, snapping her fingers.

My God! How do I face her when she gets here? Will she even recognize me? What if she recognizes me?

Levi suddenly was queasy and his palms became sweaty. He didn't want to be around when the girl came, which meant he had to find something to do that would take him out of the office. Maybe he would say he needed to go source the decor fabrics they would need for their new client's wedding.

"Earth to Levi," Ms. Preye said.

"Sorry, ma'am. I got distracted thinking about the kind of decor fabric to get for our new client's wedding. So, if she agrees to work here, I suppose she'll be using the staff room?"

Ms. Preye considered it for a minute while Levi prayed the girl would turn down the job so he wouldn't have to face her. He had already made peace with himself about their exchange, promising to do better in future. Now that there was a possibility she would become a colleague, it made him uneasy.

"I don't think that would be a good idea. She's new here and doesn't know our standard yet so it would be good if someone showed her the ropes. For this reason, I believe your office is big enough to accommodate her," Ms. Preye said.

Levi couldn't believe how circumstances were forcing him to meet his retribution. Was there really no way he could avoid seeing this lady?

"Um, she can still work in the staffroom while I put her through."

"It wouldn't be convenient, Levi. Try to accommodate her for just three months. Once she is confirmed, she can move to the staff room. Besides, she would have to follow you everywhere to create behind-the-scenes content before the actual events. So, you need her close by," Ms. Preye said.

"Okay. I'll make room for her *if* she agrees to work here," Levi said.

"'*If*' is the keyword. I don't even know why I'm getting ahead of myself when she hasn't agreed to work here yet."

Exactly! Let's not get ahead of ourselves.

"I need to attend to pending emails," Levi said, excusing himself. As he turned to leave, Ms. Preye said, "Oh, and Levi?"

"Yes, ma'am?"

"I need you to be around when she gets here. You know, just in case she agrees to work with us," Ms. Preye said.

Wahala o.

"I had planned to go out to start sourcing for the decor fabric and materials for the new job. One can never be too early with this." Levi chucked dryly.

"Sure but it can wait. It's almost nine thirty. If you leave now, you won't get back until late afternoon. So you might as well just wait to know where things stand before you leave."

Levi nodded stiffly and turned to leave. His plans had been ruined. He didn't want to be around when the girl showed up and he'd somehow hoped she wouldn't accept the job offer. But on second thought, if she accepted the job offer, how long could he avoid her, especially when she would be working in his office? Maybe it was best they ripped the Bandaid now.

The next thirty minutes felt like eternity to him. He kept looking at Ms. Preye's office, which was adjacent to his, and when nobody showed up, he felt relieved. Shortly, a girl in denim pants and a blazer walked into Ms. Preye's office. Levi checked the time to know if it was the maid of honor. The time of the girl's arrival suggested so, but she couldn't possibly be the one. The maid of honor he had run into had beautiful, bright orange curly afro hair. This girl here had black braids and was even ten minutes early.

Levi waited for his intercom to ring as the girl who walked into his boss's office had been there for about twenty minutes. When it didn't ring, he assumed the girl in the office was a prospective client. He also concluded that the maid of honor wouldn't show up again since she was already ten minutes late and no one in their right mind would arrive late for something this important. He decided to focus on the email he had been typing since he got to his office. There was no point getting anxious over someone who wasn't going to show up.

Levi also decided that after sending out all the emails he needed to send out, he would leave for the fabric sourcing. It would take him about thirty minutes to finish sending out all five emails. That was enough time to justify that he had actually waited for the girl to show up before leaving. Just as he sent out the third email, his intercom rang.

"Levi, please come to my office."

His heart skipped a beat and a random thought flashed through his mind. He brushed it off by saying, "No, that's not her in the office. Ms. Preye most likely wants to tell me that the girl canceled on her."

When he got to her office, the girl had her back to him so he couldn't see her face. But she turned when Ms. Preye said, "Vivienne, meet Levi, your supervisor. You'll be working in his office for the next three months."

As soon as their eyes met, it felt as though she had doused him with another glass of water. The smile on her lips vanished and her doe eyes narrowed into thin slits. Levi had never felt more uncomfortable in his life. He couldn't even look her in the eye anymore. He had hoped that by some miracle, she would decline the job offer or wouldn't even show up, and since he would be out of office, they wouldn't have seen each other ever again. Which meant this matter would be permanently laid to rest. But unfortunately, here she was, shooting daggers at him with her eyes. If only he had found a way to apologize to her before now.

"Levi, meet Vivienne, our new social media manager and video content creator," Ms. Preye said.

"You're Levi?" Vivienne asked.

He nodded and stretched out his hand for a handshake, which she shook weakly then retracted her hand quickly as though he had a contagious disease.

"Have you guys met before?" Ms. Preye asked, looking between both of them.

"Yes. We *bumped* into each other at the Langfords' wedding," Vivienne quipped before he could answer. Which was probably a good thing because he didn't think any words would come out of his mouth if he tried to speak.

"Okay, that's great. Getting along shouldn't be difficult then," Ms. Preye said.

If only you knew.

Levi stood awkwardly beside Vivienne as he tried not to look at her, but he could feel her laser-like stares. Ms. Preye shuffled through some papers on her desk and handed one to Vivienne.

"That's your employment contract. Go through it carefully, sign it, and submit it at the end of the week. If you don't understand anything on the contract, ask Levi."

"Okay, ma'am. Thanks again for having me on board," Vivienne said sweetly with a big smile.

"I look forward to the amazing things you will do here, Vivienne," Ms. Preye answered, smiling.

His boss looked delighted that the maid of honor had agreed to work with them. Levi couldn't remember the last time his boss was excited about hiring anyone. This just meant one thing—the maid of honor was special.

Vivienne. Her name is Vivienne.

Ms. Preye clapped. "That should be all for now. Levi, please help her settle in."

"Sure," Levi said and cleared his throat.

As they were about to leave, the receptionist walked in to say Mr. Desmond asked to see Ms. Preye urgently but he didn't have an appointment. Levi noticed that Ms. Preye's eyes lit up when the man's name was mentioned. He was sure he'd heard her mention that name before but he couldn't remember why or when. Nevertheless, whoever the man was to his boss wasn't any of his business. Ms. Preye told the receptionist to bring him to her office.

Levi held the door open for Vivienne and she walked out without acknowledging him. She waited for him to lead the way to his office then she followed. From his office, he watched Ms. Preye fix her hair and expression as she waited for her visitor. Levi had worked for his boss long enough to know this wasn't an official visit because the man had a bouquet of pink roses in his hands. Clients came with checkbooks, not bouquets. Again, it wasn't any of his business.

"Where do I set up?" Vivienne said, bringing his attention back to her.

"Oh, sorry. Give me a sec," Levi said and smiled at her, but she just looked at him coldly.

Lord, help me.

Levi had no idea how he would even broach the subject of an apology with her since she was clearly still livid at him, but he understood why. Still, he needed to start somewhere, and he felt the best way was through his actions. He made room for her on his desk and then asked Bayo and Chuks to bring the two-seater couch in the staffroom to his office so he could replace the client seat Vivienne now used with it.

"Make yourself comfortable. If you need anything, don't hesitate to ask me," he said once Bayo and Chuks had left.

Vivienne looked at him for a while without saying anything. Then she nodded and offhandedly said, "Okay."

"Great. So, I'm going out to source for decor fabrics for a new client's wedding. Would you like to come? I mean, Ms. Preye said you're to cover behind-the-scenes content too."

"Yes, she said that. But I would like to skip this one. If you don't mind," Vivienne said.

"No, I don't mind. There will be so many other opportunities, but I just wanted to make sure you didn't decline because you are avoiding me."

Vivienne sniggered. "Don't flatter yourself, Levi. We literally work in the same office so there's no avoiding each other. However, I want to minimize how much time I spend around you. Does that make sense?"

Since they now worked together, all he wanted to do was find a way to make peace with this 5'5 girl who didn't want to breathe the same air as him. He figured it was best to just address the issue directly since his first attempt at soft pedaling it by being nice didn't work.

"Yes, it makes sense, Vivienne. Look, I know you are mad at me and you have every right to be, but I am deeply sorry for speaking out of turn. The way I acted at the party isn't the kind of first impression I want to leave people with. I'm sorry for calling you incompetent and a saboteur. I am so sorry. Please forgive me."

She was about to say something but didn't, and an awkward silence lingered between them. Levi decided to end the awkwardness.

"You are clearly amazing at what you do because I know Ms. Preye. She would never hire an incompetent person and she was quite hopeful that you would accept her offer." He paused then continued. "Again, I am sorry. I hope you can forgive me so we can work together without any friction, and who knows, maybe even become friends one day," he said and smiled.

Vivienne's features softened and she looked even more attractive than the first day he had seen her. She was quiet for a while as though she was considering whether to accept his apology or not.

Then she crossed her arms and said, "I have heard your apology but I have a question. If we hadn't crossed paths again, would you still be so bent on getting my forgiveness?"

Levi had an answer but he couldn't say it. That would just be synonymous to adding fuel to fire. For the first time since they left Ms. Preye's office, Levi looked Vivienne in the eye, but he couldn't say anything. He was remorseful for his actions but there was nothing he could do or say now to prove to her that his apology was genuine.

Vivienne scoffed and said, "I didn't think so. Let's just be civil with each other and get our jobs done because we can never be friends."

She walked out of the office and Levi sat on the couch. He buried his head in his hands and asked God to help him fix this problem.

Chapter Fourteen

Vivienne

Corporate or casual?

Vivienne held out different outfits in front of a mirror, wondering which one would make the best first work impression. She had three options: a black office dress, a black two-piece suit, and a white round-neck t-shirt with high-waisted blue denim. Her braids were neatly packed in a tight high bun and her makeup was minimal. Instead of her signature red lip, she opted for just clear lipgloss.

The first thing she did when she woke up that morning was call Ms. Preye to let her know she would be at her office by 10 A.M. Thankfully, Ms. Preye's office was just thirty minutes away from her house, even if she went by public transport. Vivienne's mom had also come to talk to her about the previous night's event. She had voiced her displeasure at the things Vivienne had said to her dad. She apologized and her mom said she was forgiven.

"So why was he here? He hasn't been to this house in over a year," Vivienne asked her mom.

"Well, it's the same reason as the last time he was here."

"And what did you say?" Vivienne asked.

Her mom, noticing the annoyance in her voice, held Vivienne's hands. "Buks, the reason I left your father sixteen years ago is the same reason I won't be getting back with him."

Vivienne nodded and smiled sadly. There was a time she adored her dad and thought her mom was the reason her dad didn't want to see them after they split. Which was true, but not exactly how she had imagined things. It wasn't until she got older that she saw her dad for who he was and she was thankful her mom had left him.

"I used to be so mad at you for leaving Dad, but as I got older, I saw why you had to leave. Even if you hadn't told us the reason you ended things with him, I would have still understood. How did you even fall in love with that kind of person?"

Her mom laughed. "Buks, your dad wasn't this bad, or should I say, I didn't know he was this bad. I met him when I was young and fell in love with him. For years, he was good to us, but everything changed when I told him I no longer wanted to be with him."

Vivienne believed her mom must have seen a few red flags in her dad but turned a blind eye to them because she was in love. Now, they were all paying for it. But she couldn't judge her mom, especially knowing the kind of household she had been raised in. Love made people do things that weren't even favorable to them. This was why falling in love with anyone was completely not in the works for her.

"Mommy, you know what? I didn't even want to accept this job offer because I wanted to give my new business the full attention it needs to grow. But after what my dad said, I needed to prove him wrong and show him that I'm not wasting away."

"Buks, you don't have to do anything you don't want to do to prove a point to anyone, not even your dad. Your worth doesn't come from what you have or don't have, or what people say or think about you." Her mom squeezed her hands gently and continued. "Your worth is who you are in Christ. Your earthly possessions, titles, or achievements are all a plus, not who you are. I pray that one day you will accept Jesus's love for you so you can see how much you're truly worth."

Vivienne swallowed hard and bounced her foot on the bed frame. It always made her uncomfortable whenever her mom or sister talked about Jesus to her. They sat in silence for a while then, her mom stood up and said, "You need to get going, Buks. You don't want to be late."

"Yes, Mommy."

Before her mom left her room, she turned to Vivienne. "Buks, I may not tell you this as often as I should and I'm sorry. But I want you to know that you are worth so much and I love you deeply. You are one of the best gifts God ever gave me."

"I love you, Mommy," Vivienne said and wrapped her mom in a tight hug.

"I love you too, Buks Buks," she said, smiling. "And you can wear my Zara perfume *again*."

Vivienne stifled laughter and cleared her throat. "Thanks, Mommy."

"By the way, wear the denim but switch the white t-shirt for a tank top. Then add a bright-colored blazer to complete the look," her mom said and closed the door behind her.

Vivienne took her mom's advice and wore a fuschia-colored blazer. The first thing she saw when she got to the office building was a big black signage with pink writings that read, *Preye's Elite Parties.* As she walked into the building, the smell of citrus lingered in the air mixed with what she was sure were perfumes and colognes of staff members and clients.

She walked up to the receptionist and said, "Good morning. I have an appointment with Ms. Preye for ten."

"Give me a second, please," the receptionist said and picked her intercom.

While the receptionist made the call, Vivienne took in her surroundings. The seating area was furnished with fine leather sofas and chairs; the walls were also adorned with contemporary African-inspired paintings, and there was a corner for refreshments opposite the entrance door.

"She'll see you now. Her office is straight ahead down the corridor. Once you get to the end, turn left."

"Thank you," Vivienne smiled and walked away.

She walked past a few offices, where everyone seemed to be buried neck-deep in their work. Besides the fact that Ms. Preye's office was the last one on the corridor, there was also a CEO tag on it. Vivienne poked her head through the door, and Ms. Preye asked her to come in.

"You're early."

Vivienne smiled and greeted Ms. Preye. Unlike the lobby, Ms. Preye's office smelled like lavender. There was a heart-shaped collage of framed pictures from events of prominent clients on the wall, and on the opposite side of it was a kissing couple silhouette wall clock. Ms. Preye closed her laptop and leaned back in her chair before speaking.

"I suppose you have made a decision, right?"

"Yes, I have." Vivienne nodded and chuckled nervously. "I would like to confirm what you told me at the wedding. Just to be sure I wasn't imagining things."

Then she reminded Ms. Preye about her business and how it would require her to be out of office on certain days, and even unexpectedly sometimes. Ms. Preye reiterated that it was fine and all she needed to do was to give a notice, no matter how impromptu.

"Any more questions?" Ms. Preye asked.

"No. Everything is crystal clear and I accept your offer, ma'am," Vivienne said, smiling broadly.

"Excellent! Welcome to Preye's Elite Parties," Ms. Preye said and stretched her hand to Vivienne for a handshake.

Vivienne shook her hands firmly while maintaining eye contact. She had read somewhere that it indicated confidence, and she wanted to appear nothing less than that. She also couldn't believe how much she would now be earning in a month. It all seemed like a dream to her.

"I'm thrilled you accepted my offer, Vivienne. As I told you earlier, you'll be on a three-month probation and you'll be working with Levi, our event coordinator. He's excellent at his job and he's also a good guy. You'll learn a lot from him."

This must be the Levi her staff member asked if I was looking for the other day.

"I'll ask Levi to come so I can introduce you guys to each other." Then she proceeded to call him on her intercom.

Shortly, Levi came, and a familiar woodsy oriental cologne hit Vivienne's nostrils. She frowned as she tried to remember who she'd met recently that had worn the same fragrance, but she couldn't. All she knew was that whoever she had met must have left a bad impression on her because she began to feel uneasy.

"You asked to see me?" Levi said.

Vivienne restrained herself from turning back to see who this Levi was. She hoped he was truly as Ms. Preye had said. The last thing she needed was another egotistical chauvinistic male around her. Ms. Preye introduced them to each other and that was when she turned to see the greatest shock of her life. Suddenly, it dawned on her why the smell of his cologne felt so familiar. But just to be sure, she looked at his neck and saw the same crucifix pendant she had seen dangling on his neck when he bumped into her. It certainly wasn't a coincidence.

Oh my goodness! He's my supervisor? He's my supervisor! So he wasn't even a waiter!

Vivienne couldn't believe what had now become her life. This was the same person who had made her feel less of herself and now she had to work with him? Not work with him. Work *under* him, if she was being practical.

"Ma'am, I was thinking I should work in the staff room. I wouldn't want to be a bother to Mr. Levi here," Vivienne said and shot him a dirty look.

Ms. Preye raised her head from the pile of papers she was shuffling through and asked if that was the only reason.

"Yes, it is. I also wanted an opportunity to get to know other staff members."

"Well, Levi doesn't mind. He and I had discussed this already. As for getting to know the other staff members, trust me, there will be ample opportunity for that."

Vivienne bit her bottom lip and nodded. Ms. Preye went back to shuffling through the papers while she turned her attention back on Levi who stood awkwardly beside her. He swiftly averted his gaze when their eyes met, and she smirked. She enjoyed watching him squirm. It was the least he deserved after humiliating her. Her new boss was happy to have her onboard, and it felt good to be wanted and needed, even if it was by a stranger. Vivienne made up her mind that she would go the extra mile to do her best for the company and to never make Ms. Preye regret hiring her.

She thought Ms. Preye's office was cold, but entering Levi's office felt like she had just arrived in the arctic region. The office was freezing but she couldn't bring herself to tell him to switch off the air conditioner or adjust the temperature. Thankfully, she had a blazer on, and if it got too cold, she would step out of the building to warm up under the sun.

Vivienne looked around Levi's office. There were no pictures or art work on the walls, not even a clock. The only interesting thing about the office was the coral-colored wall paint. Levi's office also smelled like him and she wondered if he had an air freshener of the same scent. Vivienne turned to find Levi watching Ms. Preye with a look she couldn't quite decipher. She couldn't tell if Levi liked their boss or if he was taken aback by her fixing her hair and appearance in the office.

"Where do I set up?" Vivienne said tersely, bringing Levi back to reality.

He apologized and asked her to give him a second, flashing her a smile that revealed pearly white teeth. She gave him a cold-eyed stare because even his brilliant smile wasn't enough to persuade her to like him. Levi made room for her on his desk by shifting his laptop, stack of books with a Bible on it, a small digital clock and a three-in-one picture frame. The picture frame caught Vivienne's eye and she studied it. The first picture was of Levi and an elderly couple she presumed were his parents. They all looked so happy together and she could see that he was a carbon copy of his dad.

It must be nice having two parents who still love each other even in old age.

The second picture was of Levi and a boy his age. They both looked really young and without any facial hair. She also noticed that the other boy wore a similar crucifix necklace to what Levi currently wore. The last picture was of Levi, the elderly couple in the first picture, another woman who looked exactly like who she'd presumed was Levi's mom, and a girl about her age, who was the younger version of both women. Vivienne wondered why the boy she had seen with Levi in the first picture wasn't in the last one. Whatever the reason was, it wasn't any of her business.

If someone had heard her ask for space to set up her things, they would think she had more than a laptop, water bottle, journal, and pen. Still, she was thankful for the couch because it meant she didn't have to sit opposite him or share a desk with him the whole day. She would sit on the couch and work from there.

Levi apologized for behaving rashly with her and calling her incompetent. She was about to tell him to save his apology when Fisayo's words went off like alarm bells in her head. "Vivienne, when people accept their wrongs and apologize for them, try to give them the benefit of the doubt."

So, she kept quiet. Levi must have seen it as an opportunity to keep talking. The sheen in his eyes, his furrowed brows, and gentle tone—which was a far cry from how he had sounded when they first met—coupled with her sister's words made her heart soften a little.

Vivienne ruminated over Levi's words as they both stood in the silence with nothing other than the whooshing of the air conditioner. She could forgive Levi, but first she needed to be sure his apology was genuine. If he was genuine, then she would also apologize for her actions and they could move past this. Unfortunately, she was left disappointed and angry all over again by Levi's silence which was all the confirmation she needed. This was the reason she didn't believe in giving people second chances because it was synonymous to giving them the permission to hurt her again. She felt foolish for wishing his apology came because he genuinely felt bad and not just because they would be working together and he didn't want any bad blood between them.

Three months and I'll be out of that office.

Chapter Fifteen

Levi

Over the next few weeks, Levi did all he could to get Vivienne to forgive him, but nothing worked. Right from childhood, he didn't function well in a strife-torn environment, and even if it bruised his ego, he always found ways to resolve conflicts. This was why Vivienne's constant rejection had begun to take a toll on him. Even though they spoke to each other only when it was necessary, they were able to do amazing work together.

Levi also didn't know for how long he would continue to try to earn her forgiveness and respect before he gave up. But now that the Holy Spirit had instructed him not to give up, he had no choice but to obey. Since his run-in with Vivienne, he had become more intentional about pleasing God than doing what his flesh wanted. It wasn't always an easy decision, but as a Christian, he knew his life no longer belonged to him but Christ. So, each passing day, no matter how difficult it was or what the offender deserved, pleasing God was his priority.

He had just returned home from a three-hour Sunday service, and he felt refreshed. It was a special prayer service and he took the opportunity to pray about his situation with Vivienne. At first, he didn't think it was that much of an issue that would require praying about. But after seeing how the animosity Vivienne had for him had dragged on for six weeks, he knew it was time to table it before God. After countless attempts of using his human wisdom and effort to get Vivienne to forgive him and failing at it, this time he would go in the might and wisdom of the Holy Spirit. During his prayers, the Holy Spirit led him to Galatians 6:9-10.

"Let us not become weary in doing good, for at the proper time we will reap a harvest if we do not give up. Therefore, as we have opportunity, let us do good to all people, especially to those who belong to the family of believers."

This was all the encouragement he needed because he was ready to give up trying. Levi repeated the Bible verse over and again until he could recite it by heart perfectly. Apart from helping him get through life's challenges, memorizing Scripture was something he did to strengthen his convictions based on God's word. From past experiences, Levi had discovered that each time the Lord taught him a life lesson, He would also present an opportunity for him to teach someone else that same lesson, using his life as a relatable example. Levi was so certain there would be a turn in events that, unlike other Sundays for the past six weeks, he didn't dread going to work. From tomorrow, he would approach this conflict with a renewed sense of purpose to show what it truly meant to be a Christian.

He went to his closet to sort out his outfits for the week. It was also where he took out time to pray if he wanted to fight the temptation of falling asleep in his bed while praying. Once he was done sorting out his clothes, he went to the kitchen to prepare a meal. He wasn't the best of cooks so he kept his meals simple. It was also why he went to his parents' or aunt's house to get takeout whenever he got tired of eating his concoction meals. The mangoes on his kitchen counter caught his eye and he knew it was time to take care of them. His aunt had sent them over three days earlier and he had been too busy to slice them up.

"I just hope these mangoes haven't started rotting. God *abeg*."

While his food cooked, Levi sliced the mangoes open. Thankfully, they were still fresh. He cut them into thin slices and arranged them neatly in two airtight plastic containers. He kept them in the fridge and made plans to snack on them at home that week.

Just as he closed the door of the fridge, the Holy Spirit nudged him to take one of the containers to work and offer Vivienne some.

Levi chuckled. "I have offered to buy her lunch so many times but she declined each one. Why would she accept mangoes from me?"

He couldn't understand why the Lord was asking him to offer Vivienne mangoes, but he knew trusting God always paid off even if it didn't make sense in the beginning. Levi set a reminder on his calendar to take the mangoes to work the next day. Maybe that would be the conversation starter as he had run out of things to say. His phone chimed with an Instagram message notification from Jemima.

"Levi, I apologized to her again and was honest about everything just as you advised. It still didn't go well. She said she still needs time to process the hurt and evaluate our friendship. What else can I do?"

A day after the memorial service, his cousin had sent a voice message on Instagram explaining how she had a falling out with her friend over a boy. Jemima had explained that her friend had a crush on a guy at school but it wasn't mutual. She said they got to know it wasn't mutual when he stopped them after class one day and instead of asking for her friend's number, he'd asked for hers. She had given it to him because she liked him too but had never said anything to her friend. Now Jemima's friend was mad that she had given the guy her number when Jemima knew she liked him. She had called Jemima a disloyal friend.

Levi had asked her if she thought she had offended her friend by giving her number to the guy when he asked. Initially, Jemima had said she didn't think it was a big deal since he had only asked for her number and not asked her out on a date. She had also defended her actions by saying for all she knew, he had asked for her number to ask about school stuff. He then explained to her why her friend felt hurt about the situation, especially since Jemima hadn't seen the need to apologize to her on the spot or offer an explanation as to why she had given him her number.

"I guess I can understand why she would be heartbroken and disappointed at me," Jemima had texted back.

Levi had told her to apologize and ask for her friend's forgiveness and to also be honest about her feelings for the guy and why she didn't tell her friend about her feelings for him. Jemima had reported back to him about how livid her friend was and how she didn't want to hear any apology because she said Jemima had acted selfishly. He'd asked Jemima to try again and let him know the state of things.

"She's still giving me the cold shoulder and I'm tired of apologizing to her. It's like I'm talking to a brick wall. Foluke doesn't want to see things from my point of view. And you know the annoying part, the guy in question had asked for my number so he could talk to me about borrowing my notes. Nothing more! What's even worse is that he has a girlfriend too!"

Levi asked Jemima how she felt about knowing the guy had a girlfriend. Jemima said she thought she would feel hurt but all she felt was great relief and that somehow the crush she had on him was also dead. Now that he had confirmed Jemima was being honest about her feelings for the guy dying since he was dating someone else, he sent a voice message reply to her message that had just come in.

"Jems, you can't be tired of apologizing to her. You offended her and she is hurt. Remember what I told you about my situation with Vivienne? Please don't be like me. I will suggest you give her space like she requested but pray while you are at it."

"Levi, it's just awkward because we see each other in class every day. Because of her, I have even started avoiding Martin in class."

"Martin's the guy's name?" Levi asked.

"Yes. Duh."

Levi chuckled as he pictured Jemima rolling her eyes. Then he replied to her text saying, *"Have you even told her that you and Martin have nothing going on and that he has a girlfriend?"*

"I haven't. It didn't occur to me."

"Well, tell her. It may help restore your friendship. But don't forget to pray about it before approaching Foluke again."

"I will. Thanks for your help, Levi. Let me also know how your situation plays out. It's as if offending people runs in this family."

Levi chuckled at Jemima's last text and he replied with the laughing-crying emoji. He checked his food and it wasn't ready yet. He had added too much water to the noodles so it was taking longer to dry up. He thought of going to the living room to start watching the latest season of a TV series he was following, but he knew his food would become a burnt offering if he left the kitchen. So he stayed and spent the next few minutes watching Instagram reels.

A few reels later and he stumbled on the birthday party of their most recent client. No matter how many times he watched the BTS/reveal reel as Vivienne had called it, he was always greatly impressed. The views on the video had also doubled and he couldn't be happier for her. He also hoped she could see just how valuable she was, especially based on her results in the company in less than two months. Which made him realize he had very limited time to achieve his goal before she left his office for the staff room.

Levi found Vivienne's business page from other videos she was tagged to on their company's page. He spent a few minutes there, watching every single video she ever posted on it. He also noticed her business was lacking something vital and he hoped she would let him fix it for her. The smell of burning food took his attention back to what was on the stove, and he sighed at the irony of being in the kitchen yet burning his lunch.

He got to the office the next day and said his usual good morning to Vivienne. Unlike the past few weeks, she sounded cheerful and even looked at him when she replied, "Good morning, Levi."

Lord, is this a sign?

He was taken aback by her warmth. So, instead of keeping quiet and focusing on his work as he had always done, he asked how her weekend was. To which she replied nonchalantly that it was normal. As Levi settled in his seat, the paintings on the wall caught his eye. He knew it had to be Vivienne because Ms. Preye wouldn't keep anything in his office without asking him first.

He cleared his throat. "I like the paintings. They make this office look more vibrant. Thanks, Vivienne."

"Uh, you're welcome. I thought you wouldn't notice them."

"Trust me, I notice everything even if I don't say anything." Levi flashed her a bright smile.

Vivienne's brows rose slightly and she gave a small nod before mouthing what he assumed was, "Okay."

He thought of how best to start a conversation about her business without making it seem like he was stalking her or trying to prove that he knew better than her. The last thing he wanted was to ruffle more of her feathers. He also considered offering her the mangoes first was the smartest move.

"Vivienne?"

"Huh?" She raised her head from her laptop slightly, her red-rimmed blue-ray glasses perched on the bridge of her nose.

From where she sat on the sofa across him, Levi thought she looked more stunning with the pair of glasses.

"I got something for you," he said and brought out the plastic container.

This time, Vivienne's full attention was on him and he didn't miss the frown on her face.

"For me?" she asked, and he nodded.

"Why?" she asked again.

Levi shrugged. "My aunt gave me more than I can finish. I didn't want them to go bad so I thought who better to share them with than you?" Levi said and opened the lid.

Vivienne removed her glasses and tilted her head to the side. Levi hoped she wouldn't say she wasn't interested before she even found out what it was.

"What's in it?" she asked, craning her neck to see what was inside the container.

"Mangoes. My aunt has an orchard in Abuja. Her mangoes are the best you'll ever eat," Levi said excitedly pushing the container closer to the edge of his desk.

Levi saw Vivienne's eyes light up at the sight of the mangoes. Then he thought he was imagining things because the spark he had seen in her eyes was quickly replaced with indifference. All that didn't even matter. The mere fact that she was curious enough to ask him questions was more progress than he could have imagined.

"How do you know they are the best I'll ever eat? I never even said I would try them," she said and leaned into her seat.

"Well, I meant if you wanted to try them. Look," Levi said then he picked a piece with a fork and put it in his mouth. After swallowing he said, "They're safe to eat. I didn't poison them or anything."

Vivienne rolled her eyes. "I don't think you poisoned them. I'm just wondering why you keep trying different tactics to get us to become friends even when I clearly say and show that I am not interested in being friends with you."

Levi put the lid back on the plastic container before saying, "I'm not trying to get you to be friends with me. All I want is for you to forgive me for speaking out of turn and hurting you, and to make you see that I'm not a bad person. You have less than two months left in this office and I wouldn't want you to leave while you still have ill feelings toward me."

"So, you're saying you don't want us to be friends?" Vivienne asked, slightly squinting.

"N-no, I… that's not what… No. I-I want us to be friends, but we can't be friends if you don't forgive me," he said.

"Well, your forgiveness will depend on if I like your peace offering," Vivienne said and pointed to the plastic container.

Really? Is this even happening?

Levi walked to the front of his desk and opened the lid. He gave Vivienne another fork while he held the container. She picked a small slice and he watched as she bit into it with her full red lips covering the width of the small piece. She closed her eyes, and a small hum of satisfaction escaped her lips as she chewed. Levi caught himself smiling as he watched her savor the bite.

"No way! This is really good!"

"I told you," Levi said, beaming.

"Wow! I have never had mangoes like this. What does your aunt put in her soil?" Vivienne asked as she took another slice.

Levi chuckled and gave her the whole container. "Here. You can have all of them."

"Really? What about you?" Vivienne asked, feeling hesitant.

"Don't worry about me. I have some at home."

"Okay, then." She shrugged and took the container from his hand with a smile.

Levi watched her pick another slice and put it into her mouth. "Does this mean you've forgiven me?" Levi asked in the most charming tone he could muster.

Vivienne stared at him as she continued to chew. He couldn't quite read the look in her eyes but one thing he knew was she had the most beautiful eyes he had ever seen. The movement of her lips was so distracting that it took all his willpower not to stare at them for too long. "Ask me after I eat the last piece," Vivienne said and playfully shooed him away to his seat

Levi chuckled. "Okay."

"Thanks, by the way," Vivienne said as a small smile danced on her lips.

"Anytime, Vivienne," Levi replied, smiling back.

Chapter Sixteen

Vivienne

On her first week at work, Vivienne had told Fisayo about meeting Levi again at her new job and how he had apologized to her but she didn't accept it because she believed his apology wasn't genuine.

"How do you know his apology wasn't genuine?"

"Because he wouldn't have apologized if we hadn't run into each other again," Vivienne said.

She heard Fisayo sigh at the other end of the phone and she knew a sermon was coming so she braced herself.

"Buks, the guy offended you and he apologized. I think that counts for something. You saying he wouldn't have apologized if he hadn't seen you again doesn't sound fair. Okay, what should he have done?"

"Found a way to apologize to me that same day?"

"Buks, how? Was he supposed to roam the streets of Lagos screaming your name, which I am not sure he even knew?"

Vivienne knew her sister was right, but she wouldn't give in easily. If she were the one who had offended someone in that manner, she would have done everything within her power to get in touch with them.

"No. But he could have asked his employer for my contact or even the bride. It's not that difficult to find people, Fifi. That's why we have technology."

"Well, that makes sense too. But what if there is a company policy against contacting clients for private matters? Look, I don't support what he did and said to you, but I think you should give him a chance to prove that he isn't as bad as he behaved when you met him," Fisayo said.

"I don't know what to think of all the excuses you have made for him. But one thing I know is when I asked if he would have still been as determined to get my forgiveness as he is now if we hadn't run into each other again, he had no answers for me. That's how I know his apology isn't genuine."

"I think the question you should have asked him was if he had felt bad after speaking to you in the manner that he did," Fisayo said.

"Well, I didn't ask him that and it doesn't matter," Vivienne said.

"Hmm." Fisayo paused. "So what has it been like working with him?"

"I've been here for just a week but it's been okay. He tries to start conversations but there's just nothing to talk about."

"Well, I'll ask you this question again in a few weeks. Hopefully, you'll have a different answer for me."

Vivienne scoffed and said, "Fifi, I doubt it. I really do."

"Never say never."

"Please, let's talk about something else," Vivienne said, forcing her sister to change their topic of discussion.

She asked Fisayo how school was and if she had successfully registered BGFAD. Fisayo said she had and that Vivienne would receive an email with her certificate of registration.

"Thanks, a lot, Fifi. I'll send you some money by the weekend."

"*Ehen!* That's what I like to hear. In this life, have a rich big sister *o,*" Fisayo said, hailing Vivienne in her usual sugar-coated manner.

"You should be a hype woman, you know," Vivienne said, and Fisayo laughed.

True to Vivienne's words, she sent Fisayo some money as soon as Mariam paid her and ordered a new Zara perfume to surprise her mom. This way her mom would feel more inclined to give her the old bottle.

Today made it exactly seven weeks since she started working for Ms. Preye, which meant she had five weeks left to spend in Levi's office. If she was being honest, she enjoyed and preferred working in his office to the staff room. It was quiet, clean, and always smelled good, just like Levi. She had tried working in the staff room for a day and it was hell. The incessant discussions and unsolicited pieces of advice about working for Ms. Preye was enough to make Vivienne realize sticking with the devil she knew was a better choice.

If it were up to her, she would continue working in Levi's office, but it wasn't. Maybe one day she would go up the ranks and earn a corner office just like Levi. Moreover, Levi would definitely want her to leave because she had made staying in the same office unbearable for him the past few weeks.

After speaking with Fisayo again last night, Vivienne decided to take her sister's advice to let go of any grudge she had against Levi. She remembered Fisayo saying, "Don't give anybody so much power over you that they live rent-free in your head and heart."

"To be honest, Fifi, I am getting tired of holding on to anger that's already fizzling out."

Fisayo whooped and said, "Buks, Buks, have you, by chance, caught feelings for your supervisor?"

Vivienne had vehemently refuted her sister's claims.

"We speak to each other only when it's absolutely necessary. Besides, I keep rejecting his offers to buy me lunch or give me rides home."

She also added that despite Levi being so attentive to her that she never had to ask him any questions about work because he was right there putting her through, she still didn't find him attractive.

Fisayo was disappointed at Vivienne's behavior and told her the same.

"Buks, this isn't like you. Yes, he hurt you, but I don't know you to be one to take things this far and hold grudges for this long, especially with strangers. Daddy is the only person I know you have perpetual anger toward."

"Please, don't mention Daddy in this conversation *abeg*. But you're right, Fifi. It's been so hard trying to keep up with being angry because he's been nothing but kind to me, even with my meanness."

"I'm glad you have come to this realization. Please let go and live with a lighter heart."

"Yes, ma'am," Vivienne said laughing.

"But Buks, I think you haven't found Levi attractive because you were angry at him. Many girls would have forgiven him long ago with all the effort he has put into trying to win you over."

Vivienne grunted and Fisayo said, "Seriously, Buks. Just imagine how doting Levi would be as someone's boyfriend or husband if he can be this loving to someone who is constantly mean to him."

"Well, Fifi, I'm not many girls. Neither am I looking to find anyone attractive or starting something with anyone. Love's not my thing."

"Okay then. Since you're not interested, is he single? I'm asking for a friend," Fisayo said playfully.

Vivienne laughed dryly and said, "I pity you. Do you know if he did all that just to get me to forgive him? What if he's not actually a good person?"

Fisayo clicked her tongue against the roof of her mouth. "I don't think so, Buks. Nobody has the time or patience to keep going overboard just to get someone to forgive them. It's not like he even has anything to gain. I think he's naturally a sweet person."

"Okay *o*, madam character analyzer."

They ended their conversation with Fisayo asking Vivienne how Mariam's wedding went. She said it was better than Funke's, but it was a two-day event and she was exhausted. She showed Fisayo the souvenir items she had gotten and promised to keep some of them for her when she came home for her birthday.

"Buks, I'm not sure I will make it down for your birthday."

"Fifi, why *now?*" Vivienne asked, sulking.

"It's looking like that would be our test week and I can't afford to miss any test."

"Fisayo, hurry up and graduate from that school, *abeg*. I can't have us missing important moments in each other's lives because of school," Vivienne said grudgingly.

Fisayo laughed. "Yes, ma!"

As Vivienne dressed up to get to work, she was happy that Ms. Preye's company wasn't the event planning company Mariam and her husband had hired which meant she didn't have any serious work tasks to get to. A few minutes later, Levi walked in. and greeted her in his usual, "Good morning, Vivienne."

Which she responded to in a tone that was too happy for even her ears. She also couldn't help but notice that he looked particularly good. There was something different about him that morning. It certainly wasn't the bright red turtleneck he wore, or was it?

Why am I even noticing this?

Vivienne shook her head and got back to work. Her sister might have successfully planted a seed in her heart but she wouldn't let it grow. The last thing she wanted was to notice anything else about Levi. There was an awkward silence between them but she pretended not to notice as she continued to type away at her laptop. Then Levi called her name and it amazed her how quickly her head snapped up as though she had been waiting for him to say her name all morning.

She closed her laptop and looked at Levi, who held out a container of mangoes he had brought for them to share. Mangoes were her favorite fruit and it took little convincing from Levi to get her to accept his peace offering. She watched as his brows shot in excitement and as his lips broke out in a smile. The sweet, tangy tropical smell of the mangoes danced around her nostrils. Her mouth watered at the thought of what the ripe sweet-smelling fruit would taste like.

Vivienne wondered how he could still be so persistent after weeks of rejection. Maybe Fisayo was right. He was probably a genuinely good person.

She put a piece into her mouth and her eyes closed in response to the divine taste on her tongue. She was glad she'd listened to Fisayo about letting go of her grudge against Levi. If she hadn't, she would have missed out on these out-of-this-world mangoes.

Levi must have felt pleased with her reaction because instead of sharing them with her as he said earlier, he told her to take the whole container. She did a little internal dance, happy to grab the container from his hands, but she didn't want to appear selfish.

So she said, "What about you?"

He told her he had some at home. She shrugged and collected the container from him with a smile she was sure showed her thirty-two teeth. She settled into her couch more and began eating another slice of mango when Levi asked, "Does this mean I'm forgiven?"

Vivienne studied his face as she chewed. His head was slightly tilted, his brows drawn together and his eyes had a lost puppy look. He had the most endearing, boyish look of contrition she'd ever seen, and it made her heart flutter.

Why does he have to look so handsome? It would have been easier holding on to this grudge if he wasn't handsome or kind.

She already had an answer for him but she needed a distraction to break off whatever was going on in her head while they stared at each other. It was a new and weird feeling for her and she had no interest in exploring it.

Soon it was lunch break, and Levi invited her to lunch. She declined, saying she was full from eating the mangoes. Then he asked if she wanted anything to take home, and she said she didn't. She and Levi just got off on the right start, and she felt letting him buy things for her wasn't right.

When Levi left for lunch, Vivienne took a few minutes to go over everything that had happened that morning. She couldn't believe how far a little forgiveness could go. It made her consider forgiving her dad for all he had done to her, but on second thought, she didn't think her dad deserved her forgiveness. Because unlike Levi, he had never made any attempt to show that he was sorry for how he had treated her all these years. He didn't even think he had done anything wrong to her, so forgiving him was out of the question.

By the time Levi got back, she had scheduled one week's worth of social media content for Preye's Elite Parties and even started editing video clips from Mariam's traditional wedding. When Levi opened the door, the smell of his cologne entered the office before he did.

"Hi," Levi said.

"Hey," Vivienne replied.

"I got you a donut just in case you get hungry later." Levi raised a small box mid-air.

Vivienne knew that box too well. It was from her favorite ice cream place, which was ten minutes away from the office. She felt uncomfortable accepting the donut, but at the same time, she didn't want to reject it so Levi wouldn't think she was still holding on to the past.

"You didn't have to, Levi. I feel very uncomfortable about accepting this."

"Don't worry. It's just one donut. You can buy me lunch tomorrow if it'll make you feel better," Levi replied, proffering the box in his hand to Vivienne.

"Thanks, Levi. Tomorrow's lunch is on me."

"Careful, girl. I've got expensive taste," Levi laughed. "Which reminds me." He paused as he adjusted his seat. "You haven't posted any wedding content recently."

"On PEP's page or my business page?"

"Yours."

"Oh. I haven't uploaded the wedding content from Saturday and yesterday. I haven't even edited them."

"Okay. 'Cause I was wondering,"

"How did you know I haven't posted any content recently? Wait! Are you following my business page?"

"As a matter of fact, I am," Levi responded, smiling.

"How come I didn't notice?"

"Well, it's probably because my username isn't my real name."

He showed Vivienne his Instagram profile. His username was KingPriest and his bio read, *"Child of God. Saved and redeemed. Spreading the love of Jesus Christ one person at a time."*

"Ah! Makes sense," Vivienne said.

"Which leads me to what I wanted to talk to you about. I watched all the videos on your page and they are amazing. But something's lacking."

Vivienne was genuinely curious. As far as she knew, she had done the necessary things to make sure her business started on the right professional track. From getting it registered to drawing up a contract for her clients, she was quite sure she had done the needful.

"Okay? What's that?" she asked.

"You don't have a website. At least, I didn't find the link to one on your profile."

"Oh, that! Yes, it's in my future plans. Right now, I can't afford to hire a website designer. Those guys are crazy expensive."

"I can help you though. That's if you'll let me," Levi said casually like it was no big deal.

"Really?" Vivienne asked, wide-eyed, and Levi nodded.

"How much is it going to cost me?" she asked, scratching her chin.

She wasn't about to accept any more freebies from Levi. Even if she couldn't afford to pay him once from her savings, she would come up with a payment plan.

"It's going to cost you a few extra hours after work for about a week."

"I'm not sure you understand, Levi. I meant, how much am I going to pay you for the website?"

"I heard you. And I said a few extra hours after work. We don't have any new clients until next month, which is a week from now. So I can finish your website in a week if you are there to provide all the details I need to set it up immediately."

"So, you don't want me to pay you for your service?" Vivienne asked, a frown plastered on her forehead.

"Technically, it's not a service. See it as a, uh…" Levi looked at the ceiling as he racked his brain for the right word to use. "As a favor. Yep, that's it. A favor."

"No. This doesn't sit right with me. I'd like to pay you," Vivienne said.

"And I said that I don't want you to pay me. See this as an extra peace offering."

Vivienne stared at Levi for a few minutes then she said, "Can I think about it, Levi?"

"Yes, but don't take too long. One day's already gone."

Chapter Seventeen

Levi

Over the next few days, Levi and Vivienne spent extra hours after work building her website. It had surprised him when she accepted his offer the next day. Still, he was happy she'd agreed to let him help her. He had chosen a simple but classy template for her website and made sure it contained just the necessary details high-end clients would want to see. It also helped that he had a degree in business administration. Now that he could see the end result, he couldn't wait to put finishing touches on the website and he would be done with it. Levi was proud of his work but more elated with the compliments and thank yous he got from Vivienne all week.

"Wow! This feature image is so stunning! How did you do it?" Vivienne said when she came back from the restroom.

Levi had waited for her to leave before he uploaded it because he wanted to surprise her when she got back. His initial plan was to upload it at home the night before then show her the finished website the next morning at work, but the designer hadn't delivered the picture at the agreed time. So he had to look for the next best opportunity, which was when she left for the restroom.

"I didn't do it. I'm good at many things but certainly not graphic designing," Levi said. "A graphic designer friend who owed me a favor did it for me. It's funny how he said the same thing about you when he saw your pictures."

"That I'm stunning, *abi?*" Vivienne said, flicking her hair side to side.

Levi nodded. "Yes, you are stunning. Very stunning."

They locked eyes, still smiling at each other. Levi wasn't one to play coy when it came to paying people compliments, especially ladies. It was something Josh had taught him about making a good impression on people. Vivienne cleared her throat, breaking the silence that hung between them. "Well, I'm glad I snapped those pictures when I did. Otherwise, I wouldn't have had anything to use."

"I know right! Personal pictures and videos of you performing your duty as a pro maid of honor or bridesmaid are important for your job. Also, if you can get your clients to do video testimonials talking about their experience with your service, it will help to cement prospective clients' hiring decision," Levi said.

"This makes so much sense, Levi! Thanks a lot. I deeply appreciate all your help. And please help me thank your friend for the feature image too," Vivienne replied, smiling broadly.

I certainly won't be doing that.

What he also wouldn't do was tell Vivienne that his friend had asked for her number. The way he'd gushed about how stunning Vivienne was and how every picture was a back-to-back hit was enough to annoy Levi. Over the next few hours, Levi gave Vivienne a tour of the blog's backend and frontend. By the time they were done, it was almost 9 P.M.

"So, this is it! BGFAD now has a website," Levi said, smiling, and Vivienne whooped.

"All thanks to you, the man of many talents." Vivienne curtsied.

Levi playfully took a bow and they laughed. Then he said, "Remember what we discussed regarding your blog?" Vivienne nodded and he continued. "Great. You should use it to educate the visitors on your website, who may eventually become clients, about why they need your services. So, topics like, '*Who is a professional bridesmaid and why you need one,*' '*Why your professional bridesmaid is the best video content creator for your wedding,*' are excellent blog starters to help your clients become familiar with your business and even feel pressured to hire you."

"Let me write down those topics before I forget," Vivienne said, typing away furiously on her phone with a rhythmic staccato. "I'll think of more later," she added.

"Sure. I'll just pack up so we can order some food and go home. It's getting late," Levi said.

"It's not that late," she said, looking up from her phone briefly. "Besides, we both don't live far from here."

She stopped typing and put her phone in the side pocket of her thigh-high denim skirt. "Also, I was thinking I could add videos from some of the weddings in the blog post about pro maid of honors as wedding content creators."

"Yes, Vivienne! That's actually smart. Add pictures where you can too. Then after those two topics, you can write about other wedding-related blog posts."

"All right. Noted."

"So, I'll send the link to your website and the backend login details to you on WhatsApp. Then you can add the website link to the bio on your social media profile and start writing your blog posts," Levi said as he zipped his laptop bag.

"Thank you so much, Levi. You have no idea how much I appreciate what you've done for me," Vivienne said, smiling broadly.

"You're welcome, Vivienne," Levi said, smiling back.

Spending these extra hours after work with Vivienne made him see other sides of her he wouldn't have likely seen if they weren't spending time together. For starters, she was super funny, and what made it more endearing was that she didn't even know it. Nobody had made him laugh as much as she did since Josh died and it felt good. As he stood up from his seat, he felt slightly dizzy so he sat down again.

"Levi?!" Vivienne shrieked and rushed to his side. "Are you okay?" she asked, touching his head and face with the back of her palm.

"I felt dizzy and my head hurts badly."

"Do you want to go to the hospital? Maybe get some tests done? Why am I even talking about getting tests done? You most likely have malaria. It's a normal everyday Nigerian illness," Vivienne said, still touching his forehead and neck.

Levi looked up at Vivienne who leaned over him. Her brows were drawn in a tight, furrowed line that etched deeper as she scanned his face. He laughed and held her shoulders.

"I'm fine, Vivienne. It's not like your eyes can x-ray me and see what's wrong."

Vivienne withdrew her hand and stood straight. "You must be really fine since you can still laugh and your tongue is dripping with sharp sarcasm."

Levi chuckled. "Or maybe I'm just hungry. Let's order something to eat."

"No. We are going out to eat today," Vivienne said and grabbed her bag.

"Why don't we just order in? I'll pay," Levi said and held the door open for her.

"Nope! We are going out. Mainly because I can't afford to order any more meals since you have a really expensive taste!" She walked through the door and Levi followed behind.

Vivienne turned sharply to speak to him, and he almost bumped into her, but she didn't seem to notice because she continued speaking while walking backward.

"Ah, Levi!" Vivienne clicked her tongue as she shook her head. "In these few days of ordering food, my bank account has seen premium *shege.*"

Levi burst out laughing. Vivienne rolled her eyes and turned her back to him, still walking. To be fair, he had warned her that he had expensive taste, but for her sake, he had allowed her to buy him lunch from wherever she could afford. Surprisingly, the food was just as good as the ones from the expensive restaurant he ordered from.

"But I warned you. You said you could handle it," Levi said when they got to the parking lot.

Vivienne scrunched her nose. "And I still can. What is expensive about jollof rice or *eba* and seafood okra? It's just that I am being frugal so spending extra money is *peppering* my body."

She seemed to consider her next words for a few seconds as they walked to his car. "But you are worth it, *sha,* because I would definitely spend more if I were to hire someone to build such a stunning website for me."

The dimly lit parking lot cast a gentle glow over Vivienne, highlighting her features in a soft, flattering way. Shadows danced across her face, making the curve of her cheekbones more pronounced and the subtle arch of her lips made her look delicate. She leaned on his car and shifted her weight on one leg, making her silhouette appear more feminine and effortlessly elegant.

"I'm worth it?" Levi asked, cocking his head to the side with his gaze fixed on Vivienne. His voice had also taken on a deeper, lower tone.

Was I just being flirty?

"Yeah," Vivienne replied, her voice barely audible.

They stood in the quiet parking lot, eyes locked. Neither of them moved. Levi's heart beat rapidly with unspoken, unexpected emotions. He tried to speak but he couldn't find the right words.

"We should get going," Vivienne said, snapping them out of the moment they just had.

"Yeah. Sure," Levi replied and rubbed the back of his neck. "So where are you taking me to eat today?" He opened the front passenger door for Vivienne, and she got in. When she was seated, he leaned on the door and added, "And I don't want rice or *eba*, *abeg*. Give me something light. Or should I order pizza?"

"Levi, will you die if you allow me to spend my money on you for one more day? What do you mean by, 'Should I order pizza?' Relax. I gotchu," Vivienne said, waving her wallet.

Levi raised his hands as he laughed.

"My bad. Please spend your money on me." He closed the door and walked to the driver's side.

Just before they drove out of the compound, they saw Ms. Preye arm-in-arm with Desmond, walking to his car as they laughed.

"Ms. Preye has been working late every day this week. And every time, it's either Mr. Desmond comes to pick her up or they spend time talking and eating in her office," Vivienne said.

"You noticed it too, I see," Levi said and started the car.

"Yeah. But you know what's funny too?" Vivienne asked and crossed her arms. Levi shook his head before putting the car in reverse. "At some point I thought you liked her," she continued.

"Who? Ms. Preye?" Levi asked, shocked.

"No. Me," Vivienne said through pursed lips, giving Levi the side eye.

"Wait. Why would you think that I liked her?" Levi asked as they drove out of the compound.

"'Cause on my first day here, I saw you watching her as she fixed her hair to welcome Mr. Desmond. I couldn't quite place the way you looked at her, but it appeared to me like you were interested in her."

Levi laughed heartily while Vivienne watched him with her top left lip raised and curled. The look she gave him was even funnier than her assumption. When he calmed down he said, "Sorry, but this is funny. You are funny. I don't like Ms. Preye at all." He turned to look at Vivienne briefly before looking back at the road ahead.

"I mean, she's great and all but I don't have any interest in her." Levi paused. "I like someone else," he said, staring deeply into Vivienne's eyes.

She stared back the first few seconds and averted her gaze as she tucked an errant hair behind her ear. The loud blast of a car horn got Levi driving again. One thing was for sure, he liked Vivienne but he wasn't sure if she liked him too. For all he knew, she could just be reciprocating what she thought were his acts of kindness toward her and nothing more. Levi also knew he had to be careful with his heart because despite wanting to find love and start a family, it needed to be with someone who loved the Lord and shared the same family values as him. To him, those were more important than any physical attraction he would have with a woman. Right now, he didn't know anything about Vivienne or her relationship with God. But he was determined to find out.

Levi cleared his throat and said, "Where exactly are we going?"

"With what?" Vivienne asked, puzzled.

"Where are we going to eat?"

"Oh, that!" Vivienne tittered. "It's not far from here. Keep going straight and turn left after the next T-junction," Vivienne added, avoiding eye contact with him.

"Got it," Levi said and smiled at her.

They talked about their next event, which was the wedding of the former governor of a western state in the country.

"Were you among the pioneer staff members for PEP?" Vivienne asked Levi.

"Not at all. I joined three years after they had begun operations. But none of the pioneer members are here, except the HR manager," Levi replied, and Vivienne nodded. "In my three years of working here, I have seen firsthand how Ms. Preye has grown her brand to be the number-one luxury event planning company in Lagos."

"I hope my professional bridesmaid business will become even half as successful in the future."

"It will. You'll see," Levi replied.

Vivienne's phone rang, and she quickly fished it out of her side pocket but froze when she saw the screen. The phone continued to ring and Levi looked at her to find out why she hadn't answered the call. There was no movement from her as she continued to stare at the phone blankly. Then she ended the call. The phone rang again, jolting her out of the daze she was in. This time, she didn't hesitate to end the call. She apologized for the interruption, and Levi said it was fine even though he wondered why a phone call would make her so edgy. They tried to resume their conversation but her phone rang for the third time, interrupting them. This time, Vivienne hissed and switched off the phone.

"Is everything okay?" Levi asked, unable to hide his curiosity.

"Yes. It's just my dad," Vivienne answered nonchalantly.

Levi was taken aback by her tone and aloofness toward answering her dad's calls. He couldn't wrap his head around why she would act so disgruntled that her father was calling her. He tried to ignore his uneasiness about the situation, reminding himself that it wasn't his business. Yet, somehow, he couldn't let it go.

So he said, "If you don't mind me asking, why did you ignore your dad's calls?"

"He's not calling to tell me anything good or important. I might text him later."

"But what if he needs something urgently? It's late and I think your dad calling you at this time means it must be pretty serious."

"Levi, please. Can we drop this subject? I know my dad, you don't," she said, looking at him pointedly.

Levi didn't miss the anger that flashed in Vivienne's eyes before she turned away to face the window. It was the same look he had seen when they bumped into each other months ago.

"Okay. I'm sorry."

"It's fine. We're almost there. It's the next left turn," Vivienne said, still not looking at him.

They drove the rest of the way in silence, and Levi wondered why talking about her father got her fired up. Still, he thought of what he could do or say to cheer her up again.

Chapter Eighteen

Vivienne

When Vivienne's phone rang, her first thought was that it certainly had to be her mom calling to ask when she would be home. But then she saw the caller ID and froze for a minute, staring at the screen in disbelief. Her father hadn't called her in over two years, and it made no sense why he would call her out of the blue.

Unless he is calling to shame me about my job… Again.

Her body became stiff and she ended the call. The last time she saw him or heard anything from him was the night of Funke's wedding when she met him at home. Since then, it had been crickets from his end. Her father called again and she ignored it until she eventually switched off her phone after his third call. Wondering why her father would call her repeatedly so late at night made her stomach queasy and her palms sweaty.

Vivienne was pissed at how much power he had over her. One minute she was happy, talking about her future aspirations for her business, the next minute her father calls and ruins her mood. She also didn't appreciate Levi trying to convince her to answer her dad's calls when he knew nothing of her relationship with him.

But since her last conversation with Fisayo about her bitterness toward Levi, she had decided to take her sister's advice about not letting people live rent-free in her head and heart. Now, she was more conscious about the way she reacted to things and people who annoyed her. Vivienne had also decided that nobody was worthy enough to ruin her mood or day. She mentally shook herself back into the bright mood she was in before her father's call came in.

Vivienne had made it a point of duty to buy dinner for Levi every day for the past five days to thank him for the website he was building for her business for free. Today, instead of ordering in, she suggested they go out to eat since they finished earlier than usual. She hadn't told him exactly where they were headed, but it was to her favorite roadside snack stand. She would buy some hot *puff puff* and enjoy herself as usual, shoving her father out of her mind as she shoved the hot dough into her mouth. Then they would end the tour at her favorite ice cream place.

Spending the past few days with Levi showed her a lot about him. Fisayo was right—he was a genuinely good person. She had watched him help other staff members with their tasks and even personal needs. One time, she saw him giving Bayo some money, and even though she couldn't hear their conversation, it was clear that Levi had helped him sort out his financial difficulty.

Something else she was also afraid to admit was that Levi had managed to make her feel again. It was the same excitement to see someone every day, being hyper aware of their presence and smell, the giddy feeling when they do something nice for you or call your name. All of it was scary and brought back painful memories for her. Levi also made her feel safe and cared for, which was something she lacked from her dad—the very man who should have made her wellbeing his life's mission.

Remembering the way Levi had looked at her earlier when he said he liked someone else had made her stomach do a thousand flips. Nevertheless, experience had taught her not to assume she knew a man's feelings for her simply by what he did. Her first and only experience with feeling this way was in her second year at the university when a transfer student became close to her. He started by borrowing her notes and asking her for tutorials.

Then he would reciprocate her kindness in different ways, including buying nice gifts for her. He did all the right things a man interested in a romantic relationship with a woman would do. However, he never asked her out, and when she confronted him about their situation months later, he said he thought they were just friends who did nice things for each other. After that experience, her motto became, *"If he doesn't say it, don't assume it."*

Vivienne could see the familiar crowd hovering around the snack stand as they got closer. The air around smelled like sweet fresh dough in cooking oil. The yellow light bulb dangling from the ceiling of the stall cast a warm, diffused glow through the smoke and fumes swirling from the large frying pan and firewood. It was always a welcome sight that meant the snacks were piping hot.

"It's here. You can park here," Vivienne said excitedly.

"Oh! Okay," Levi said, looking a bit taken aback by her excitement.

"Do you want to come with me?"

"Nah. I'd rather wait in the car. Being around hungry, impatient customers isn't my thing, but I'll come running if you need me."

"Okay." Vivienne hopped down from the car and skipped to the woman's stall. It was her usual spot whenever she craved a snack, which was quite often. She had become a regular and the woman never failed to let her know.

"Good evening, Ma. How market?" Vivienne asked the woman who was swiftly scooping, wrapping, and handing snacks to waiting customers.

"My better customer welcome o. Market dey fine, thank God."

"Abeg, give me one thousand five hundred naira puff puff."

The woman had *puff puffs, buns,* plantain balls, fried yam, fried sweet potatoes, and spicy sauces. But the *puff puffs* were her favorite. They were also the cheapest at thirty naira a piece which meant she would get a lot for a small amount. The woman wrapped up Vivienne's order and gave it to her.

"Madame, this your puff puff don small o. Wetin happen na?" Vivienne said, eyeballing the snacks in the transparent plastic bag.

"Hmmm, my sister. Na the country wey we dey. Everything don cost now. Before, I de buy bag of flour for twenty thousand naira. Now dem dey sell am forty-four thousand."

Vivienne perfectly understood the state of the country's economy. It was biting down hard on everyone so much that even the rich complained. Levi had told her some of their clients had to either double the budget for their events or cut down on the things they wanted. This made Vivienne wonder how the poor even survived.

"Na true sha. Things don cost for everywhere. But you for maintain the former size, come increase the price."

"Ah, my sister. Who go buy am? People like as e dey cheap. If I increase price, many people no go fit buy am, especially small children wey dey go school."

"True talk. E make sense."

"God dey. Him go help us survive. Thank you o," the woman said cheerily.

"Bye, bye, Ma."

The aroma from the fried sugary dough filled the car as Vivienne got in and closed the door.

"It smells really good," Levi said, eyeing the plastic bag.

"Wait till you try it. But I must warn you that it's quite addictive. This place and our next stop are the things finishing my salary."

"If that's the case, I'm not interested," Levi said and started the car.

"No *o*. I can't be the only one addicted to this thing. You must join me," Vivienne said, waving a piece of *puff puff* in front of Levi's face.

"Fine! I'll join you." Levi laughed.

"Now, that's more like it," she said and threw the *puff puff* into her mouth.

"Where to next?" Levi asked.

"Waffles, Cones, and Cream," Vivienne said with her mouth full.

Levi chuckled. "No wonder your salary finishes quickly."

Vivienne shrugged and threw another piece of *puff puff* into her mouth. She raised the plastic bag and told Levi that if he didn't drive fast, all the *puff puff* would be gone by the time they got to their next stop.

When they got to the ice cream place, they placed their orders and got a table. Levi had chosen a simple strawberry and vanilla flavor mix while she had ordered rum and raisin with sweet cream, waffles, and coconut shavings as the topping.

"Your ice cream is so plain. No single razzmatazz," Vivienne said to Levi as they sat down to eat.

"What can I say? I'm a simple man."

Vivienne scoffed. "Or you are not just adventurous. I have worked with you for almost two months and one thing's for sure. You have a routine and you stick to it. Same thing with when we order food. It's always the same thing. *Eba*, rice; *eba,* rice."

"Seems like you have been studying me," Levi said, looking impressed by her findings.

"Well, you are a pretty easy read. If you were a university course, I'd definitely get an A."

Levi nodded and continued digging into his ice cream. Vivienne pushed the *puff puffs* to him and asked him to take a bite before eating his ice cream.

"Good, yeah?" Vivienne asked wide eyed.

Levi nodded, slightly opening his mouth to relieve himself from the frostbite.

"Do you want to try mine? You're halfway through yours already," Vivienne asked, lifting her cup of ice cream.

"Doesn't yours have rum in it?" Levi asked and she nodded.

"I'll have to pass. Alcohol makes me light headed. Plus I don't want to add anything to this headache I'm nursing."

"Your head still hurts?" Vivienne asked, looking worried.

"Yes, but a little. I just need to get enough sleep."

"Or maybe you are dehydrated. Should I get water?"

"Nah. It's not that. I'm just really tired."

"Okay. Let's go. I can finish this on my way home. Let me order a ride home," Vivienne said, bringing out her phone.

"No, take your time. I'll drop you at home too. We live fifteen minutes away from each other."

"Are you sure?"

"Yes," Levi said, and she nodded.

Levi had the same soft look in his eyes that he had earlier at the parking lot, and her heart fluttered.

"Vivienne," Levi said, his voice lower as he held her gaze deeply. His eyebrows were drawn together in a semi-unibrow, which made his forehead crease.

"Mhm?"

"I'm sorry about what I said earlier when your dad called. I don't know what your relationship with him is like and I shouldn't have insisted on you doing what you didn't want to do."

Vivienne didn't know how to react, especially not with the way he looked at her. So she waved him off without maintaining eye contact as she chewed her waffles.

"It's okay. You probably have a close relationship with your dad. That's why it seemed strange to you that I continually ignored my dad's calls. I get it and it's fine."

"Yeah. You're right. My dad and I are really close."

Vivienne nodded and licked her lips. "I figured it out from the pictures on your desk. My dad and I haven't had a good relationship for years, and I'm used to it. It's a miracle I still have his name saved as Dad in my phone."

"It's that bad?" Levi asked, wide-eyed.

Vivienne felt a little hurt that her estranged relationship with her dad was so alien to Levi who obviously had a loving and present father. She wished things were different with her dad, but they weren't and she had learned to cope with it.

"Yep! He hasn't been present in my life since I turned eighteen simply because I refused to study what he wanted me to study. He has called me every name in the book and made me feel less of myself."

She scraped the last bit of ice cream in her cup and licked the spoon.

"It's the reason I found it hard to forgive you when you called me incompetent because my father tells me that every chance he gets."

"Oh my God. I'm so sorry, Vivienne."

She blinked away the sheen in her eyes as quickly as she could and shrugged.

"It's okay. I mean, I am okay and doing well for myself. I have a pretty good-paying job and I can rub my success in his face."

"I know I cannot relate to not having a present and loving father. But despite having a great relationship with my dad, I have an even better father-son relationship with my Heavenly Father. No human relationship, no matter how close, can fill our need for love from God, the Father."

Vivienne watched Levi talk about his relationship with God with so much excitement. His eyes lit up as he talked about God's faithfulness and love. She couldn't relate to what he said because she didn't have a relationship with God and she also didn't think God was all that loving if He told His people to do things that hurt them just to please Him. But that was a topic for another day.

"Along with the stuff I'll send to you tonight, I'll also send you the link to a song by Daniel Bentley titled, 'Daddy dada.' You're Yoruba, and you know what it means right?"

"Yeah. It means good Daddy."

"Right. When you listen to the song, you may understand what I said about God being the best father anyone can ask for."

Vivienne didn't want to tell Levi that she wouldn't be listening to the song because she didn't care about knowing God as a father because she wanted nothing to do with Him. Instead, she nodded and said they could leave.

"I'm sure I look like Winnie the Pooh with the number of *puff puffs* I ate tonight," Vivienne said as she stood up.

Levi was lost for a minute but when he got that she was talking about how her crop top had gone up a notch higher from having eaten too much, he laughed heartily, attracting curious stares from other customers. The both of them covered their mouths with their hands as they giggled out of the ice cream place.

Back in his car, they talked about cartoons from their childhood. Vivienne told him how she and her sister would reenact some scenes from their favorite cartoons.

"One time, my sister and I decided that the best scene to act would be the one where Jerry set Tom's tail on fire."

"What?!"

Vivienne chuckled. "Yep! We obviously don't have tails so we decided to use our hair. Okay, my hair. Things got out of hand and my baby sister couldn't put out the fire quickly enough."

Levi looking at her and back at the road, wide-eyed, was even funnier than the story she was sharing.

"My dad was so pissed I had ruined my long hair. He said I would wear it burned and uneven like that, but my mom wasn't having it. She brought out his clipper and shaved my head *bololo,*" Vivienne said, chuckling.

Levi gasped. "No way!"

Vivienne nodded, laughing at the memory, but back then it wasn't funny.

"I was so ashamed of going to school with absolutely no hair on my scalp. I had to lie that I had cancer and was undergoing chemotherapy so nobody would bully me. And it worked," she said, smiling.

"What?" Levi laughed. "Wait, how old were you that you knew all about cancer and chemo?"

"I was nine, and I used to watch lots of Western movies so I knew more than the average nine-year-old."

"What a story! I can't even imagine you being bald,"

"Have you seen an egg before? That was me."

Levi laughed. "You're so effortlessly funny, Vivienne. You remind me of my cousin, Joshua,"

"He must be cool then."

"Yeah. He was," Levi said with a wistful look in his eyes.

"Oh. Sorry. What happened to him, if you don't mind me asking?"

"We were involved in a car accident and he died."

"Oh my goodness! I'm so sorry, Levi," Vivienne said and touched Levi's hand on the gear stick.

Levi acted surprised by her touch, but he seemed to welcome it. She also expected him to say more about his cousin's passing, but he steered the conversation in another direction. The way he avoided talking about his cousin told her that he didn't want to go into all the details of his death with her. She understood and didn't push for the conversation to happen. Soon, they arrived at her house and she thanked him for bringing her home.

"See you on Monday?"

Vivienne chuckled. "Sure."

They stood in front of his car, staring at each other for a few awkward moments. She wanted to bid him goodnight and go inside her house, but she didn't because it felt like Levi had something to say. He had removed his hands from his pockets and moved closer to her but did or said nothing, except tap his foot. Vivienne scanned his face for any hints and all she could pick were his nerves. She wondered why saying goodnight to her would make him nervous unless he wanted to do more than just say goodnight. Whatever it was, she didn't want to find out to avoid giving him the impression that she liked him.

But you like him, don't you? As a human being, of course.

She did an internal eye roll, dismissing the voice in her head. It was the same way Fisayo had managed to plant the seed that got her thinking Levi was attractive. Deciding that she wouldn't entertain the intrusive thoughts or Levi's weirdness anymore, Vivienne said, "Goodnight, Levi, and thanks for the ride."

"Goodnight."

His hands were back in his pockets and he looked less nervous than he had earlier. She chuckled, waved at him, and went into her compound.

Chapter Nineteen

Levi

Vivienne opening up to him about her relationship with her father had shocked him deeply. He felt sorry for her—that she had to live with the burden of feeling unloved and uncared for by the person who ought to love her the most. It also made him want to be there for her now more than ever.

Aren't you getting way ahead of yourself?

Levi brushed off the thought as he felt he was doing the right thing. He was also thankful that he had been persistent in trying to earn her forgiveness after hurting her. It now made sense why she was angry and hostile to him for that long. Nobody would be happy being around someone who constantly reminded them that they are not worth anything.

Lord, how can I help her?

Since he got home Saturday night, this had been the question in his heart. Levi couldn't imagine life without a good relationship with his father. Everything he knew about being a kind and intentional man, he'd learned from his dad. His dad had also been the one who taught him about Jesus from a tender age and helped him grow as a Christian over the years. He also saw the way his dad loved his mom to bits, and he longed for that kind of love. One that withstood storms and fought for the happiness of their home, no matter what it took.

Levi had once asked his dad how he knew his mom was the one for him. His dad had told him that apart from being physically attracted to his mom and having the same ideology about marriage and family, she also shared the same faith as him, which was the most important aspect. Every other thing they didn't agree on, they had found a compromise to make their relationship work.

For him, the physical attraction for Vivienne was there, but he wasn't sure if they shared the same faith or beliefs about marriage and family. This was something he needed to find out if he wanted to pursue a relationship with her. It would also be his first relationship ever, and the thought gave him butterflies. But how would he even pursue a relationship with Vivienne if he couldn't man up to hug her two nights ago?

Levi groaned as he remembered how he had moved toward Vivienne and did nothing but stand awkwardly in front of her. She must have thought he was crazy, but in his defense, not hugging her was safer than trying and getting rejected. He chuckled as he imagined what Joshua's response would be if he heard him thinking this way. Josh had always told him to live a little, take risks and remain persistent despite rejection. He never took his cousin's advice seriously, which was why he never dated anyone in school.

It was Monday morning, but he was already looking forward to visiting his parents this weekend so he could catch up with them and seize the opportunity to snap new pictures with his dad for the Father's Day father-and-child photo contest at PEP. Maybe talking to his dad would help him get more insight about his growing feelings for Vivienne.

Speaking of Vivienne, why is she late?

"Is everything to your liking, Mr. Levi?" the owner of the venue asked.

"You have a beautiful space and it ticks most of our boxes. However, there are a few things you will have to sort out if we will use your space."

"Of course! Those things will be sorted out for you once you've paid a deposit," she replied.

Levi thanked her and said he would get back to her once they made a decision. He took down notes on his iPad, and when he was done, he checked the time—9:30 A.M. He had thirty more minutes to spare, after which he would go to the next venue and text Vivienne to meet him there if she didn't answer his calls.

As he brought out his phone to dial her number again, a throbbing headache hit the left side of his head and he instinctively held it. He also broke out in sweats, and it was strange because the hall was air-conditioned. Levi walked slowly to one end of the hall where a chair was and sat on it. He had been nursing rebound headaches since he got home after dropping Vivienne off last Saturday, and he knew it was time to go to the hospital.

When he regained himself, he dialed her number. This time, he heard her ringtone in the hall and he turned to the entrance where the sound came from. Like a model out of a magazine cover, Vivienne strutted into the hall. Her hair was back to being the bright orange, curly and bouncy afro. Even though he had seen her wear her hair this way before, she looked more stunning to him that morning.

"I'm so sorry I'm late," Vivienne said, as she hurried to where he sat.

Levi was speechless. His eyes were fixed on Vivienne and he forgot he had just been nursing a headache before she walked in. Vivienne smiled at him and touched her hair.

"Hi," she said, holding his gaze.

"Hi," Levi said, smiling back at her.

"Sorry I'm late. But how did you even get here so quickly?"

Because I looked forward to seeing you, especially after I goofed on Saturday.

"I left my house earlier than usual and came here first," Levi said.

"Oh. That explains it." Vivienne nodded.

"Yeah," Levi said, touching his head again when the headache took another swing at him.

"Are you okay?" Vivienne asked.

"Yes. I have a slight headache, but I'll be good."

"Sure?" Vivienne asked, and he nodded.

"You had a headache on Saturday. Are you sure you don't need to go to the hospital?"

"I'm fine, Vivienne. Just take your pictures and videos so we can go to the next venue. We are a little behind schedule."

"Okay then. Give me five minutes max."

"Sure."

Levi watched Vivienne get to work, and he was sure he had never felt more strongly about anyone before. He had liked a few girls in the past but it never materialized into anything more than a friendship. So he had stopped trying to pursue anything romantic with any girl, no matter how much he liked her. But Vivienne was different. Something about her was enthralling, and he was willing to risk the outcome of exploring it.

"You're sweating profusely, Levi," Vivienne said, pulling him out of his daydream. He hadn't even noticed her presence until she touched his forehead.

"You're also burning up!" Vivienne said as her eyes grew as wide as saucers.

"I don't feel good either," Levi said, reeling forward.

"We need to get you to a hospital now. Can you drive?" Vivienne said, holding his shoulders as she squatted in front of him.

Levi nodded, looking into her eyes. It was intense yet filled with so much compassion. He relaxed his shoulders and touched her right hand on his shoulder with his left hand. Since he moved out of his parents' house, he was used to fending for himself and making sure others around him were okay. So someone else caring for him made him feel good, and he didn't want it to end.

She stretched her hand and asked if they could leave. Levi nodded and stood up, holding her hand. They got to the hospital and booked an appointment for him to meet with a doctor. He explained his symptoms and he was asked to run some tests. The results came back saying he had malaria fever and would be given some medication.

"Does my treatment involve injections?" Levi asked with raised eyebrows.

The doctor chuckled. "No, but you have to take intravenous Artesunate immediately."

"Are you scared of injections?" Vivienne teased him on their way to the ward from the doctor's office.

"This has nothing to do with whether I am afraid of injections or not. There is just no way I am sticking my butt out for someone to pierce with a needle!" Levi said with so much seriousness that Vivienne laughed, holding her sides.

She wiped the tears away and said, "Levi, nobody sticks their butt out. We usually just stand still for the nurses to do their thing. If showing half your butt to a stranger bothers you so much, think about women who have to show their private parts to strange people in the name of birthing a baby."

A nurse came in and prepped Levi for the IV medication. When she was sure he had settled in and the fluid drip rate was perfect, she left the ward. Levi thought about what Vivienne said before the nurse came in. She was right, but it still didn't change his dislike for injections.

"You're right, *sha*. I didn't even think about that. Geez! It takes a lot of courage to do that."

"I guess so. However, in that state of birthing pain, I don't think any woman is thinking about how many people will get to watch her give birth. All she wants is for the baby to come out quickly and safely."

"Sounds like you are prepared for it already. I mean, especially since you don't have an issue with sticking your butt out for a nurse to stab with a needle."

Vivienne laughed heartily again. "Well, I don't know if I am prepared to have kids, *o*. I like them and will probably want some in the future except I don't want to raise one all by myself."

Levi sat up straighter. "What do you mean by raising them yourself? Won't you get married so you can raise your kids with your husband?"

"Uh, that's the thing. I don't want to get married," Vivienne said.

Levi was taken aback and his brows shot up in response. He wasn't expecting her to say she didn't want to get married. Now, he definitely wanted to find out why.

"Why's that?"

"For starters, I don't believe in love. I think it's just a way of romanticizing basic human instincts like physical attraction or the need for companionship. Secondly, love, for selfish people in particular, is all about convenience or need. Nothing more. Finally, I haven't seen any examples of what a good marriage looks like around me and I certainly don't want what my parents had."

Levi was speechless for the second time that day. He felt like a deflated balloon. The woman he was interested in having a future with wanted nothing to do with love or getting married. He had never experienced heartbreak before, but the way his chest hurt made him think he was experiencing one.

"Are you okay?" Vivienne asked, scanning his face.

Levi swallowed hard and shook his head. She asked if he wanted her to call the doctor and he said he didn't. So many thoughts ran through his mind including Josh's advice about not backing down in the face of rejection and Songs of Solomon 8:4.

Do not arouse or awaken love until it so desires.

Levi was conflicted about what to do. He didn't know whether to pursue his feelings for Vivienne—especially because something about the way she acted around him and spoke to him made him so sure she liked him too—or leave things to play out according to fate.

What if she's just being nice?

Levi didn't think Vivienne was just being nice. There was more to her actions toward him than playing nice. Still, one lingering thought remained. What was her relationship with God like? Did she even have any? He hoped Vivienne was a child of God because it would make things less complicated for him. He couldn't even imagine trying to win her affection—maybe even succeeding—only to discover she wasn't saved. It would ruin everything for him.

"I'll call Ms. Preye to let her know we're at the hospital," Vivienne said, indicating she was leaving the ward.

Levi nodded, and she left him to his thoughts. Again, Songs of Solomon 8:4 crossed his mind, but this time, it didn't matter to him. He had made up his mind and there was no giving up on his part. He would do everything humanly possible to show Vivienne how much he cared about her and how much she deserved to be loved. He would be the one good example of what true love was and he would prove himself to her no matter how long it took.

Chapter Twenty

Vivienne

Vivienne was in the salon dying her hair back to its ginger color when Fisayo called her to say their dad had been trying to reach her the previous night to no avail. She told her sister that she had nothing to say to their father which was why she didn't answer his calls.

"Buks, didn't Mommy tell you?"

"Tell me what?"

"Daddy is sick."

There was no way her mother would have told her anything because her mom had already gone to bed when Levi dropped her off that Saturday night. By the next morning, before she woke up, her mom had gone to church for Sunday service. Now, it was already noon and she was at the salon, and she didn't even know if her mom was back from church yet.

"Okay? I'm not sure why he was calling me because the last time I checked, I'm not a doctor," Vivienne said.

"I know, Buks. Daddy called me to say that he really needs to speak with you. He didn't sound fine at all."

"He'll be fine, Fifi," Vivienne tutted.

"No, he won't," Fisayo said and broke down in tears.

Though she couldn't share Fisayo's sentiments toward their dad, it worried her that her sister sounded frightened and sad. Whatever was wrong with their father wasn't something minor, otherwise Fisayo wouldn't call her or sound so upset.

"Fifi, what's wrong?"

Fisayo blew her nose and sniffled. "Buks, Daddy's dying. He has acute liver disease."

"What? How? Are you sure? Did you see the doctor's report?" The questions rolled out of Vivienne's tongue faster than her brain could process them.

One thing was for sure, her father was a manipulative person who liked to use every form of blackmail to get what he wanted. She had seen this play out many times to the point that nothing about him surprised her anymore.

"Mommy went to see him yesterday. She called me on video from the hospital and we spoke to the doctor together," Fisayo said and sniffed.

Vivienne's heart pricked when she learned she was the only one in her family who didn't know about her father's illness. But at the same time, she understood why her mom and sister might have been hesitant to tell her about it.

"Buks, you need to go see Daddy as soon as you can. He refused to tell me or Mommy why he wants to see you," Fisayo said.

"Fifi, I can't. I am the happiest I have ever been these past few weeks, and Daddy's not responsible for that. He and I already have bad blood, and I don't want it to get worse or ruin the little happiness that has managed to find me."

"Buks, from what the doctor told us, Daddy has a slim chance of surviving this. The treatment isn't working and the only solution is to get a liver transplant. We don't even know how much time he has left. What if he dies and you never got to see him? Wouldn't you regret not hearing what he had to say to you?"

"Fifi, please," Vivienne said tersely. "I don't like the emotional blackmail. What makes you think I will regret not resolving my issues with Daddy if he dies?"

"Because you are a good person, Buks. You're just angry at Daddy and until you learn to forgive him, he will always be a weight on your heart or a stumbling block preventing you from experiencing the love and happiness you rightfully deserve." Fisayo paused as she waited for Vivienne's retort but there was none so she continued. "Buks, Daddy hurt you and you have every right to be angry. But I also know that you unconsciously carry this hurt around and it's the determining factor for most of your life's decisions. You can't live like this forever. You deserve better."

"I don't know, Fifi. But I'll think about it."

And she had. Vivienne thought about what her sister said to her throughout that day and if she was being honest with herself, Fisayo was right. She'd started attending wedding parties to spite her dad, and even though it ended up being the foundation for her growing business, the motive behind it wasn't right.

She'd also accepted Ms. Preye's job offer just to prove to her dad that she too could be successful. More so, the only reason she'd been so mad at Levi for weeks was because his words reminded her of her father's actions toward her.

Hearing her mother pray for her dad all night also didn't help. Her conscience pricked her, making her question if she truly wouldn't regret not resolving her issues with her dad if he died. It also made her wonder how her mom could forgive and even pray for him after everything he did to them. Maybe it was time she asked her mom for some advice because Fisayo was right. Everything she did was to prove her father wrong.

"Driver, *o wa o!*" Vivienne said once she realized they were at her bus stop.

Monday mornings were always hectic and she was already late for work. Thankfully, she was on her way to meet Levi at an event center instead of going to the office. Thinking about meeting him at work made her heart flutter. Each day, she looked forward to spending more time with him, and right now, it was the one good thing she had going for her.

It's funny how I went from loathing him to looking forward to spending my day with him.

Vivienne brought out her phone to check the time and saw two missed calls from Levi. She hadn't heard her phone ring throughout the bus ride. True to her suspicion, her phone was in silent mode. She turned off the silent mode and hurried into the hall. Just as she got to the entrance, her phone rang again. It was Levi.

When he turned to face the entrance, she could swear her stomach took a deep dive and tingled at the same time. Levi looked striking in his black V-neck polo that showed off his crucifix necklace and tan corduroy pants. Vivienne waved her phone at him before ending the call. She apologized for coming late, but it didn't seem like Levi heard her. Even though she had put in effort to look extra nice that day, she didn't expect her knee-length floral sundress to have such an effect on him.

His reaction made her feel warm, and she smiled at him. She thought about telling him he looked good, too, but decided not to.

"Hi," Levi said, smiling back at her.

Vivienne apologized for coming late again, and Levi said he was worried when she didn't pick or return his calls. She didn't want to tell him her phone was in silent mode so she said the bus was too noisy for her to hear anything. Levi grimaced and touched his head.

"Are you okay?" she asked him, and he told her it was a slight headache. The same thing he said on Saturday.

Vivienne wasn't comfortable with his answer but let it slide. However, she decided that if Levi showed any other signs of discomfort, she would drag him to the hospital if she had to. She got to work filming the venue and taking pictures. If they decided to use this hall, it would form part of the behind-the-scenes and before and after content for PEP.

When Vivienne got back to where Levi sat, she found him sweating profusely, which was strange. She touched his forehead and was shocked at how hot it was. Her mind flashed back to her dad in the hospital and she felt a guilty prick on her heart. But Vivienne brushed it off.

Being so close to Levi and her hands on his shoulders made her all too aware of his presence and her actions. She had never been this openly affectionate with anyone other than her mom and sister. The way Levi stared at her as though he could see her soul or read her mind made her heart race. She traced his jawline with her eyes and then moved up to his lips. A soft smile danced on their natural curve and Vivienne wondered what they would feel like against hers.

Stop it!

"You're worrying too much, Vivienne. But thank you. I'm glad you're here with me," Levi said, ending her wild imagination.

"You're welcome," she said and stood up before she would embarrass herself. She didn't even notice Levi had put his hand on hers until he gave it a gentle squeeze.

Levi eventually agreed to go to the hospital and he was quickly placed on intravenous medication. She excused herself to go inform Ms. Preye of the situation. Their boss asked if Levi was okay and Vivienne said he was. Then she asked Vivienne to come back to the office when she was done with Levi. Somehow, she had hoped Ms. Preye would tell her to take the rest of the day off to be with Levi. But who was she kidding? She wasn't his spouse or family member nor was she a doctor. So her presence wasn't exactly needed.

When she returned from her call with Ms. Preye, she found Levi asleep so there was no point in staying back as she had purposed to do before making the call. The crucifix pendant on Levi's neck had moved to the side and she adjusted it for him. She held the tiny pendant, studying it for a while. It reminded her of the arguments she and her mom had about going to church when she decided to stay far away from God.

Vivienne placed the cross gently on his neck to avoid waking him up, then she covered his legs with a blanket. Seeing Levi sick and being by his side made her rethink how she felt about her dad. Here she was sitting by a stranger in a hospital when her dad was probably alone in the hospital.

He has other kids. They will be there for him.

Vivienne told herself she had every right to be angry and not be there for her dad since he wasn't there for her when she needed him the most. If she was by Levi's side now, it was because he had done enough to show her that he cared for and valued her. Before leaving the hospital, she sent Levi a text saying she had informed Ms. Preye that he was ill and that she had to get back to work. She also said she would try to come see him after work if he was still at the hospital by then. Otherwise, she would visit him at home the next day.

On her way back to the office, she called her mom and told her Fisayo called her the previous day to tell her their dad was sick. She also asked her mom why she didn't tell her, and her mom said she didn't know how Vivienne would feel about it. She told her mom it felt weird that they lived in the same house but she found out about her dad's illness from Fisayo who was in school. Her mom apologized and asked Vivienne if she wanted to go with her to visit her dad that evening, which would be good since he had been asking to see her.

"I don't think this evening will be possible. My supervisor and I had some work to do together, but he fell ill. Now I have to do the work alone."

She didn't want to tell her mom that she had no intentions at all to visit her dad at the hospital. The last thing she needed was her mom trying to convince her to forgive her dad or hear what he had to say at least.

"Okay then. Whenever you feel up to it, we can go together," Vivienne's mom said, and they hung up.

True to her assumption, when she got to the office, Ms. Preye gave her a list of venues she had to visit the next day since Levi wouldn't be coming to work for the rest of the week. Two of the halls were on the island while the other two were on the mainland. Looking at the list, she mentally planned her schedule.

Vivienne got home late that night, and she found her mom praying for her dad in the living room. She prayed for God to heal him and for him to accept Jesus as his savior. She prayed in tongues for a while and then switched back to praying for her dad's salvation in English and Yoruba. She wanted to talk to her mom about her conflicting emotions on whether to visit her dad in the hospital or not. At least, if anyone would understand how she felt, it would be her.

After speaking to her mom that afternoon, she felt so uneasy— as though she was doing something wrong. No amount of pep talk could shake away the weird feeling or justify why not visiting her dad was the right thing to do.

Just when she thought her mom had finished praying and was about to go meet her in the living room, she started another round of prayers. This time, she was the prayer point. Somehow, it felt intrusive listening to her mom pray about her so she plugged her AirPods and put on some music from her favorite playlist.

The first song that played was "I like Me Better" by Anthony de la Torre and Lana Condor. It reminded her of Levi, and she smiled thinking about him. She didn't think it was right to call him late at night so she sent a WhatsApp message instead.

"Hey. How are you feeling?"

Almost immediately, his reply popped up. She didn't think he would be awake but she was glad he was.

"I'm good and home now. I've been waiting for you to call or text me, though."

"Sorry. I got busy. I had to get back to work."

"Yeah. I saw your message. I was hoping I would wake up to you by my side, not a text message saying you had to leave."

Levi added the crying emoji and she replied with the laughing crying one.

"Guess what?"

"You're taking the day off to come see me tomorrow?"

Vivienne chuckled and rolled her eyes.

"You wish. Ms. Preye is having me go check out those venues in your stead tomorrow."

"Oh my God! It's going to be super stressful for you. What if I come to pick you up tomorrow and we go together?"

Inasmuch as she would like to spend the day with Levi, she didn't think it was wise for him to risk his health.

"Are you crazy? Or did you forget you are an invalid?"

"Na wa o. Small malaria and you are already calling me an invalid. I feel fine already even though I have to finish the rest of my medication."

"You're clearly not feeling fine. If you were, you wouldn't be offering to chauffeur me around Lagos."

"So, how do you think I will cope if I don't see you the rest of this week? I'm used to spending half of my day with you. No, scratch that. I like spending my day with you."

Vivienne's stomach did multiple flips, and she caught herself grinning. She rolled on her bed and switched positions many times. She felt giddy like a high school girl talking to her crush, the popular kid every girl wanted to date.

You don't like him, Vivienne. I repeat, you. do. not. like. Levi. He's not attractive and you're not interested in falling in love. You don't even believe in it!

Despite chiding herself, Vivienne typed that she liked spending time with him too. She was about to send the message to him,

183

damning the consequences, but then she thought of all the things that could possibly happen because of it. So she deleted it and sent,

"Just focus on getting better first, then you can think about work."

"Well, you're right. I can drive you around when I get back to work. By the way, I'll send you a list of things to ask and look out for when you visit those venues."

"That'll be great. Thanks, Levi."

"Anything for you, Vivienne."

Her thoughts flashed back to the wild thought she had about kissing him earlier, and she shook her head. Before she had any more crazy thoughts, it was best she went to bed.

"Goodnight, Levi."

"Night. Talk soon."

He added the upside down smiling emoji and she replied with the thumbs up emoji.

"It's nothing. I just need companionship. That's all," Vivienne said and threw the duvet over her head.

"Buks Buks. Are you sleeping?" her mom said, poking her head through the door.

"No, Mommy. Come in." Vivienne sat up.

"I had a feeling you wanted to talk to me," her mom said and sat on her bed.

"Actually, I did. But you were praying and I didn't know when you would finish."

"I knew it," her mom said, smiling at her. "I prayed for you too."

"I heard you, Mommy. But I don't need saving."

"Everyone needs saving, baby," her mom said with so much compassion.

Vivienne cleared her throat and turned away. Her mom touched her cheek tenderly. "Buks, how are you?"

She looked at her mom and tried to put words to the emotions she felt, but she couldn't. She just moved closer to her mom and hugged her. They held each other for a while, and her mom eventually broke the silence by apologizing for not telling her about her dad.

"It's fine, Mommy. I understand, and that's what I want to talk to you about. How did you manage to forgive Daddy after all he did to you? Mommy, it hurts me every time I remember the things Daddy has said to me, but at the same time, I feel so bad that I don't want to go visit him at the hospital. It doesn't even help that Fifi called to tell me to forgive him and then I come home and hear you praying for him."

Her mother waited to make sure Vivienne had finished talking before she spoke.

"First of all, Buks. You feel bad because you are a good person. You still have a conscience and I'm extremely happy about that. Second, there is no way I could have forgiven your dad even if I wanted to. You know how much pain and humiliation your dad put me through because I left him to follow Jesus. It was the Holy Spirit who helped me to forgive him. It was difficult but ultimately, obeying God paid off."

"How, Mommy? How has following Jesus paid off? We were at Daddy's mercy for survival for so long. Then, when I turned eighteen and refused to do his bidding, he cut me off completely. That plunged you into deeper hardship. So, how did Jesus help you? Why didn't He save us from suffering since you left Daddy to follow Him?" Vivienne asked, her voice breaking.

Her mom had tears in her eyes as she held Vivienne's hands. "Buks, the answer is simple. It's Mark 8:34-37. Yes, leaving your dad was difficult but I had to because I was with a married man. I was breaking up a family because of my selfishness and love for wealth and comfort. But when I found Jesus and gave my life to Him, I no longer lived for myself. So, even if it was hard for us, knowing that I was pleasing God gave me hope and comfort. It also gave me the peace of mind I never enjoyed even while I was with your father."

Vivienne's mom sniffed and continued. "Buks, you have no idea what it feels like to live like a prisoner. When we initially started the affair, your father would ask me to play dead whenever his wife called."

Vivienne's brows shot up and her eyes widened in shock. She had no idea her mom had lived this way at some point. All she knew was that her dad had another family and she couldn't see her half-siblings.

"When his wife eventually found out about us, I had just given birth to you. It made me live in constant fear that one day she would find me and hurt us for ruining her marriage. There were also times I would beg your dad to come see us and he would tell me that he was with his family as if we weren't his too. Buks, I didn't want you girls to grow up around that kind of example, and I am glad I found Jesus when I did."

When Vivienne's parents split, she was eight years old. She knew it was because her mom had become a Christian and didn't want to continue her relationship with her dad. It wasn't until she turned thirteen that she knew the full details. Still, it didn't stop her from being mad at her mom for sending their dad away and making life difficult for them. Hearing her mom's side of the story made her see things differently now. She couldn't imagine having to take insults from her dad just to fend for herself.

"Right now, I just want your dad to accept Jesus into his life before it's too late."

Vivienne also remembered following her mom to church grudgingly after her parents split because she had no choice than to obey until she turned eighteen and stopped going. At that point, a relationship with her dad was non-existent as she had already told him off. Her mom had tried her best to settle the conflict between them but it only created more problems. Her attempt at peacemaking only made Vivienne more rebellious as she stopped going to church, knowing it would hurt her mom since building a relationship with God and making sure her girls were raised that way meant everything to her.

"But what if he doesn't want to?" Vivienne asked.

"Then I'll keep praying for him just as I am praying for you, Buks. It is my deepest desire that one day you will experience God's love and accept Him into your heart," her mom said with a small smile playing on her lips.

"Mommy, I don't want anything to do with a God who forces His followers to make decisions that bring them pain and poverty," Vivienne said defiantly.

Her mom chuckled. "One day, you'll understand, and I pray it's soon."

Chapter Twenty-One

Levi

Levi couldn't contain his excitement knowing that Vivienne was just five minutes away. He decided waiting for her by his apartment gate was best since it was quite late already. He shifted his weight from his right foot to the left. He had been waiting outside for over ten minutes, but he didn't mind. All that mattered to him was seeing Vivienne.

He had pulled out his phone to call her when he saw her bright orange hair pop out of a car. His heart skipped a beat and his face broke into a smile.

"Vivienne!" he said, waving her over.

She turned and waved back, beaming at him.

Levi met Vivienne by the car, and this time, he didn't hesitate to hug her. He asked the driver how much his fare was. Vivienne told him she had paid already and that it wasn't much. He insisted on reimbursing her and she gave him a side eye.

"Where's your apartment, *abeg*?"

Levi chuckled and led the way with Vivienne following behind.

"*Ahan! Oga* Levi. You're a big man *o,*" Vivienne said, looking visibly impressed.

"Please, *o.* I am just managing.

Vivienne scoffed playfully. "Managing indeed. A whole boss like you. Your place is quite nice and it smells good too. Or did you spray perfume because I was coming?"

"Yes *o.* I have to impress you so that you will come again," Levi teased back.

"Well, your scheming might just work. But it will also depend on how nicely you treat me today," Vivienne said as she settled in comfortably on one end of the two-seater sofa.

"Say no more. I'm at your service." Levi took a bow.

He asked her what she would like for refreshment. She said she was fine and didn't expect him to have anything ready since he was recuperating.

"Vivienne, you don't rate me at all. I have ordered all your favorite things. At least, the ones I know," Levi said and walked into the kitchen.

"Huh?"

Shortly, Levi came back with a large tray containing ice cream from Waffles, Cones, and Cream, pizza, *ofada* rice and *ayamase* sauce, and a pack of mango juice.

"See how you've succeeded in making me feel silly for bringing just apples and grapes for you."

Levi laughed. "No vex, *abeg.*"

"But wait *o*. For you to have the energy to do all these, you must be feeling very fine," Vivienne said, still looking surprised by everything Levi had laid out on the table.

"As a matter of fact, I am. Also, it doesn't take much energy to order food *now*."

"I see. So how are you feeling?" Vivienne asked.

Levi sat down, facing Vivienne on the other end of the sofa.

"I feel great and well-rested actually. But it's only the second day, and I feel tired of this break already. I should tell Ms. Preye that I feel fine enough to work. Or maybe I should just show up at the office."

Vivienne angled her head to one side as she looked at Levi in disbelief.

"What?" he chuckled.

"Why do you like stress, for God's sake? You have no idea what I would do to get a week off right now."

"You can ask for a short leave. Maybe two or three days," Levi said and bit into an apple.

"Right. But how will you survive without me in that office?" Vivienne asked, smirking.

"You're right. I won't survive because as I haven't been around you in almost forty-eight hours, *na die I dey so.*"

Vivienne laughed and called him a clown. Her laughter sounded like music to Levi's ears. It was airy and it made his heart feel light and warm. He couldn't help but smile as he watched her talk about the funny things that had happened at work since he was away.

The way she threw her head backwards and clutched her chest as she laughed made her extremely attractive. She took a slice of pizza and bit into it with her eyes closed. Levi watched as she licked the pizza crust off her lips.

Levi cleared his throat. "So, how did the venue inspection slash hunt go? Was my list helpful?"

At this point, he would ask any random question just to distract himself from watching Vivienne like a creep.

"Yeah. It was a lifesaver."

"I'm glad you found it helpful. Apart from work, what's up with you?"

Vivienne shrugged and said there was nothing going on with her except work and that the website he had built for her had lots of blog traffic. She also said she had weddings booked for the end of the month and mid-July.

Levi watched her avoid eye contact as he commended her on the success of her business. He sensed something was wrong with her, and he hoped she would feel safe enough with him to talk to him about it. He thought about asking her what was wrong but decided not to. He would just keep talking to her about random things until she felt comfortable enough to open up.

They talked about other colleagues in the staff room. Vivienne said she dreaded moving there but had no choice as her three-month probation in Levi's office would be over in four weeks.

"I can talk to Ms. Preye about letting you stay longer."

Vivienne shook her head. "I don't want you to. Please don't."

"Okay. I won't."

The discussion veered to their families and Levi couldn't help but notice how Vivienne meticulously avoided bringing up her dad even when the conversation was about their childhood memories. If he remembered correctly, they didn't become estranged until she turned eighteen. So it felt weird that she didn't mention him, and her body language also gave her away.

"I'm done for tonight. If I eat any more food, I'll puke," Levi said and wiped his mouth with a napkin.

"Which means more for me," Vivienne said with a smile that didn't reach her eyes.

He smiled back and watched her swirl the juice in her cup as she stared into space. Then she dropped the cup and turned to him.

"Levi, can I ask you something?"

"Yeah. Sure!" Levi said and shifted in his seat.

"You're a Christian, right? I mean you believe in God and you obey His commands, right?"

"Yeah. I do."

"Okay," Vivienne said and let out a deep breath. "Do you think God is fair with His commands?"

Levi was puzzled by the question, and it must have shown because she said, "Let me rephrase my question. Do you think God is being fair when He asks you to give up something you really want just to prove that you love Him?"

If her first question had puzzled him, this rephrase had thrown him off balance. Deep down in his heart, he knew the reason she asked this question was either of two things. Either she was struggling with her faith or she didn't have a relationship with God. For his peace of mind, he wanted to know where she stood.

"Are you a Christian? I mean, have you accepted Jesus as your Lord and Savior?" Levi asked, hoping she would say she was.

"No, I'm not a Christian. I don't have a relationship with God and I don't want one."

Levi nodded as he silently prayed for the Holy Spirit to give him answers of peace for Vivienne. He would be lying if he said he didn't feel defeated that she didn't want to have a relationship with God because he liked her a lot and cared about her deeply. But right now, the situation at hand was weightier than the hopes he had for a future with her.

"So, here's the thing. Let's assume your child has a toy with button batteries and this toy makes them so happy. As a parent, will you allow your child to play with that toy while the batteries are still in it?" Levi asked and she shook her head.

"You would either take the toy away or remove the batteries because you know how dangerous they can be for a child, right?" he asked and she nodded.

"In the few minutes you had the toy to remove the batteries, your child would most likely cry or throw a tantrum. Will you damn all consequences and let them play with the toy while the batteries are in it just because you don't want them to cry?"

"I guess not."

"Right. This is similar to how God acts with His children. When God asks us to give up something we believe is good or comfortable for us, it is because He has better things planned for us in the future. Most times, we won't even know or understand why God has asked us to do or not do something. We might even call Him unfair, but at the end of the day, He is a good father whose ways and thoughts are higher than ours, and He makes all things work together for our good. Even if we or the people around us can't see it happening."

Vivienne appeared to be in deep thought about everything he'd just told her, and he hoped that his answer was enough to help her get the clarity she needed.

"You know, I asked my mom this same question in a way that applied to her situation with my dad. Her answer was pretty much the same as yours."

"Vivienne," Levi said and held her hands. "Sometimes, being a Christian can be difficult. It's not all roses and butterflies. I'm still learning to let go of my desires to follow God's will for my life."

"Really?" she asked, and he nodded.

"So, what's your experience with this?" she asked.

"For starters, I want to have a family as soon as possible, and I want to build that family with a woman who shares the same Christian faith and beliefs about marriage as me."

"So, what's holding you back?"

You.

"I have met a few nice Christian girls who should fit this bill but there's always something lacking. And just when I thought I may have found someone, I discovered she isn't interested in two of the most important aspects of my life—God and marriage," Levi said, looking intently at Vivienne.

"Hmm." Vivienne removed her hands and turned away.

They stayed silent for a while and Levi wondered if indirectly telling her that she didn't fit the bill of the kind of woman he wanted to spend the rest of his life with was a smart move.

"My dad is sick and I can't bring myself to go visit him even if I feel guilty that I haven't," she blurted out.

"Is it because you're still angry at him?"

"Yes. But at the same time, I feel excited that he even wants to see me. Let's even assume that I go. What will I say when I see him? What if he says something negative to me? Or what if he even asks for my forgiveness? How can I forgive him?"

Her voice was hoarse, and Levi knew she was fighting back tears. It hurt him that she was hurting so much, and he wanted to do what he could to help her. Levi moved closer to Vivienne until they were shoulder-to-shoulder. He put his arm around her and she rested her head on his shoulder.

"I don't know how things will play out if you decide to go visit your dad. And yes, forgiving someone is hard, but you don't have to do it alone. You can ask God to help you."

Vivienne chuckled. "I don't think God would want to help someone who wants nothing to do with Him."

"Oh, He definitely would, Vivienne. You have no idea just how much He's waiting for you to talk to Him."

Vivienne raised her head from Levi's shoulder and looked up at him. Levi could see a tiny streak of tears on her nose and he brushed it away with his thumb. She smiled weakly at him and put her head back on his shoulder.

He was out of things to say as he battled thoughts of whether to let Vivienne find God for herself or help point her in the right direction. It brought back memories of how Joshua had felt lost and angry at God after his dad died and how Josh had told him to stay away from him because he felt Levi was being too pushy with trying to help him understand the way God works.

"Vivienne, holding onto a grudge is like drinking poison and expecting the other person to die. You can't live this way for the rest of your life," Levi said.

"We'll have to see about that." Vivienne stood up. "I have to go now, Levi. It's getting late."

"Please, let me take you home."

Surprisingly, she didn't argue. The ride to Vivienne's house was silent as they were occupied with thoughts of their own. When they got to her house, she asked Levi to come say hi to her mom.

"I don't think that's a good idea."

"Well, it will be rude if you don't, especially since this is the second time you've dropped me off at home."

Levi agreed, and she led him into the house. He met an older-looking version of Vivienne, watching TV in the living room. There was absolutely no doubt that she was Vivienne's mom. On the walls were also picture frames of Vivienne, her mom, and sister. There were none with her dad in it.

"Mommy, this is Levi, my supervisor,"

"Good evening, ma'am. It's nice to meet you," Levi said, bowing slightly.

"Nice to meet you as well, Levi. Please make yourself comfortable."

"Thank you, ma'am."

"You look oddly familiar, Levi. Have we met before?"

"I don't think I have had the pleasure. But maybe you've seen me in church or at a wedding I coordinated."

"I don't go out much so it must be at church. What church do you attend, Levi?"

"I attend CTRCC, ma'am."

"Mommy, that's your…" Vivienne cleared her throat. "He attends CTRCC too," she said slowly.

"Oh really! That must be where I saw you." Her eyes lit up. "Are you in a service unit?"

"Yes, ma'am. I'm in the follow-up unit."

"Aha! I knew I had seen you before. It's really lovely to meet you, Levi. And I'm deeply grateful to you for helping Buks with her business website, and all the free counsel too. Thank you so much."

"Not at all, ma'am. I'm happy she even let me help her, especially since we didn't meet on a great note. You raised an amazing daughter. You should be proud."

"I am really proud of her. Thank you, Levi. I'm sorry but you'll have to excuse me, Levi. I was only waiting for Buks to get home before retiring for the night."

"It wasn't a problem, ma'am. Thanks for having me."

"Buks Buks, get him some refreshments before he leaves. Thank you for bringing her home, and it was nice to meet you, Levi."

"Likewise, ma'am," Levi said with a smile.

"Goodnight, guys."

"Goodnight, ma'am."

"Night, Mommy."

"Buks Buks?" Levi said once they were outside.

"Yeah. That's what my mom and sister call me."

"I like it. It has a cute ring to it. I should start calling you Buks Buks too."

"Levi, you've not earned the right to call me Buks Buks yet."

"Yet? Does that mean I'm getting closer to earning it?"

"Levi! Start going to your house."

"Okay. Okay!" Levi laughed.

Before he got into his car, he said, "Vivienne,"

"Yeah?"

"Everything will be fine. Just remember what I said."

Vivienne nodded. "I don't think I'll be getting any sleep tonight. So, it will definitely be keeping me up."

"Well, if you need anything, I'm just a phone call or WhatsApp message away," Levi said, and she nodded.

"Goodnight, Vivienne."

"Goodnight."

When he got home that night, he thought about what his recent discovery about Vivienne meant for him. First, she had told him she didn't believe in love or want to get married. That was quite manageable because with persistent effort and time, she would most likely come around. But now, she said she didn't have a relationship with God nor wanted one. How would he convince her that God isn't who she thinks He is?

Levi didn't know where to start from or how to go about his new mission, but one thing he knew he wouldn't be doing was living with the regret of not doing enough. For years, he blamed himself for not doing enough to get Josh to come back to Christ, and now that he had a second chance, he sure wouldn't blow it.

Chapter Twenty-Two

Vivienne

A few days went by and Vivienne eventually went to visit her dad at the hospital. Her mom and sister were elated when she told them that she was ready to see him. Talking to Levi that night had played a big role in her decision. When he left, she had taken time out for some deep introspection and came to the conclusion that she was tired of holding onto anger against her dad and trying to prove him wrong. She also admitted that she wouldn't be okay if her dad died without her forgiveness.

Initially, she felt she needed the closure of her dad asking for her forgiveness because she was still hurt by all the things he had done to her. But after watching the videos and reading articles Levi sent to her on forgiveness, she made peace with forgiving him even if he didn't ask for it. She had even passively told God to help her forgive her dad because she didn't think she could do so on her own. Vivienne hadn't even considered it a prayer because she hadn't prayed in years. To her, it was just a passing statement which seemed to have worked because seeing her dad lying helplessly and frail in the hospital bed filled her with so much compassion for him.

Her father had become a shadow of himself. His skin and eyes had a yellow coloration, his feet and ankles were swollen, he looked drained, and there were visible spider-like blood vessels under his eyes. The great and proud Adekunle Adetokunbo hanging on to whatever was left of his life brought tears to her eyes.

"Bukunmi, you're here," her father said, sounding weak and breathless. "I'm glad you are here, Bukunmi. I can now die peacefully."

"Don't say that, Daddy. You'll be fine," Vivienne said, fighting back the tears that threatened to spill.

"Your mother keeps saying the same thing. She keeps praying for me to get better and for me to accept Jesus into my life." Her dad coughed then waited a while to regain himself before he continued.

"I tell her it's too late for my soul to be saved. I'm on the brink of death and I deserve it for all the hurt I have caused you."

"Kunle, it's not too late. Remember the story I told you about the thief who was crucified with Jesus? He asked Jesus to save him just before he was killed. As long as you're alive, you can still be saved, Kunle," Vivienne's mom said.

"Bukunmi, do you think your mother is right?"

Vivienne looked at her mom and back at her dad. She nodded even though she didn't know what she believed.

"Well, I told her that I will accept her Jesus if you forgive me."

"Daddy, but that's a crazy thing to do. What if I never forgive you?" Vivienne asked, upset that her dad would do something so irrational.

"*Ma binu si mi, omo mi.* Your mom keeps saying God can do the impossible, and I think the most impossible thing for me is you forgiving me."

Vivienne let go of the tears she had been holding when her dad called her his child. All these years she had acted strong and unbothered by her father's cruelty to her; meanwhile, her inner child was broken and in need of fatherly love and affection.

"Well, Mommy was right. I have forgiven you, Daddy."

"Really?" her dad said and tried to sit up, but she told him to lie down and he did.

She watched as tears spilled from the corners of his eyes and hoarse-sounding sobs escaped from his lips. "Bukunmi, please forgive me. I…"

"It's fine, Daddy. I have forgiven you," Vivienne said, cutting her dad off mid-sentence.

"Please, let me apologize properly even if it's the last thing I do today."

Vivienne nodded and sniffed.

"For years, I projected my anger and childhood trauma on you," her dad said weakly. He paused to catch his breath before saying, "I was eighteen when my father, your grandfather, disowned me. Back then, farmers were the most successful people, and he wanted me to take over his trade, but I had other plans. I wanted to go to the university to study law. This didn't sit well with him so he asked me to choose between going to school and taking over the farm. I chose to study and he disowned me."

Vivienne's father coughed again, and he signaled for a drink of water, which her mother gave to him. When he had drunk his fill, he looked at Vivienne as fresh tears spilled onto his cheeks. With all the strength he could muster, he reached for her hand. She moved her seat closer to his bed and held his hand.

"He said he wanted nothing to do with me, that I was a disgrace to the family, and nobody in his lineage would be mediocre. In return, I told him I would be more successful than he ever was, and I never wanted to be called an Agbaje. So, I changed my surname to my grandfather's first name and I became Adekunle Adetokunbo."

Her dad heaved a shuddering sigh. "I needed to prove to my father that I could be successful without being a farmer, and I did it. Although, surviving was extremely brutal but I vowed to best my dad and my determination didn't stop even after he passed away. So, when you said you didn't want to become a lawyer like me, I saw it as you trying to jeopardize my years of hard work."

"But that wasn't what I was doing, Daddy," Vivienne said tearfully.

"I knew it, but I just couldn't see past beating my father. I treated you horribly and I am so sorry, Bukunmi. Please forgive me. Please," her dad said and broke down again.

Vivienne got up from her seat and hugged her dad as they cried in each other's arms. Her mom was by her side, rubbing her back as she too sobbed quietly. Even though she had forgiven her dad, it felt cathartic hearing him ask for her forgiveness.

"I've forgiven you, Daddy. I just want you to get better so we can make up for the lost years. I miss you," Vivienne said amid sobs.

"I miss you too, and I'm so proud of all you have accomplished, Buks Buks. I feel so ashamed and embarrassed at all the names I called you."

Vivienne left her father's embrace and sat down. She didn't want to put too much strain on his body as he was still very weak.

"It's all in the past now. Just get better soon," Vivienne said, and her dad nodded.

"Victoria," her dad called her mom.

Vivienne stood up from her chair so her mom could sit in it and be closer to her dad.

"Yes, Kunle," she said.

"Please, pray for me. I want to keep my promise of accepting Jesus into my life now that God has done the impossible for me."

"Oh, Kunle! That's so wonderful," Vivienne's mom said gleefully.

Her mom brought out her Bible and read Romans 10:9-10. When she was done, she explained how God created the first humans—Adam and Eve—with the intention of having direct access and fellowship with Him forever, but when they sinned, that access was cut off. From that time, mankind was doomed for eternity and could only have access to God through priests and prophets, who in turn had to be holy before approaching God to intercede for mankind.

"Each time man sinned, they had to atone for their sins through blood sacrifices of blemish-free animals. God wanted to save mankind from eternal damnation and to restore fellowship with them through a once-and-for-all atonement of sin by the blood sacrifice of someone who had never sinned before. That person is Jesus, the son of God." Vivienne's mom paused to make sure she still had Kunle's undivided attention. When she was certain that was the case, she continued.

"Jesus, who is God, came down to earth in the form of man through a virgin, Mary, to die for the sins of mankind and to restore direct access and fellowship with God just as God had intended at creation. Now, anyone who believes that Jesus is the son of God and that He came to earth, died and rose again so they can be saved, and confesses Jesus as the Lord and savior of their lives, is assured of an eternity with Jesus."

Vivienne listened intently as she was intrigued by everything she heard her mom say. Her mom went over everything she had said earlier a second time. When she was done, she asked if her dad understood and he said he did. Then she asked if he believed that Jesus died on the cross for his sins and rose again on the third day to give him an eternity with God.

"I believe," he said weakly.

Her mom lifted her hand in worship as she thanked God for saving Vivienne's dad.

"Kunle, please repeat after me. Lord Jesus, I repent of my sins and surrender my life to you. Wash me clean; I believe that Jesus Christ is the Son of God." She paused, waiting for him to finish before continuing.

"I believe that He died on the cross for my sins and rose again on the third day for my victory. I believe this in my heart and confess with my mouth that Jesus is my Savior and Lord."

As soon as her dad said the last word, her mom whooped and continued shouting, "Glory to God! Thank you, Jesus!" Then she broke out in another round of thanksgiving after which she prayed for him.

"Buks, I'm now a Christian!" her father said as enthusiastically as he could and she smiled at him weakly.

Her dad's excitement made her curious to know if someone had been preaching to him before now seeing that he accepted Jesus without hesitation. But then, he had mentioned placing a condition on his conversion. One he deemed miraculous when it was met.

Now she was left wondering if she should do the same and there was only one thing on her mind—for Levi to accept her the way she was. Vivienne was shocked at herself for thinking about wanting Levi to accept her despite her estrangement from God and her aversion for love and marriage.

Unless…

Oh shoot! I like him. I like Levi!

Chapter Twenty-Three

Levi

Levi was tired of tiptoeing around Vivienne's obvious avoidance of him. She now spent less time in his office and her reason was that she was trying to get used to the staff room in anticipation of the coming week. He would also send her WhatsApp messages, and she would leave them unread unlike before when she replied to his messages almost immediately.

Something was wrong but he couldn't figure it out, and the only way to find out was to confront her about the situation and how he felt.

"Vivienne, why do I feel like you've been avoiding me lately? You haven't left this office, yet it feels like you have. Did I do something wrong?"

"What?" she asked, surprised.

Levi repeated his question and waited for her to answer.

"No, Levi. I've just been busy."

"That's it? Are you sure? Because I feel like there's more and it has something to do with me."

"There's nothing more, Levi. I've been both busy and emotionally drained with life lately."

"Well, you can talk to me if you want to. I'm here for you."

Vivienne nodded. "Thanks."

Levi felt more at ease knowing Vivienne's recent behavior had nothing to do with him. He went back to planning the itinerary for the next event, which was a wedding ceremony and reception on Vivienne's birthday. If the wedding hadn't fallen on a weekday, he would have asked to take her to dinner, but it had, so he had to make other arrangements.

"I eventually went to visit my dad at the hospital," Vivienne said, making Levi jerk his head in surprise.

"Wow! That's great news, Vivienne. I'm so happy for you," Levi said, beaming.

"I guess I have you to thank for the endless devotionals, videos, and articles you keep sending to me," Vivienne said and pursed her lips.

"You don't mind them? At some point I began to think I was sending too much."

"I guess, it's okay." Vivienne shrugged. "I'm learning a few things about God, and let's just say it's been interesting. But I have yet to make up my mind about Him."

"Sounds like you are having a change of heart," Levi said, smiling with his chin resting on his hands.

"I never said that."

"It sounds like it."

Vivienne shook her head and got back to work. It pleased Levi greatly that his not-so-subtle evangelism with Vivienne seemed to be working. Over the last few weeks, she had asked him questions about salvation, faith, grace and other Christian-related topics. He had answered them to the best of his knowledge and also sent her sermons or articles that could help her understand more. It made him feel better knowing he wasn't blowing up this second chance.

"Levi?"

"Yeah?"

"You once told me your cousin died in an accident. Didn't his death affect your faith?"

"No, it didn't. However, I must say that I feel I could have done more to help my cousin."

"What do you mean?"

"Our parents raised us in the way of the Lord from as early as we could speak, and we continued that way until Josh's dad died a few months after we turned twenty-one. He became angry at God and asked me so many times why God would allow his dad, who had served Him faithfully all his life, to die. He questioned if God truly answered prayers because we had prayed for his dad to recover but he never did," Levi said, blinking back tears.

"I tried to talk to him about God's faithfulness even though I had questions of my own. But each time, I was met with Josh's rebuttal of how God was healing other sick people and even raising the dead, yet He let his father die. I did all I could to pacify Josh and make sure he didn't lose his faith, but nothing worked. It was as though the more I tried, the further he stayed away from God and me," he continued.

"That must have been so tough."

"Yes, it was." Levi sniffed.

"Were you ever able to find answers to Josh's questions?" Vivienne asked.

"I thought I had the answers until recently when I spoke to my aunt, Josh's mom, about how I felt. In her words, she said God is more interested in our eternity than how long we live here on earth. She also said that no matter what happens to us now, good or bad, it is all for our good in the long run. We may not understand why, but it doesn't change the fact that God is good."

Vivienne looked lost, and he couldn't blame her.

"Mind-boggling, I know," Levi chuckled. "Even now, I still struggle to understand things like this sometimes, but what helps me is that I have learned to trust and obey God blindly."

"What was Joshua like?"

"We were like two peas in a pod and looked so much alike that we could pass for twins. In fact, we told people we were twins, especially because our birthdays were just days apart. Our mothers are twin sisters so you can imagine the joy they felt knowing they were expecting at the same time. They raised us together and did everything for us together. My mom used to call Joshua her firstborn," Levi said fondly.

"Sounds sweet. You guys must have been so close, especially because you are an only child."

"Yes, we were. In fact, I didn't even feel like an only child because I was always around Josh and Jemima, his sister."

"So, how did he die? If you don't mind me asking."

"No, I don't," Levi said.

He thought about how best to summarize Josh's death in a way that wouldn't leave him emotional.

"Two years after Josh's dad died, his mom decided she wanted to turn his remembrance to a mini family vacation. It was scheduled for every Easter, and we had to travel out of state to their house in Abuja. That year, my aunt and parents traveled before us because we had a test to write. Josh and I were supposed to catch a late flight and meet them in Abuja later that day, but we missed our flight. It was my fault.

"Instead of calling our parents to inform them of our missed flight, I somehow convinced Josh, against his better judgment, to take a night bus. He didn't feel good about it but I brushed aside his fears. Josh was the kind of person you couldn't convince to do something he didn't want to do but again, for some weird reason, he agreed to travel by night bus."

Levi told her how their bus had gotten attacked by kidnappers two hours to the end of their journey, which was in the early hours of the next morning. He said their driver did his best to avoid the kidnappers as they shot at them. They eventually escaped but the damage had been done as their tyres got hit and they ended up in an accident. Levi said the last thing he remembered was Josh holding his hand as the driver lost control of the bus.

"By the time I came to, there were strange people all around me. I tried to open my eyes but they felt glued. There was a cut on my head that had bled all over my face and shut my eyes. I remembered Josh was with me and I called out for him, but he didn't answer. Then I heard someone say, *'One of those twins don wake up. Make we comot am from this motor, carry am go hospital.'* The moment I heard them mention hospital, everything came rushing back in and I started shouting Josh's name, but he still didn't answer."

Levi told Vivienne he grabbed one of the men and asked for his brother. The man empathetically said his brother didn't make it, but they had called his mom and she would meet them at the hospital. He said that was when it hit him like a ton of bricks that Josh had died.

"I must have passed out again because when I opened my eyes, I was in the hospital, and the first person I saw was Josh's mom. I can still remember the fear and guilt that washed over me when I saw her face. I asked after Josh again hoping to get a different answer, but I didn't get it."

Levi said his aunt told him his cousin had passed away and that the rest of what she said to him that day was a blur.

"Vivienne, my mom was so angry at me that she couldn't even look at me. For the next one week at the hospital, all she did was ask if I was okay or had eaten. She never asked what happened and I knew it was because she was hurt. Many times, I would pretend to be asleep while I watched her crying for Josh's loss and thanking God I didn't die too. After my discharge from the hospital, I tried to take my life thrice but I was unsuccessful. It was too much for my mom to handle so my aunt asked her to bring me over."

"Wow! Your aunt is such an angel. I can't imagine dealing with such a terrible loss and still caring about other people," Vivienne said, deeply touched by his story.

"She is and I don't know what I would have done without her in my life," Levi said with a wistful smile.

Levi touched his crucifix pendant. "She also gave me Josh's Bible and this necklace saying he would've wanted me to have them."

His attempt at not getting emotional had failed. Levi dabbed at the corners of his eyes with his sleeves. "I miss Josh so much it hurts."

"I'm so sorry about Josh, Levi."

Levi nodded. "It's fine."

"Fun fact is that I applied to work here at PEP because Joshua and Ms. Preye have the same name."

"Really?" Vivienne asked.

"Yep."

"That's cool. Thanks for sharing your story with me, Levi."

"You're welcome," he said with a smile.

They stayed silent for a few minutes until Levi looked at the clock on his desk and saw that he was behind time for the errand he had to run. He packed up his bag and said to Vivienne, "I have an errand to run for Ms. Preye and I may not be back today. So, I guess I'll see you tomorrow at the wedding?"

"Yeah." She nodded.

"All right. Bye."

Vivienne waved him goodbye and he left the office.

The next day, Levi left for the wedding venue hours before everyone else ought to be there because he hadn't been able to supervise things by himself. He had put Bayo in charge of the supervision to attend to other duties, and Levi hoped he had done a good job, otherwise there would be chaos as they had four hours left until the wedding. This particular client was a double-edged sword in the sense that both the wedding ceremony and reception would be in the same hall, so he had his work cut out for him.

It was also Vivienne's birthday and he had a surprise for her. His initial thought was to get her the trending money bouquet but knowing how she felt about receiving favors or monetary gifts from people, he decided a bouquet of flowers was the better option. Still, he wanted flowers that would show he liked her and was interested in pursuing a relationship with her in the near future. When he called the florist, they had advised him to go for red roses and he had bought two dozen roses to signify her new age.

Per his plans, Levi arrived before everyone else and it gave him ample time to thoroughly inspect everything they had set up. Bayo had also done a great job because the hall looked spectacular. The couple had chosen a bright coral color and white daisies as the main features of their decor while the rest was left to Ms. Preye and her team to decide.

A few hours later, Bayo and a few of PEP's logistics team arrived, followed by the vendors who began to set up for the wedding. Levi thanked Bayo for a job well done and told the team to get breakfast before the wedding began. Then he texted Vivienne to know if she had arrived at the couple's hotel to shoot content for PEP. She said she was in the middle of it and would leave in an hour.

Levi decided to use his free time to study his Bible since he didn't do that before leaving the house. His Scriptural focus for the day was Proverbs three. Verse seven stood out to him more, and it felt like the Lord was drawing his attention to something he was doing wrong lately. He said a quiet prayer, asking the Lord to direct his steps and to expose the errors of his ways.

When he was done praying, he met the caterer and grabbed a plate of coconut rice and a turkey wing. Levi knew the food would be exceptional because they hired the same caterer as often as they could. Once he was done eating, he went around the hall to ensure the MC and DJ were ready to go. The wedding was to start in an hour and there was no room for error. When he confirmed that they were ready, he asked the DJ to play wedding-themed instrumentals to liven up the hall.

Levi ticked items off his To-Do list with a satisfactory smile. Just then, Vivienne walked in and tapped him on the shoulder. "Excuse me, Mr. Levi."

"Yes?" Levi turned, expecting it to be someone else only to come face-to-face with Vivienne.

"It's even you," Levi tutted.

"See the way you're acting as if you're not happy to see me," Vivienne said, side eyeing him.

"Actually, I am," Levi chuckled.

"I thought so."

"*Ahan!* We're even twinning," Levi said, referring to their outfits.

They both wore white shirts while Levi had on black chinos pants and Vivienne wore blue denim pants.

Vivienne chuckled. "Not really, but it's close."

"Why are you even wearing sunglasses inside the hall?" Levi asked, puzzled.

"It's part of the aesthetic of my look today. Without the glasses, I'll be just meh," Vivienne said.

Levi laughed. "I see."

"I'll talk to you later. I need to start filming this hall. I can tell everyone to leave the hall, right?"

"Sure. I'll also tell Bayo to help you get them out," Levi said.

"Okay, thanks." Vivienne turned to leave.

"Don't you think you should go grab some food first?" Levi asked.

"There's no time for that. Besides, I already ate something before coming."

Levi nodded. "Okay. I'll see you at the end of the day, right?"

"Yeah. Bye." Vivienne waved and left.

The wedding ceremony started, and it was beautiful as expected. Levi made sure he didn't miss the vow exchange, which was his favorite part. Both the groom and bride were teary-eyed as they said their vows, and it made him emotional. Throughout the wedding ceremony, he and Vivienne exchanged looks and smiled at each other, but he still didn't fail to notice how quickly she averted her gaze each time.

After the wedding ceremony ended, the reception began shortly. This time he was too busy to hang around or notice Vivienne. The few times he saw her was when she had to film close to where he was, and as expected, she was also too buried in her work to notice him. Once the groom said the vote of thanks to his guests, those who didn't want to stay for the after-party began filing out.

Levi heaved a sigh, knowing he could now rest on his oars a little. He couldn't wait for the after-party to end so he could surprise Vivienne with her birthday present. He delegated a few tasks to his team members and went to his car to rest a little. When the DJ announced that the after-party was coming to an end, he sent a WhatsApp message to Vivienne, telling her to meet him in the parking lot.

He checked the bouquet to make sure they were still in perfect shape and the handwritten card which read, *"Dear Vivienne, you're special and every moment with you feels like a gift. Here's to more. Happy birthday,"* was still in the bouquet.

When he saw her coming, he got out of the driver's seat and waited for her by the front passenger door with the roses hidden behind him.

"I'm so glad this wedding is over. What a day!" Vivienne said breathlessly.

"Me too. Were you able to film enough content?" Levi asked, glad she hadn't noticed that one arm was behind his back.

"Yes. Matter of fact, more than enough. My phone's memory is almost full," she replied.

Then she noticed he had an arm behind him and said, "What's up with your arm?"

"Happy birthday, Vivienne," Levi said, bringing out the arm.

He gave her the bouquet of roses, and her eyes lit up as she held it. Her smile was bright, and Levi found himself smiling too. It felt good to see her light up with a smile, which was something he hadn't seen in a while.

"You know today's my birthday?"

"Yes, I've known for a while, but I didn't say anything earlier because I wanted to surprise you."

"Thanks, Levi. I love them," she said and smelled the flowers.

Then she pulled out the tiny card in between the roses and read the note. Vivienne cocked her head to the side; mischief danced in her eyes and a small smile spread across her lips.

"Do you like me, Levi?"

Levi moved closer to her and said, "What do you think, Vivienne?"

Still looking at him intently, she shrugged and said, "I don't know. You tell me."

Levi chuckled and nodded. His eyes traveled from her eyes down to her lips and then back to her eyes. "Yes, I like you, Vivienne. Very much so."

Vivienne's lips parted as though she wanted to say something, but she didn't. She looked away and shook her head. This wasn't the reaction he expected from her. They had spent so much time together, and he knew for sure that he wasn't the only one who had caught feelings.

"What? You don't like me?" Levi asked, his forehead creasing in a frown.

"That's not the point," she said and put some distance between them.

"I'm confused, Vivienne. You're not saying you like me back nor are you saying you don't like me."

"What I am saying is, this *thing* between us can't work," she said, swirling her free hand between her and Levi.

"So, there's a thing! Meaning you like me too. But I'm still not sure what the problem is."

"Levi, how can you not see what the problem is for goodness' sake?"

Levi was taken aback by her tone, but she didn't seem to notice or care.

"You said you want a girl who shares the same faith and has the same beliefs about love and marriage as you. I am none of those things. How's that hard to see?" Vivienne added angrily.

Levi felt as though he had been doused with a bucket of frigid water when the situation at hand dawned on him. He watched as her eyes filled with tears, and without thinking, he moved forward to hug her but she put her hand out stopping him.

"Vivienne, this isn't even an issue! Yes, I know you still have reservations about marriage and having a relationship with God, but it's something we can work on together. You're even already making progress. We can make this work," Levi said, hoping Vivienne would see reasons with him.

"What progress?" Vivienne asked, clearly confused.

"For starters, I believe you like me too and there's nothing you can say to convince me otherwise. So, that's settled. Second, you have been asking me some pretty intelligent questions about God, repentance, salvation, and faith. Questions that only someone who is researching to make up their mind about God would ask. If that's not progress to you, then what is it?"

"Curiosity, Levi. Curiosity! Yes, I like you too. So?" She shrugged. "Does it change the fact that I don't have a relationship with God, which is the most important thing to you? Also, you've been trying to change me into your ideal woman, but I'm not! If you like me, then like me for me. Accept me the way I am because I like the way I am and I don't want to change. Also, you're wrong because I still don't want a relationship with God," Vivienne said, and her voice broke.

Levi was shocked by her outburst, but at the same time he finally understood why verse seven of Proverbs three stood out to him that morning. He had been acting wiser than God by playing the role of the Holy Spirit in Vivienne's life, trying to convince her into wanting a relationship with God. He regretted not seeking the Lord first before embarking on his savior journey or acting on his romantic interest in Vivienne. Now everything had backfired and it was too late to salvage the situation. His heart was breaking into a million pieces and he felt suffocated.

"I'm so sorry, Vivienne. I acted selfishly because I care about you deeply and I also wanted a relationship with you. I went about it the wrong way and I shouldn't have. I'm sorry."

He saw her relax, and then she wiped away a teardrop. Neither of them said anything for a while. Levi could swear he could hear his heartbeat in the silence.

"Maybe there's a chance this could still work," she said and moved closer to him. "You won't try to change me and we see where this leads us."

"Vivienne," Levi said and held her free hand.

He didn't know how to say this in a way that wouldn't hurt her, especially not when she looked at him with so much hope. Despite how much he wanted to be with her, he knew obeying God was more important. There was a reason the Bible instructed believers not to be unequally yoked with unbelievers, and he wasn't about to risk his relationship with God to find out why.

"I'm not looking to see where things go with you. You're worth way more than that. I want marriage and a family with you. But I know that for a relationship to stand the tests of time, both partners need to have something in common. For me, that common denominator is Christ and…"

"That's something I don't have, right?" Vivienne interjected and let out a small laugh, then she withdrew her hand.

"I wish things were different but they aren't. You know how I feel about you, but having a relationship with Christ is much more important to me. I'm deeply sorry, Vivienne," Levi said hoarsely.

He could feel the tears that had gathered on his eyelids, threatening to fall. He clenched his jaw and took a deep shuddering breath as he blinked the moisture away.

"And this is exactly why I don't want anything to do with a God who forces people to make decisions that bring nothing but pain to them. Just like He made my mom end her relationship with my dad, he's making you choose between Him and your happiness," Vivienne said and shoved the bouquet back into Levi's arms.

"Vivienne, neither of us will be happy in the long run if we aren't on the same page."

"Fine! Then go be with a Jesus-loving Christian girl and leave me alone," Vivienne said and stormed off the premises.

"Vivienne!"

Levi tried to go after her, but his feet didn't carry him. He stood in the warm evening breeze, speechless and heartbroken, as she walked away, leaving him alone in the heavy silence.

Chapter Twenty-Four

Vivienne

Vivienne's heart and head ached from so many emotions as she rode to the hospital to meet her mom. Thoughts and scenarios of how things could have played out differently crossed her mind. Since the day she visited Levi at home and he told her he wanted to start a family with a girl who shared the same faith and beliefs about marriage as him, Vivienne had decided it was best to distance herself from him to avoid getting more emotionally attached. But it hadn't been easy staying away from him, not when she spent the most part of her day with him and he never stopped being kind to her.

As much as she hated to admit it, she liked Levi way more than she wanted to, and it hurt her to think that she wasn't good enough for him. She'd made up her mind to avoid him at the wedding and just go home after, but seeing him made her change her mind. He had been so excited to see her, and when he asked if they would see each other after the wedding, she couldn't say no. If she had known the night would turn out as horribly as it did, she wouldn't have stayed back to talk to him.

Also, to think that it was her twenty-fourth birthday, one she had looked forward to celebrating all year. But right now, she was far from being in the celebratory mood. As she got closer to the hospital, the fear that her dad had passed away crippled her. When she walked into the ward where he was admitted, she met her mom standing on the other side of the bed. Her hands were on her mouth and she looked like she'd been crying. A doctor stood over her dad, checking his vitals so she couldn't see his face.

"Mommy?"

"Buks," her mom said, and she hurried over to where Vivienne stood.

They hugged each other and Vivienne asked, "Is Daddy okay?"

Her mom nodded frantically as tears streamed down her face. Vivienne couldn't decide if they were happy or sad tears.

"Mommy, what's wrong? Is Daddy okay?"

Her blood ran cold as she feared the worst had happened. She and her dad had spent the last six years at loggerheads, and now that they had reconciled, they wouldn't have the luxury of spending time with each other to bond again.

"You won't believe it, Buks, but your daddy is completely healed!"

"What?"

It didn't make any sense to her. The last time she had come visiting, which was a few days back, the doctor had told them he needed a new liver urgently because he wasn't responding to treatment. Now, her mom was saying the same person who was on the brink of death had been miraculously healed.

"This doesn't make any sense," Vivienne said, peeking over her mom's shoulders to see her dad, but the doctor was still in her view.

"I know! Oftentimes, miracles don't make sense."

Vivienne's mom told her that she had been home when she received a call from the doctor asking her to come down to the hospital as soon as she could. When she got there, he told her that Kunle no longer had symptom of liver failure. He said they had run all the necessary tests and the results had come back negative for acute liver failure.

"It hasn't been long since I got here and I called you shortly after."

Vivienne couldn't believe it. She didn't know if her dad's conversion had anything to do with his healing, but one thing she knew was that she was grateful for his second chance at life.

"Doctor, can we talk to him? Is he okay?" Vivienne asked.

The doctor turned to the both of them and he said, "Yes, your dad is okay. He's just resting, and he needs it. His body has been through a lot. If you want to wait for him to wake up, that's fine. But if not, you can come back tomorrow. By then, we should be getting ready to discharge him if he maintains this progress."

"Wow. Thank you, Doctor. We'll wait," her mom said.

So they sat by her dad's bed and waited for over an hour. When he didn't wake up, they decided to leave and come back the next day.

The next day, Vivienne made sure she arrived an hour before the resumption time so she could pack her stuff from Levi's office and move to the staff room. When she got there, Bayo and Chuks said it was high time she moved into the staff room because they needed a pretty face around. Even though she wasn't in the mood for jokes, she smiled and chipped in their conversation when her attention was drawn to it.

During lunch break, she went to Ms. Preye's office to tender her resignation. It was a decision she'd made after coming back from the hospital. She didn't want to be in the same office space as Levi to avoid being constantly reminded of what she wanted but couldn't have. Her last day was the next day and she was thankful she wasn't a confirmed staff member yet, otherwise she would have had to give them a month's notice. When she gave Ms. Preye the letter, she asked Vivienne if there was anything she could do to change her mind. Vivienne thanked her for the opportunity and work experience at PEP but that her mind was already made up and she needed to quit for personal reasons.

"It's been a pleasure knowing and working with you, Vivienne. Your impact at PEP has been tremendous and I appreciate you for it," Ms. Preye said with a smile.

"Thank you, ma'am. I loved working here and I will miss PEP," Vivienne said, swallowing the lump that had formed in her throat.

She loved her job and wished she didn't have to quit, but the odds were not in her favor. It was also easier to quit her job now because she didn't have to prove anything to her dad anymore.

"If you ever need a recommendation, don't hesitate to contact me. You're also still running your pro bridesmaid business, right?"

"Yes, ma'am."

"All right then. I'll be sure to refer you to my clients who need your services."

Vivienne thanked Ms. Preye and left her office feeling downcast. As she walked out, she saw Levi staring at her from his office. He waved at her but she ignored him and headed for the staff room. Shortly after she settled back in to finish the work from the previous days' wedding, a familiar scent—none other than Levi's cologne—enveloped the staff room.

"Oga, Levi. This one wey you come our staff room so. Hope no problem o," Chuks said sarcastically.

"Shut up! Na everything wey your eye see, your mouth go talk? Shey na you boss come find for this office? Aproko," Bayo said, rebuking Chuks.

Vivienne pretended not to hear the exchange as she tried her hardest to concentrate on what she was doing. The noisy staff room suddenly fell quiet and she knew why.

"Hi," Levi said when he got to her desk.

She raised her head from her laptop. "Hi."

Levi looked at her like he was studying her, and she didn't have the patience or emotional capacity to play any games.

"What do you want? I'm busy, Levi," Vivienne said without looking at him.

"I didn't see you in our office. So, I came here to find you. Did you leave because of what happened?"

"No, Levi," Vivienne said and raised her head to look at him. "My three-month probation ended yesterday."

Vivienne purposely didn't tell him that she had turned in her resignation. She wanted him to find out after she had left. That way it would be too late for him to try to convince her to stay.

"Oh. I forgot about that," Levi said and paused. Then he added, "I also came to give you this."

He dropped the bouquet on her desk and Vivienne pushed it back toward him, shaking her head.

"I don't think I should accept this anymore, given the circumstances."

"They are yours, Vivienne. What happened between us has nothing to do with the roses. Please accept them."

She took the roses off the table and said, "Thank you," in a barely audible voice.

"It's no problem. Vivienne, can we talk?" Levi said, his voice softening as his eyes searched hers, a hint of desperation lingering in his tone.

She shook her head. "There's nothing left to say, Levi. We've both said how we feel and where things stand between us, and I don't think anything has changed. Or has it?"

Levi shook his head sadly, and she replied, "Exactly. There's nothing left to talk about, but I wish things didn't turn out this way. For what it's worth, you're a great guy and you don't deserve this."

"You don't think you deserve me?" Levi asked, and Vivienne gave him the stink eye.

"I'm sorry. I wish things were different too," Levi said.

"Yeah, me too. Thanks for the flowers again. Goodbye, Levi."

This time, it was her turn to watch him. A flurry of emotions played across his face. His eyes had a deep level of sadness she hadn't seen in anyone before; his face looked strained and he rubbed the knuckles of both hands against each other.

"Bye, Vivienne," Levi eventually said, then he turned to leave.

As soon as he left the staff room, the chattering resumed. This time in hushed tones. Vivienne had bigger problems to deal with than to concern herself with petty office gossip about her. Her heart broke into a million pieces as she watched Levi walk back to his office. His shoulders were slumped and she could still picture how hurt and sorry he was a few minutes ago. It broke her heart more that he was hurting too, but there was nothing either of them could do about it.

When she got home that evening, she met her mom in the living room. She greeted her and tried to escape to her room. But her mom stopped her to remind her that they had to go visit her dad later. Vivienne said she would change her clothes and be right back. She hastened to her room so her mom wouldn't know she had been crying, but it was too late. Her mom asked her why she was behaving strangely and she said it was nothing. She wasn't buying Vivienne's response so she got up from her seat and walked to where her daughter stood with her back to her.

The first thing she saw was the flowers and she said, "Buks Buks, those flowers are beautiful! Who are they from?"

"They're from Levi, Mommy."

"Okay? But why do you look sad? Did something happen?"

Vivienne shook her head and said she didn't want to talk about it. Her mom insisted that they talk about it because she didn't like the way Vivienne's eyes were swollen and red. Tears streamed down Vivienne's face, and her mom led her back to the sofa. She laid Vivienne's head on her lap and stroked her hair. Vivienne could do nothing but cry, and her mom told her everything would be okay.

When she calmed down, her mom made her a cup of hot tea and asked her to talk whenever she was ready.

Halfway into the cup of tea, she told her mom about her and Levi's story from the first day they met. She told her how she had loathed him for what he said to her, how she found out she would be sharing an office with him, and how he was consistent in earning her forgiveness until he eventually did.

"He sounds like a wonderful person," her mom said, still stroking her hair.

"He is, Mommy and that's what makes this so difficult," Vivienne sniffed and then blew her nose into a napkin. "I never wanted to fall in love or get married mainly because of how I saw Daddy treat you. But I met Levi and my perspective about love began to change. Unlike the guys who were interested in me, Levi was genuinely kind and did things for me because he cared."

Her mom sat quietly and allowed her to keep talking. Vivienne stayed quiet for a few minutes, and all she did was drink her tea. When she slurped the last drop, she turned to face her mom. "The only reason he says he can't be with me is because I don't want to have a relationship with God. Does that even make sense?"

"Oh, Buks. I know you're hurt and probably don't want to hear the truth, but Levi is right. I'm sorry you're hurt and you feel this way, but he did the right thing. Your dad didn't find it funny when I told him I was ending our relationship. I told him God wanted me to live a sanctified life and His will for me wasn't someone else's husband. That's the reason he became hostile to us—because he was hurt and couldn't handle it maturely."

"But why does God make people choose? Why can't we just do what makes us happy?" Vivienne asked and broke down in tears again.

Her mom drew her in for a hug. "Because what makes us happy may not always be the right thing to do. Levi honors your heart and he wants to protect you from getting hurt in the future. Honestly, I don't see you guys being happy long-term if you go ahead to start a relationship when you're both on different pages."

"But it hurts, Mommy. Why did I fall in love with him?"

"Buks, love is a beautiful thing and I am so glad you've experienced what it feels like to be in love with someone."

"I even feel so embarrassed telling him that maybe we could try to work out a relationship without him trying to change my mind about God. He said no," Vivienne said and blew her nose again.

"I'm sorry, baby. Everything will be fine. If it's God's will that you guys will end up together, then at the right time, it will happen. But if not, you'll meet someone else and fall in love again."

"I don't want to fall in love again. It hurts too much."

Her mom chuckled. "Yes, it hurts when things don't go the way we want, but at the end of the day, they always work out."

Vivienne's mom excused herself and went into her room. When she came back, she gave Vivienne the red prayer journal she had seen earlier

"Here, read this."

Vivienne asked her mom if she was sure she should read her private thoughts and prayers. Her mom said it was fine because all the prayers in the journal were about her. She also said Vivienne could take her time to read it. Then she gave her daughter some privacy.

Vivienne spent hours reading prayer points about her dating back to three years prior. Her mom also documented how her attitude was at the time of the prayer request and if she thought her daughter was improving or not. By the time she got to half of the book, she could see how her attitude toward her mom had changed over the years. They had gone from quarreling over her not going to church anymore to being so close to each other that there were no secrets between them. Her mom was her best friend and Vivienne was grateful she had cared enough to want a relationship with her that she had prayed about it every day for a year.

It eventually dawned on her that though she may not have a relationship with God, He was still mindful of her because how else could she explain Oluchi asking her for a favor that ended up as a job offer from Amara days after her mom had prayed about it? What could she say was the reason she began to develop feelings for Levi if not that her mom had prayed for her to experience genuine love and happiness?

Tears streamed down Vivienne's face as she realized she had been wrong about God all this while. The last prayer point in her mom's journal was her asking God to draw Vivienne closer to Himself. She prayed that He would reveal Himself to Vivienne in a way that leaves her doubtless about His love for her. Vivienne closed the journal and curled herself on the sofa. She couldn't bring herself to go to her room as there was too much weight on her heart. All she did was let her tears flow freely.

Chapter Twenty-Five

Levi

One week had gone by since Vivienne quit her job at PEP without telling him. At first, he had been angry and disappointed that she didn't tell him even when he went to give her the bouquet. But eventually he understood why she quit and it saddened him that he would no longer see her around.

Levi tried to get in touch with her but she wouldn't pick his calls or reply to his messages on any social media platform. So he decided to give her some space, which ended up being a bad idea because when he tried her number over the weekend, the response was that she was unavailable to pick his calls. He initially thought it was network problems so he kept trying but the response was the same. On social media he tried sending her messages and that was when he discovered he had been blocked as he could no longer see her profile picture.

He still didn't want to believe she had blocked him. So, when he got to work that morning, he asked Bayo to help him call Vivienne with his phone. True enough, he could hear the ringback tone and she even answered the call. Bayo covered up for him saying he was calling to know how she was doing and that they missed her. When Bayo finished speaking with her, Levi tried her number again and it gave him the same response from before.

"Oga Levi, e be like she block you. Sorry," Bayo said.

Levi thanked him for his help and went back to his office. The tightness in his chest became worse and he was certain that there was no way to salvage his relationship with Vivienne. The day he went to return the bouquet to her, he had gone with the intention of asking them to remain friends. However, when he saw her, he realized it was a bad idea. So he didn't bring it up and when she said there was nothing else to talk about, he couldn't have agreed more.

Seeing the couch in his office and knowing Vivienne wanted nothing to do with him hurt him deeply. Still, he decided to leave the couch there so he could have something to remember her by. In the middle of his melancholy, his phone rang and he knew that tone very well. It was his aunt. She was the only person in his contact list who had a special ringtone.

"Hi, Auntie. Good morning, Ma."

"Levi, my boy. How are you?"

Levi didn't know if he should tell his aunt the truth about how he felt or to lie and say that he was fine. He didn't think lying was necessary, especially since he could just say he didn't want to talk about it.

"I'm not fine, Auntie."

"I sensed it. Why else do you think I'm calling you? Well, it's also because I haven't heard from you in a while and I miss you."

Levi chuckled and said, "I miss you too, Auntie. I don't have any excuse for not calling or visiting lately. Matter of fact, how about I come see you this evening?"

"That's wrong timing *o*. I'm on my way to the airport. I'm going for a mini vacation."

"Really?! Oh, Auntie. I'm so happy and excited for you! *Ahan!* Auntie, Auntie," Levi hailed his aunt, and she laughed.

"Josh really rubbed off on you with his flattery," his aunt said, still laughing.

"He did *o*. The only thing he couldn't pass on to me were his dancing skills. I still can't dance to save my life," Levi chuckled.

"We are in the same boat, Levi."

Levi chuckled and said, "So, where are you off to?"

"I'm going to visit Jemima in school and spend some time touring Ontario with her."

"Nice. Bring back something for me *o,*" Levi said.

"I will but don't try to change the topic, Levi. What's wrong? Work or girl problems?"

"Auntie Jessy. What girl problem?" Levi teased his aunt.

"*See this one o.* You think you're too young to have girl problems? Aren't you almost thirty?"

"Auntie! I'm just twenty-seven!" Levi said, alarmed by his aunt's exaggeration of his age.

"And so? *Wo,* Luke was your age when we got married and I need to see my grandchildren before the Lord comes back or calls me home."

Levi laughed. "I've heard you but that you'll have to wait longer to see your grandchildren."

"Why *now?*"

Levi asked his aunt if she remembered their conversation about the girl he had told her he offended at a wedding party. She said she remembered. Then he told her how they started working together and later developed feelings for each other.

"We didn't start out as friends, but she eventually forgave me for what I did and I think spending so much time together made it easy for us to fall for each other. This isn't discrediting the fact that she's so kind, thoughtful, funny and fierce," Levi said wistfully.

"She sounds like a great person, Levi. Pardon me, but I still haven't heard what the problem is here."

"I was getting to it, Auntie. Vivienne is wonderful and I care about her deeply. However, she doesn't share my faith and beliefs about love and marriage nor does she plan to."

"Oh, I see. That's a big problem, Levi. I'm so sorry about that, but I believe everything is working out for your good. Does your mom know?"

"She knows who Vivienne is. I told her about Vivienne when I fell ill and she took me to the hospital but I haven't told her about my current situation," Levi said.

"It's called heartbreak, Levi, even though you guys weren't dating."

"You know what, Auntie? I can't help but feel like I have made the same mistake I made with Josh a second time, even though it's actually the opposite."

"How's that?"

Levi said that when Josh started having doubts about God and his faith, he did his best to convince him that God was still good and had a plan for his life. Levi said he continued encouraging and preaching to Josh until he got angry at him and didn't want to speak to him. Then he later apologized to Josh and stopped preaching to him so peace could reign.

"I remember the falling out you guys had because Josh told me about it. I had told him to settle his differences with you because you guys are brothers and cannot avoid each other," Levi's aunt said.

Levi said they settled their differences but Josh died shortly after and he has carried the burden of thinking he should have never stopped preaching to Josh. Now, in Vivienne's case, he had pushed her too much because of his selfish desire of wanting her to develop a relationship with God so they could be together.

"I should have taken things slowly with her and given her time to want to know God on her terms. Now, her resolve against God is stronger than it was before. What if something happens to her when she is yet to receive salvation? How do I live with that?"

"I have heard all you said, Levi. But the truth is, some things are beyond our control. Yes, we might want to do something for the Lord and can even have good intentions, still it doesn't stop us from asking God for guidance. And even after we do this and things don't turn out as we expected, let's still be thankful for the opportunity

God gave us to plant seeds in the person's heart. Remember that Paul planted and Apollos watered, but it was God who gave the increase."

Levi thought about what his aunt said and it made perfect sense to him.

"And about Josh. What he didn't tell you was that the day he told me about your falling out, he also told me he was beginning to see reasons with what you had been preaching to him about. Josh said that he wanted to start going to church again and know God better for himself. He said he was tired of fighting God and we prayed together that day. Shortly after, you guys had an accident and he died."

Stunned was an understatement for how Levi felt. For years, he had carried the burden of thinking he should have pressed harder in convincing his cousin to restore his relationship with God. Only to just find out Josh had actually reconciled back to God.

"Levi? Are you there?" his aunt asked, sounding worried.

"But why… Why didn't he tell me?"

"I had no idea he didn't tell you. If I had known, I would have told you myself. I'm so sorry, Levi."

Levi told her he felt relieved knowing that Josh was with the Lord. His aunt reminded him that Josh never stopped being a child of God just because he had doubts and stopped going to church. He just needed someone to answer the questions he had, which Levi had done even without knowing.

They talked some more about his situation with Vivienne, and his aunt said if God wanted them to be together, things would fall into place for them.

"I have to go now, Levi. They just announced the boarding for my flight."

"Bye, Auntie. Have a safe trip."

"I will. Stay safe, okay? I love you."

"I love you too, Auntie."

Chapter Twenty-Six

Vivienne

Over a month had passed since Vivienne quit her job at PEP. She didn't realize how much her daily routine would change now that she no longer had a 9-5 job. Even though BGFAD was doing well, she still missed her job.

Lately, Vivienne spent her time writing articles for her blog and contemplating whether to unblock Levi or not. It also didn't help that he had no social media presence so she couldn't stalk him even if she wanted to. She missed him terribly, and there were times she thought of stopping by at PEP just to see him. But she knew it would only make things worse for both of them.

Two days after she and her mom went to visit her dad on the night of her "break up" with Levi, he got discharged from the hospital. That day, Vivienne was supposed to go with her mom but she had to finish up a client's dress so she ended up going alone. When Vivienne got to his ward, she met a woman and two men, who she presumed were in their early to mid-thirties.

"Sorry, I can always come back," Vivienne said and turned to leave.

"No. Bukunmi, come back. These are my sons, your half-brothers, and my wife," her dad said casually.

Vivienne's eyes went wide, and she stood frozen in that spot. Her father could have warned her that they would be there. What if her mom had come with her—how would his wife react upon seeing the woman who caused her so much pain in her marriage? Vivienne's armpits began to sweat, and she wished she would just disappear.

She swallowed hard and greeted her father's wife, and to Vivienne's surprise, she responded warmly. She looked at her half-brothers, who were obviously older than her, and they both smiled at her. She must have tried to smile back to no avail because her lips felt stiff and heavy. Both men were spitting images of their dad, except the younger one was light-skinned like his mom.

"Hi. I'm Deji, and that's Damola, my younger brother," the older one said, stretching his hands to Vivienne for a handshake while Damola waved at her.

Vivienne looked between him and Deji before shaking Deji's outstretched hand and saying a weak, "Hi."

"Daddy has told us so much about you," Damola said with a smile.

What did he say, for God's sake?

"Oh!" Vivienne said.

"I take it that you're just learning about our existence just as we are yours," Deji said.

Vivienne shook her head and said, "No. I've always known Daddy has other children. I'm just shocked to meet you guys out of the blue and under these circumstances."

"Really?" Damola asked and she nodded.

"So why didn't you and Fisayo try to meet us?" Damola asked again.

Vivienne shrugged. "I'm not sure how it would have turned out. Illegitimate children don't go about looking for their half-siblings."

There was an uncomfortable silence in the room. Vivienne cleared her throat. "I'm sorry. I meant to say Daddy and I just got over our differences. We weren't on good terms for almost a decade."

Deji scoffed and said, "You too?"

Vivienne nodded and then asked, "What was your offense?"

"Let's just say he and I are interested in different career paths," Deji answered.

Vivienne scoffed. "Sounds about right. Again, I'm sorry for interrupting your private moment. I can always come back."

"No, it's okay. I told Kunle to ask you and your mom to come because we wanted to meet you," the woman said.

"Huh?"

"Yes. We wanted to meet our sister," Deji said.

"Sisters," Damola chipped in.

"Yes. We wanted to meet our sisters."

"Oh. I'm sorry. It just felt strange that you said you wanted to meet us," Vivienne replied, embarrassed.

"I hear Fisayo is studying to become a lawyer," Damola said, looking impressed, and Vivienne nodded with a smile.

"She must be Daddy's favorite then," he added.

Her dad, who had been quietly watching the exchange between his children, said, "That's not true. I love you guys equally."

Vivienne and her brothers looked at each other and laughed in unison. It was oddly scary how they all had the same laughter even though the pitches varied.

"You have no idea how much we wanted a sister, and now we have two," Damola said excitedly.

"Let's stay in touch, Bukunmi. We've missed out on a lot already. We don't have to miss special occasions anymore," Deji said.

"We'd also like you to meet your nieces and nephews someday," Damola added.

"I'd like that very much. Thank you," Vivienne said, tearing up.

"It was nice to meet you, Bukunmi. Tell Fisayo we said hello," Damola said, and Deji nodded.

"Yeah. Likewise," Vivienne said.

Even after they left, Vivienne stood in that same spot, stunned by everything that just happened.

"Bukunmi, won't you say hi to your dad?" her father said, bringing her out of her standstill mode, and she went over to hug him.

By mid-afternoon, her mom joined them at the hospital. Vivienne told her all that had happened in her absence. She had expected her mom to be antsy, but she wasn't.

"Mommy, how come you're not worried Daddy's wife wanted to meet with you?"

"Buks, a clear conscience fears no accusations. I also apologized to your father's wife years ago for causing her pain after I ended things with him."

Her parents spent the rest of the day studying the Bible together. Her dad had asked her to join them, but she declined, saying she needed to go home to get some rest.

Since his discharge from the hospital, Vivienne and her dad had hung out a few times. She took him to Waffles, Cones, and Cream for a treat, and he had teased her, saying she hadn't outgrown her sweet tooth. He also bought her an expensive set of jewelry and shoes for her last birthday.

Something that was apparent to Vivienne was how much her dad had changed since giving his life to Christ. He was more patient and compassionate, and every chance he got, he talked about the goodness of God in life. He told everyone who cared to listen how God healed him and restored his relationship with his daughter as he invited them to church. Vivienne couldn't believe that the same man who had been hostile to her for years now radiated an unexplainable peace and joy.

She opened her laptop to schedule blog posts for the rest of the month, but with the Bible study going on in the living room, she couldn't concentrate. So, she plugged in her AirPods and selected her favorite playlist. It had songs she had added because their lyrics made her feel warm and hopeful about love. Now, they reminded her of Levi, how she felt about him and their nonexistent relationship. Her heart pricked but she was determined to not drown in her sorrows.

The first song on the playlist was "Anyone Else But You" by Anthony de la Torre and Lana Condor. It was the perfect description of her situation with Levi. She drowned out the lyrics of the song as she typed. Vivienne scoffed at the irony of writing an article about planning the perfect wedding when she wasn't even in a relationship. A few more songs played, and sometimes she sang along to distract herself from the rising emotions the article was coaxing out of her. Soon an unfamiliar song played, and she checked to see if the songs in her playlist had ended and the streaming platform had shuffled her to other random songs. But they hadn't.

It was the song Levi had sent to her a while ago. The one she had refused to listen to. Vivienne let the song play, and unlike the others she had played earlier, she couldn't listen to it passively. She stopped typing and soaked in the lyrics of the song. It talked about what a good father God is and how He never lets one down. Tears flowed from her eyes as the reality of the song hit her.

Vivienne remembered her conversation with Levi the night he had sent the song to her and her mom's prayer journal. Everything her mom had prayed for concerning her had come to pass. If she was being honest, God had been good to her even when she didn't deserve it. She got out of bed and went to the living room to look for her mom. Her mom was just coming back in from seeing her church members off.

"Mommy, can I talk to you?" Vivienne asked, impatient.

"Buks, *shey kosi?*"

"No. Mommy, do you think God will still want anything to do with me?"

Her mom took Vivienne's hand and sat her down beside her. Then she bowed her head and muttered under her breath. Vivienne couldn't hear what she was saying, but she could bet that her mom was praying. When she raised her head, her eyes were wet. But they were filled with so much joy.

"Buks. God wants everyone, no matter what they have said about Him or done to others. God wants you to come to Him much more than you can imagine."

"I'm ready, Mommy. I want Him in my life," Vivienne said as fresh tears spilled from her eyes and her lips quivered.

"I have watched you and Fifi live with so much joy and peace over the years. Even when things are bad, the both of you remain unfazed. At first, I thought it was because you didn't have any internal demons you were fighting like unforgiveness. But it became clear that wasn't the case when Daddy gave his life to Christ." She paused and took in a shaky breath.

"He has changed so much! There's something different about him and I know it has everything to do with accepting Jesus as his Lord and Savior. Mommy, I want what you, Daddy, and Fifi have. I want Jesus in my life too. Can you help me?"

Her mom nodded as tears flowed freely from her eyes. She hugged Vivienne and said, "Thank you, Jesus," repeatedly.

She read Romans 10:9-10 and asked Vivienne to repeat the prayer of salvation after her. When they were done, her mom prayed for her and they sat in the silence holding each other.

"Mommy, can I skip going to church for a few weeks?"

"Buks, going to church plays an important role in our salvation journey. It certainly helps strengthen our faith and convictions about God when we fellowship with our siblings in Christ. Besides, you are a new convert. You need to be taught the word of God."

"But that's why I have you."

"Buks, I am a part of the body of Christ, not the full body. You need to be around other Christians and maybe even make new friends. I can allow you to skip church for just one week. After that, we're going together," her mom said sternly.

Vivienne had hoped her mom would agree to her request, especially because Levi attended the same church as her. She didn't know what his reaction would be seeing her in church after not being able to reach her for so long.

I guess I'll just have to rip the Bandaid when the time comes.

"I need to tell Fifi the good news. I'm sure she'll be thrilled," her mom said and hurried to get her phone from where it was charging.

"Hello, Fifi. I have good news for you!" her mom said once her sister answered the call.

Chapter Twenty-Seven

Levi

Two months had passed since he last saw or heard anything about Vivienne. The only way he had an idea about what she was up to was through her blog posts. Though he occasionally felt sad about how things had turned out between them, he was happy she still used the website he had built for her.

It was the last Sunday of the month and a thanksgiving Sunday. Everyone was dressed in nice traditional outfits that represented where they were from. Levi was dressed in his complete Isoko traditional attire down to the cowboy hat, coral beads, and walking stick. He'd even gone to his parents' house to prepare for service so that his dad could help him tie the wrapper. As soon as he stepped into the church premises, compliments poured in about his outfit and warm smiles from both men and women. Someone said he looked like royalty, and he was flattered because that was the look he had intended.

The sermon ended and it was time to welcome the first-timers.

"Today, we have some very important people in our midst. They are people who are worshiping with us for the first time today. We prayed for you and now you're here. Please stand and let us welcome you with Jesus's joy," the pastor announced and the congregation clapped.

A few people stood up and Levi spotted someone with bright orange afro hair on the other end of the church. His heart skipped a beat as he was sure it was Vivienne.

Somebody pinch me!

While the pastor addressed the first-timers, Levi stretched his neck as far as he could to see the woman's face, but he couldn't. He couldn't wait for the pastor to ask them to file out so he could see her face clearly. His heart beat increased and his stomach swirled in anticipation. Levi could barely contain his excitement that Vivienne was in church because it meant one thing—she was now saved.

The pastor ended his welcome address and told the first-timers to follow the gentlemen and ladies holding greeting placards as they had some information to share with them. Levi eagerly stepped aside, waving his placard excitedly as he directed the first-timers around him to the exit door on the side. Instead of going with the first-timers in his front, he waited for the lady he had seen earlier to come closer just to be sure it was Vivienne. But she wasn't the one. His stomach sank.

Apparently, she's not the only one with an orange afro.

Nursing his disappointment, Levi went with the rest of his follow-up unit members to address the first-timers. By the time they were done with the welcome address, the service had ended and many of the congregation had dispersed. They stayed behind to pray for the first-timers, asking God to help them abide in His word even as they go back to the reality of their lives.

After their prayers, Levi and his unit members shared the grace and dispersed. On his way out of the church building, he heard someone call his name. He knew that voice any day but he didn't think it was possible. He shook his head and continued walking.

"Levi!"

This time he knew for sure that it was her. That husky, high register was unmistakable. It was Vivienne. Levi turned sharply and came face-to-face with her.

"Did I ever tell you that you walk fast?" Vivienne said, panting. "And these heels don't make it any easier."

Levi couldn't believe his eyes. Vivienne was standing right before him—in church! What were the odds? What happened? He had so many questions for her, but that wasn't important. All that mattered was that she was here, talking to him.

"You look nice, Levi. As always," she said, smiling.

"I tried reaching you, Vivienne, but you blocked me everywhere," he blurted out, ignoring her compliment.

"I'm sorry. But it was the right thing to do at the time."

"Right," Levi said and shook his head to clear it. "It's so good to see you again, Vivienne."

"Likewise. How have you been?"

"Good. We miss you at PEP though."

"I miss you guys too."

Levi didn't miss the spark in her eyes and they shared a knowing look. "So, what are you doing here?"

"This is my church now," Vivienne replied cheerfully.

"Your church?"

Vivienne nodded. Levi was too stunned to say anything because he had assumed his persistence in trying to get Vivienne to have a relationship with God had cemented her resolve not to have one with Him. But apparently, he was wrong.

"Does this mean you're now a Christian? Saved?" he asked, waiting for her to verify.

"Yep! Hard to believe, huh?" she said, chuckling.

Levi shook his head and said, "No. Not at all. I'm just pleasantly surprised and genuinely happy for you. Congratulations!"

God, you did it! Thank you!

Levi did an internal happy dance as he smiled broadly.

"Thanks!" she said, smiling.

He had missed seeing her smile, hearing her laugh and her jokes. He even missed her bright orange afro and sassy attitude.

"What happened to your hair?"

"Nothing. I decided to be more incognito today. It's also the reason I didn't stand up when first-timers were called."

Crafty.

Levi chuckled. "It was good seeing you again, Vivienne. Though I have to go now but we'll definitely be seeing each other around."

"Levi, before you go, I came to talk to you because I wanted to apologize to you. I'm sorry about how things ended between us and for blocking you."

"There's nothing to forgive, Vivienne. I also played a huge part in how things ended between us. So, I should also apologize."

"So can we start all over?" she asked, her eyes big and hopeful.

Levi smiled and nodded. He wanted nothing more than to have Vivienne in his life again, even if it was just as friends.

"Hi, I'm Vivienne," she said and stretched her hand for a handshake.

Levi chuckled and shook her hand. "Hi, Vivienne. I'm Levi, and it's nice to meet you."

Epilogue

Two Years Later

The wedding guests were seated with their mini umbrellas in the sun-dappled garden, filled with the fragrance of blooming blush-pink roses and jasmine. The officiating pastor stood on the altar which was set behind a floral arch, adorned with cascading blush-pink roses and greenery.

Levi stood in front of the arch as he waited for his bride to walk down the aisle. The processional hymn along with the soft rustling of leaves and the chirping of birds enhanced the beauty of the serene atmosphere.

Vivienne walked down the petal-covered aisle with her parents on each arm. Her form-fitting gown and cathedral-length veil flowed gracefully behind her as she walked to meet Levi, whose eyes sparkled with emotion. Vivienne thought her heart would burst from all the happiness. Seeing her half-brothers and their families in the crowd warmed her heart deeply and she couldn't be more thankful for the life she now had.

The officiating pastor welcomed the guests and introduced them to the purpose of the gathering.

"Today, we are here to witness the wedding solemnization between Vivienne Oluwafiebukunmi Adetokunbo and Levi Ogheneovie Edegware. We're gathered here to celebrate their love and commitment as they embark on this sacred journey together. In this moment, we honor not just their union, but also the joy and blessings that come with it." The pastor paused and flipped a page on his book before continuing.

"As we witness the couple exchange their vows and join them in prayers, let us be a living testament to the love, faith, and support that surrounds them. May this day be a reflection of their love, an inspiration to us all, and a cherished beginning to their lifelong journey together in Jesus's name."

The guests chorused, "Amen!"

"Let us pray."

After the opening prayer, the pastor preached a sermon about God's intention when he created the institution of marriage. He preached from Ephesians 5:21-33, encouraging the couple to follow God's commands regarding marriage. Then he said it was time for the exchange of vows, starting with the groom.

"Oluwafiebukunmi, the one God used to bless me. From the moment I first saw you, I knew there was something different about you. Though we had our share of ups and downs, which may or may not have included you running into me and spilling a drink on me," Levi said, and the guests laughed. "Still, you found your way into my heart, which is no surprise because you are super gorgeous, strong, independent, fierce, kind, extremely smart, and the most amazing woman I have ever met." Levi paused and smiled.

Vivienne had promised herself she wouldn't cry and ruin her makeup, but seeing Levi so emotional, tears in his eyes and his hands shaking, made her shed a few tears. Fisayo pressed a soft napkin into her hands and she dabbed Levi's eyes with it before dabbing hers, which made their guests *awww*.

She placed her hands on Levi's shaking hands and mouthed, "It's okay."

Levi smiled at her and continued reading his vows. "Today, before God, our family and friends, I vow to never stop proving to you that my love for you is more than words. It's a promise to cherish and protect you, through every doubt and every moment. It's a journey I have chosen to take with you because you've shown me the most beautiful kind of love. One that I desired to have for so long."

After Levi was done saying his vows to Vivienne, it became her turn to do the same.

"First of all, it was Levi who hit me and spilled *his* drink on himself. Just putting that out there," Vivienne said, and everyone laughed while Levi shrugged. Then Vivienne cleared her throat and read her vows.

"Dear Levi. My chocolate knight in shining armor and the absolute love of my life. You have made me feel safe, cherished, wanted, and completely seen."

She paused and drew in a shaky breath. "You also gave me the greatest gift: helping me build a relationship with the Lord. You were also instrumental in helping me restore a long-lost relationship and I'll always be thankful for your not-so-subtle evangelism."

The guests laughed again. Vivienne blinked rapidly and fanned her face with her hand.

"I said I wasn't going to cry. This makeup took hours!"

Levi laughed and held her hand then he mouthed, "I love you, Buks Buks."

And she whispered, "I love you too."

Seeing Levi's eyes fill up with tears as he looked at her with so much love made Vivienne let go of the tears she had fought from spilling.

"Levi, with you, I've found not just a husband, but my home and heart's greatest joy. Today, I vow to stand by you in all things as you follow Christ; to love you fiercely and to honor you—the man who has given me everything I didn't know I needed. I will be your support, your joy, and your forever love, always and completely."

A few of the guests sniffled as Levi and Vivienne exchanged wedding rings in the name of God, the Father, Son, and Holy Spirit.

"Levi, you may now kiss your bride," the officiating pastor announced cheerfully and a few of the guests whooped.

Their eyes locked, and a shared sense of anticipation and affection filled the air. The world seemed to momentarily fade away, leaving just the two of them in their newlywed bubble. Levi dabbed the tears on Vivienne's cheeks and leaned in to her. As their lips met in what would be their first kiss, a gentle caress, filled with the promise of love and the climax of their vows bound them together.

When Levi pulled her closer, Vivienne melted in his arms and put her arms around his neck. They broke off their kiss with a laugh as they stared at each other for what seemed like a lifetime.

"I love you so much," Levi whispered to Vivienne.

"I love you too, babe," she replied, touching the side of his face.

They turned to face their guests who cheered for them and the pastor said, "For the first time, I present to you Mr. and Mrs. Levi Edegware. Hashtag the Levites 2024."

Vivienne showed off her ring and then they walked hand in hand out of the garden. They stopped when they got to the end and faced each other again.

"I'm glad you chose to do life with me, Levi," Vivienne said.

Levi watched Vivienne's eyes fill with tears and he could swear that his heart would burst open with all the love he felt for her. He raised her chin slightly and leaned forward. With a big smile he said, "Even if it took a thousand years, I would have waited for you, my love. I am undeniably yours, Buks Buks."

Vivienne giggled. "I like the way you call me Buks Buks."

Levi's lips met hers again and they were lost in each other's arms until they heard another round of cheering across the other end of the garden.

(Cue in Worth the Wait by Spencer Crandall)
THE END!

Thank you so much for reading, Ready to be Loved by You. I hope you enjoyed it and that it blessed you too. If you'd be so kind, please rate my book and write a review on Goodreads and Amazon.

If you ever create a video review on IG or TikTok or anywhere else, please tag or add me as a collaborator. I'd love that very much. My handles are the same everywhere **@enewerome_author.** Also, I'm open to being interviewed on your blog, podcast or book club. You can reach out to me via this email: storiesforchrist@gmail.com

 Besides being a nonfiction ghostwriter and book editor, Enewerome strives to make her life count by doing the one thing she was put on this earth to do—write books that glorify Jesus Christ and spread the message of salvation one story at a time. Enewerome lives in Abuja, Nigeria, with her husband and toddler.

Thank you once again. Until I see you with my next book, which is going to be the first book in a three-part standalone series. If you'd like to read the blurb, flip to the next page.

IS AN UNFORGIVABLE BETRAYAL—AN AGE-LONG FAMILY SECRET—POTENT ENOUGH TO KEEP TWO HEARTS APART?

Nothing had prepared eighteen-year-old Orevaoghene 'Revie' Igbide for her first heartbreak with her best friend, Zik. The worst part? It was payment for a crime neither of them were guilty of. A decade later, she's set to marry Linus, her knight in shining armor and a charismatic pastor, who isn't perfect but can give her what she desires most in life—marriage.

After years of going on forced blind dates set up by his mom, Isaac 'Zik' Nwachukwu still hasn't found the one. The reason is simple. His heart belonged to someone else. When the cracks in Revie's relationship with Linus begin to widen, Zik's steadfast love forces her to confront feelings she thought were long gone for him. Still, she is reminded of why they can't be together but left with the difficult choice of sticking with Linus or throwing caution to the wind to be with the love of her life.

A final tragedy ending Revie's engagement to Linus might just be Zik's perfect second chance to fight for his one true love. But can they overcome the hurdles of their family's secret or will they let it tear them apart a second time?

Available on Amazon and Kindle Unlimited